The Second Red Ridge Pack Novel

CIRCLE OF LIES

Sara Dailey & Staci Weber

TRUTH OR DARE

"I just don't get you," I blurted. "Are you really interested in me, or is this all just a game? Because I'm not into games." There, I'd said it. I'd admitted that I thought he liked me and opened myself up for ridicule. Still, I felt a bit relieved.

Aiden stood there shell-shocked. "Really, a game? You think I'm playing some sort of *game* with you?"

"Isn't that what guys like you do? You have every girl in school eating out of your hand, so you want the one who isn't standing in line waiting her turn to hang on your arm. That's a game if I've ever seen one."

"It's not like that. Why would it be like that?" He eyed me, and a new expression crossed his face. "Why is it so hard to believe that I like you? I, Aiden Wright, like you, Teagan Rhodes."

"Because life doesn't work that way," I snapped. Then I marched away without turning back.

The Second Red Ridge Pack Novel

CIRCLE OF LIES

Sara Dailey & Staci Weber

www.BOROUGHSPUBLISHINGGROUP.com

CIRCLE OF LIES
Copyright © 2014 Sara Dailey & Staci Weber

Digital edition created by Maureen Cutajar

www.gopublished.com

ISBN 978-1-941260-51-7

For Teagan, Cameron, and Gavin. Three of the coolest kids ever.

ACKNOWLEDGMENTS

This book would not have been possible without a lot of support from our families. Many thanks to our parents and in-laws for keeping our kids entertained and out of our hair while we spent the hot summer months writing this book.

To Shari Hassell: Thanks a million for being our beta reader. We know it's good if you like it. You rock! A special thanks to Jordan Mantell, who continues to wow us with his beautiful poetry. We also have to thank the teachers at Creekside, who diligently helped us with our title dilemma. Thanks to Andy Cole for thinking of *Circle of Lies*!

To all the fabulous folks at Boroughs Publishing: Thank You! Y'all are truly a special group. Michelle, you are our hero! Many, many thanks to our amazing editors Jill Limber and Chris Keeslar. Without Jill, we would have had something like two hundred semicolons in this novel, and thanks to Chris we were able to sneak a few back in. Shh! Don't tell Jill. We know that this is a much stronger novel because of the two of you. We are so blessed to be a part of such a wonderful team.

Last but certainly not least, a special thank-you to John Weber and Jeremy Dailey for letting us do what makes us happy!

CONTENTS

I cannot stop this

I cannot stop you

You are my losing battle

A fight I can no longer muster

You are a sweetness my lips have never tasted

A pleasured twinge pulsating, breathing on its own

Bleeding a warmth within me, melting my past

Writhing into a dream of every moment, unable to wake my shining
eyes

My walled-in mind shattered into a million pieces of defiant passion

Enduring, edging your way into my spirit

You have become my inhale, my exhale

My love, my own.

—Jordan Mantell

1.

PETER

March 12th. El Paso, Texas, near the border of New Mexico. Two hunters found by park rangers ripped to shreds. Cause of death: animal attack. Species of animal unknown, but most likely extremely large. Authorities warn visitors to be cautious.

May 27th. Santa Fe, New Mexico. A rancher went to check on his herd and found over a dozen of mauled to death and partially eaten. Species of predator unknown.

September 2nd. Las Cruces, New Mexico. Missing girl. Age 10. Went missing from the family's backyard. No clues or suspects at this time. Family reported seeing what appeared to be a large wolf nearby days prior to disappearance.

Peter Marshall stared at his notes on the wall map for a few moments before he placed the last tack. It sank slowly into the board. He took a step back.

November 17th. Silver City, New Mexico. Unidentified body found just outside of town. Victim was male and presumed homeless. Cause of death: decapitation—likely by an animal. Head appeared to be ripped from body by unusually large claws.

He'd been so sure there was a pattern to these attacks, and now he knew he was right. There were too many unsolved incidents surrounding one state in particular, one particular area. He turned and started packing his belongings. He was headed to northeastern New Mexico. The answers he sought would be there.

2.

Teagan

"I'm taking off, guys. Have a great Thanksgiving," I yelled to my coworkers as I pulled off my Sephora apron and slid into my winter coat.

"See you later, Teagan. Happy Thanksgiving!" Janie replied as she finished up restocking the lip gloss.

I'd been kind of hoping that we would be busy, that the store managers would be forced to ask me to stay and work a double, but no such luck. Guess all the shoppers were waiting for Black Friday. I really could have used the extra money, but more importantly, the work would have kept me out of the house a little longer. Holidays are not so fun around there these days. It's safe to say this is my least favorite time of year.

New Mexico. I don't know if I'll ever get used to the weather here. And I used to think it got cold in San Antonio! I guess when you grow up in Texas, you don't really know the true meaning of winter. As I stepped outside the mall, a rush of cold November air hit me so hard it forced my teeth to chatter uncontrollably. Zipping up my coat, I ran as fast as my frozen legs would carry me to my beat-up Toyota Corolla, circa sometime before I could walk. I always hear kids talk about how much they love their junked out "classic" cars, how those cars have character. Well, my car doesn't have character. It's a piece of shit. The damned thing's heater doesn't even work. But, at least I have something, and when you have to buy it for yourself at seventeen you can't afford to be picky.

I could only imagine what it would be like to depend on dear ol' Dad for transportation.

By the time I got home little icicles were forming on my eyelashes, and as I walked up the front steps to our house I saw that evidence of my father's ever-growing habit littered the porch. By the look of things, he should be fairly close to passing out if not already face-down on the couch. A girl could hope. An entire case of empty beer cans and countless cigarette butts surrounded the wooden rocking chair that my mother bought just before she disappeared.

"Disappeared." That's the belief my father holds on to—or at least he pretends to hold on to it. Me, I know the truth. Only a fool wouldn't see what really happened. She was miserable at home, hated my father, and had clearly found someone new. Her sudden interest in late-night drives were enough proof for me, but I'd followed her anyway one night just to be sure and ended up at a Motel 6 near the highway. No, she just up and left one day. We moved to Red Ridge, New Mexico, and in just over a month Mom went MIA. No goodbyes, no see-ya-laters; she was just suddenly gone. Life isn't a soap opera where beautiful, mysterious captors abduct women with miserable lives and carry them off to happier ones, though. No, women have to choose to leave. They pack a bag, snag your favorite family portrait from the mantel and just walk out of your life. Out of their children's lives. Out of everyone's life.

So, that's what really happened. Only an idiot like my father would believe anything else. Hell, he likely believed that Paris kidnapped Helen of Troy. No way. Helen just took off with that hot younger guy, leaving her sorry-ass husband Menelaus alone. Life would be so much easier if my father would just accept that Mom chose to leave. Then maybe, just maybe, he could move on.

I have. I sometimes wonder, though, if the face that launched a thousand ships left a daughter alone with a drunken father. Who knows? Maybe she did. My Greek mythology is a bit rusty, as Mrs.

Shultz wasn't the most fascinating teacher ever when we studied it in class last year.

The inside of our house wasn't much better than the porch. More empty beer cans, full ashtrays, and the dishes from the night's dinner welcomed me back, which meant Dad was really messed up. Being a retired Army captain, he's anything but messy. The house was always clean and orderly, *sir!* Unless he was drunk. And he never, ever smoked in the house. Something must have really set him off.

I put my bag down and hung my coat in the hall closet. The sooner I picked this place up, the sooner I could lock myself in my room and just crash.

"Oh…hey…when did you get in?" Dad asked as he stumbled inside from the backyard.

"Just now, actually," I replied as I grabbed a trashcan. Trying to avoid confrontation, I walked around the kitchen and living room picking up the mess. Unfortunately, this only seemed to irritate my father.

"Don't do that. I'll do it tomorrow," he slurred.

"Dad, tomorrow is Thanksgiving. I need to clean up so I can attempt to cook this year. I told you that, remember?"

"I know damn well what tomorrow is," he grumbled. "You think I can't remember what tomorrow is?"

There was no use trying to talk to him like this. Instead, I handed him the trashcan and said, "Fine. Have it your way. I was just trying to help."

He didn't reach for the trashcan, so I let it drop to the floor and spill out even more evidence of his drinking binge. At first he looked shocked, but that shock soon turned to rage. Maybe I shouldn't have done it, but come on, who was the parent? I was sick and tired of trying to make things better all the time when all he did was screw things up.

He just stood there, anger boiling inside him. I saw it in his eyes just before he snapped. He kicked the trash aside and tried to grab my arm, but I stepped out of the way just in time and Dad lost his balance and fell to the ground. He wasn't hurt, though, just defeated. The look of failure on his face as he lay there was almost worse than the anger. I reached out to help him up, but he wouldn't let me.

"Don't touch me! Just leave. Leave like your goddamn mother did," he yelled.

"Come on, Dad. Let me help you," I said.

"Get out! Get the hell out of my house!"

So I did. I grabbed my bag and coat and left.

Leaving the house like this wasn't new to me. It's not like it happened every day, but I'd walked out quite a few times over the past couple of months so I knew where to go and how long to stay away. The 24-hour diner on the other side of town was always open, so I figured I'd go there and order myself a nice, greasy burger and a few sodas. I was hungry, and in a few hours my father would be good and passed out. Then I would drive home and pretend that nothing ever happened. Just like I did every other time Dad kicked me out.

3.

Aiden

"He should be fine…"

"…a few weeks…

"…muscles already healing…"

"Oh, thank God!"

I could hear bits and pieces of conversation, the drone of voices around me but I couldn't speak. I couldn't open my eyes, couldn't move my body. I didn't know how I'd ended up in this weird semi-conscious state, either. It was like one of those shows on TV where the person is having surgery and is supposed to be unconscious but he's not, not completely anyway, and he can hear and feel everything. But I wasn't in any pain; not really. And there didn't seem to be any surgical tools maneuvering around my body, so thankfully I wasn't in the middle of an operation. I just sort of felt…numb. My mind was fuzzy and my arms and legs were too heavy to move.

Suddenly, memories came flooding back: sitting at the dining room table, finding out from my mom that I'd soon be a werewolf. Yeah, a *werewolf.* Moving to New Mexico because of it, to be with a group of the same. A pack, they called themselves. A pack with an alpha as their leader. My younger sister Alli being abducted by Kendall Stuart and Dylan Christianson. Finding Alli and then realizing that I wasn't able to shift. Apparently, not being able to get all wolfy when necessary was what had landed me in this hospital bed. Whatever happened after that was just a blur.

My mom and dad were here. I could feel them hovering over me, but as hard as I tried I didn't have the strength to let them know that I was okay, that I could hear them. Instead, my mind wouldn't stop replaying the last few weeks of my once normal, now crazy life. As if living on an estate in the middle of the freaking woods, populated by people who can turn into wolves at will wasn't weird enough, my younger sister "mated" with our alpha's son, which was what got her dumb ass kidnapped and almost killed.

Interrupting my thoughts, I felt Mom push back my hair from my forehead just like she used to when I was a little boy, and she gently kissed the top of my head. A single teardrop landed on my cheek. I wished I could open my eyes and see her.

"We have to tell him."

"Oh, God. I can't believe this is happening."

"How are we ever going to get through this? What if he hates me for not telling him the truth?"

I tried again to speak, to answer the voices, to tell my mom that there was no way in the world that I could ever hate her, but I couldn't move much less say anything. What could she have to tell me now? Last time she'd had a big announcement it was that Alli and I were freaking werewolves. Could anything really get more shocking than that? What else could she have kept from us? Maybe we were hybrid werewolf-vampires. Or witches! Not zombies, surely. I laughed to myself, indulging a grim kind of humor. But, what could be left unsaid that might actually make me hate her?

A warm tingle suddenly started in my arm and ran straight to my head. The voices in the room were no longer clear. It was as if my parents were slowly moving away, step by step. I called out to them but knew my words were only in my head. No one could hear me no matter how loud I screamed. But I kept screaming. The experience was straight out of a horror movie.

Somebody hear me! I'm here. Awake, sort of! Damn it, I'm—

And then there was silence.

*****

I was roused from what must have been an incredibly deep sleep by the touch of my sister Alli's hand, and by her whispers in my ear. I recognized her voice. I had no idea how much time had passed.

"I don't know if you can hear me, Aiden, but I'm here. We're all here. We need you to wake up. We need to know you're okay. We love you."

Before she could finish speaking, I could hear a change in her voice, a familiar change which meant only one thing: tears. She sobbed and laid her head on my chest. More than anything I wanted to comfort her, to hold her tight and tell her I was fine. I hated this, hated just lying here paralyzed, unable to tell my little sister to stop crying, that I was okay. But I could do nothing else. No matter how hard I tried, I couldn't even open my eyes.

Seconds became minutes, minutes became more. Seeing me here like this must have been too much for Alli. I felt her stand up then, still crying, and she kissed my cheek. Then she left.

More time passed. Just when I thought I'd go absolutely crazy, alone in my head, my eyes slowly opened. I had no idea what I did that was any different, but one second I couldn't see; the next I could. My mom was holding my hand and had her head down. She kind of looked like she was praying.

At the slight movement of my arm, Mom's head shot up. With tears in her eyes she saw that I was conscious; then she kissed my forehead and said, "Thank God you're awake." Before I could respond, she darted out of the room shouting, "He's awake! Everyone, Aiden is awake!"

In seconds, she was back with my dad in tow. Both parents rushed to my side, asking questions at the same time. The doctor came over and moved them both aside, again before I could respond.

"Can you tell me your name, son?" the doc asked.

"Aiden. Aiden Wright."

"Do you know where you are?"

"I'm guessing the infirmary on the estate." I couldn't imagine they would let me go to a *human* doctor. It was weird being part of a compound of werewolves, but that's where Mom and Dad moved us. Everyone here was part of the pack. That's why we moved to New Mexico. I suppose it makes sense that you'd want to be near your own, even if we weren't completely separated from regular humans. I mean, I still went to school with a bunch, though they didn't know what I was. And then there was Dad.

"Good, Aiden," the doc said. "That's real good. Do you know what happened?"

I looked down at my mangled shoulder, which was completely wrapped in some type of soft cast thing, and my arm was confined to a sling. I closed my eyes and tried to piece together what exactly had happened. I remembered seeing Kendall's phone with a cryptic text from Dylan, a text that we hoped would lead us to Alli. I couldn't imagine what would have happened if that phone hadn't accidently been left at Shari's. Then I remembered getting in the car with Cade, my sister's "mate" and the alpha's son, and as if by fate spotting Kendall's car leaving town. We gave chase, but it didn't last long. Kendall's car suddenly veered off the road and then…the crash. Three wolves burst from the wreck of that car, not three people. The last thing I saw before everything went black was one of those wolves heading straight for me.

Well, I had to say *some*thing to the doc. "Do I know what happened? My memories are a bit fuzzy, but I know it had something to do with that crazy-ass Kendall and Dylan, her junkyard dog. What happened? Let's see. Kendall's car crashed, wolves jumped out, and the fight was on. The only thing I'm sure of is that Kendall and Dylan attacked us. What happened with those two anyway? The last thing I remember was a giant wolf trying to bite my head off."

"Dylan was killed on the scene, and Kendall and her mother have been banished permanently from the estate," the doctor answered. I guess he wasn't much for elaboration. I guess it didn't matter as long as Kendall was banished and Dylan was dead.

"So, I guess this means that everything turned out okay? Case closed?"

With a small smile, the doctor nodded. He then checked me over and told my parents that I appeared to be out of the woods, but that they should take it easy on me. They rushed to my bedside, ecstatic, but just as they did Allison and Cade entered the room. Allison hurried over, while Cade hung back in the doorway. He looked noticeably uncomfortable.

Mom brushed my hair back from my face with her hand and said, "We're so glad you're okay, honey. We were all so worried."

They were huddled around my bed, acting as if I'd been brought back from the dead. I couldn't help it, I said, "I'm *fine*, guys. Y'all are the ones that look like hell. Have any of you looked in the mirror lately?" They really did look awful, and I felt the need to lighten the tension in the room. Everyone was being so damn serious.

A smile spread across each of their faces. My dad said, "Well, sounds like you're going to be just fine, son. Already back to your smart-ass ways."

There came a light knock at the door, even though it was open and Cade stood visible just inside. It turned out to be his parents. Marcus and Noel Walker poked their heads through and gave a small wave. Weird. Why were they being so tentative?

"Mind if we come in?" Noel asked. "Marcus was getting antsy."

I almost asked what the hell he had to be antsy about, but I caught myself just in time. That was no way to speak to him. He was the alpha. Rules, rules, stupid rules. I was still learning to be a good part of the pack. But it was really strange that Marcus would act tentative about anything.

Dad seemed uneasy with our new visitors, and he moved toward the window. It made me realize how strange it must be, being the only true human in the room. That just reminded me of how much he must love Mom, moving here to be with her.

Marcus made his way over to my bed, and Mom stepped aside. What was he doing here? All I could figure was that my almost being killed by another pack member was official business, so he must be in hurry to get to the bottom of it all. But when he walked up and just stood over me, I knew it was something else. Something strange. I got the odd feeling that he wanted to hug me, but thankfully he didn't.

He'd always made me a little nervous, Marcus. From the moment we first met I could see why he was the alpha of our pack. There was just an air of confidence about him that most men never possess. It was both appealing and off-putting.

After a few very awkward moments he finally spoke. "How are you feeling, son? Are you in any pain?"

"No, sir," I said. "Well, not much anyway."

"Good. Good." He smiled down at me.

"Sir, I wish I could tell you what happened, but I'm sorry. I don't remember much about that night," I admitted.

Marcus looked puzzled. Then he looked at Mom and said, "You haven't told him yet?"

"Marcus, for crying out loud. He just woke up." My dad was almost shouting.

Damn, Dad. Ballsy.

I half expected Marcus to bite his head off. To tell him that nobody speaks to the alpha that way. But Marcus just stood there with a blank face and the room fell into an uncomfortable silence, everyone looking around waiting for someone else to be the first to speak.

Alli reached out and took Cade's hand. My dad put his arm around my mom, who was beginning to shake. Marcus's wife Noel just stood beside him, her eyes glued to the floor. Everyone looked so…panicked. What the hell had happened while I was unconscious?

"What's going on, Mom?" I finally belted out. I couldn't stand the silence, the guilty look on my mom's face, or the sadness in my sister's eyes.

Mom glanced at me, and I knew that look. For a moment I could see in her eyes that whatever was about to be said wasn't good. My blood ran cold, and I wasn't sure anymore whether I even wanted to hear it.

With downcast eyes she admitted, "Marcus is right. You need to know the truth." But she didn't add anything, and no one else did either.

Little beads of sweat formed on my forehead, and if I could have managed to walk out of the room, I would have been halfway home already.

Finally, Dad moved toward my bed, having decided to be the one to speak up. "Son, you know how much I love you, right? And how proud I am of you?"

I shook my head, even more confused. "Wait. What the hell is going on here? Am I dying or something?"

"No, Aiden, you're not dying. It's just…well, the truth is…I am not your biological father." He looked around the room and added, "There, I said it. Everyone feel better?"

Better? No fucking way. Instinctively I tried to sit up, but I failed miserably and excruciating pain shot through my body. I saw nothing but stars. Then darkness.

*****

I opened my eyes to find the room empty except for Marcus, who now sat in the chair next to my bed. I glanced his way, and he gave me a half-smile then looked down at his hands.

Shit. I'd hoped it was just a bad dream, learning that Dad wasn't my real father, or maybe a delusion brought on by the drugs still dripping into my arm. But after a short pause Marcus shifted his gaze toward the door and said, "Well, that didn't go exactly how I imagined."

How he'd imagined? How the hell had he expected me to react? And why did he care?

"How about *you* just tell me what's up," I muttered. "Since you're in charge here. Someone needs to." I was unable to keep the frustration out of my voice. From what I could see, this pack was full of lies and secrets. I thought I'd moved to New Mexico to be part of a werewolf pack, not a group of liars and hypocrites. If I couldn't even trust my own family, how could I trust this almost-stranger sitting by my hospital bedside?

Marcus leaned in and seemed to be debating whether or not to take my hand. I made up his mind by pulling away. I couldn't stop him from talking, though. I couldn't stop him from saying whatever would come next.

"Aiden, I'm just going to giving it to you straight. I'm your real father. There. Now you know."

So, that was the moment I realized my entire life had actually been a lie. Complete and utter bullshit. It was crazy. Anger, hurt, and confusion swallowed me whole, and I closed my eyes and turned away. The man who raised me, who taught me to catch a ball, to ride a bike, to do all of those important things that are milestones in a boy's life was not my father. Not really. Worse than that? Marcus, this werewolf, this pack alpha, my mom's ex, was.

I couldn't look at him. Not when I didn't even know who I was anymore.

4.

Peter

The road was a dark and lonely place. Peter had nothing to keep him company except for his favorite talk-radio show, *Coast to Coast with George Noory*, and his thoughts. His thoughts were deep. On nights such as this, the memory of his Uncle Raymond came flooding back. The memory of Raymond's death.

He'd been just a boy when it happened, eleven years old when his favorite relative and the only father figure he'd ever known invited Peter on his first hunting trip. A short time later, he'd stood hidden in the protection of the woods and watched in horror as his uncle was torn to pieces. For as long as he lived, he would never erase that scene from his memory. He couldn't.

His uncle had been convinced there were werewolves living among them, humans that looked just like ordinary people but who could shift into wolf form. Raymond had spent months trying to convince him and finally decided that it was time for Peter to see for myself. The trip took them into the wilds. It wasn't long before they spotted a wolf, either—and his uncle didn't waste any time. Peter watched from a safe distance as his uncle raised his gun…but before he could pull the trigger, another wolf blasted out of the thick brush and mauled him to death.

It was stranger than that, though. The second wolf was too large and powerful to be any normal animal, and it attacked from behind. Cleverly, tactically. Then, while the life drained from Raymond's body, the wolf stared directly at Peter. Seconds later it ran into forest, and it was at that moment Peter was finally convinced: The beast was a werewolf. It *had* to be. Given his uncle's obsession, he'd spent hours on the Internet researching them, and there was no other explanation. Not for the precision with which his uncle was killed, for the human eyes of his killer or the fierce determination behind them.

He'd raced back to the hunting lodge and told the authorities what happened. He was frantic, desperate, but no one believed him. Worse, upon inspection his uncle's death was ruled an accident. But Peter still knew the truth. He knew that his uncle had done nothing to provoke the attack, and he remembered the malevolent intelligence in the beast's eyes.

He'd tried to convince his mother that what killed his uncle was no ordinary wolf but something more sinister, and then he'd tried to convince counselors and doctors. The more and more he tried the worse it got for him. First came a long line of therapists, then medication after medication, each with its own unpleasant side effects. Finally, the institution. Peter had spent six and a half years of his life locked inside a psychiatric hospital. His mom visited often at first, but as the years slowly passed her visits became fewer and farther between. By the time Peter was fifteen, the visits stopped altogether.

The horrors he'd witnessed inside the institution still haunted his dreams: the isolation, the padded rooms, the drugs, the needles, the sedatives. The beatings at night when the guards were bored. Peter clinched his eyes shut, trying to block out what else they'd done to him when he was alone at night. No one would believe him about that either.

But now, twenty-one years of age and off all medication, he was free. He'd told the people at the asylum he no longer believed in werewolves, and they'd finally believed him. But his life had purpose. He knew what he had to do. It was up to him and him alone to expose the world's werewolves. He would make the world see, and then he would make every last one of those wolves pay, every last cold-blooded killer. They would pay for the death of his uncle.

Suddenly, Peter felt a presence in the car next to him. "Hello, Uncle Raymond," he said, glancing at the passenger seat.

"Hello, Peter," a voice said back. "I hope you're ready this time. We're close to finding them. I can feel it."

"I'm ready, Uncle. I will not let you down."

"I hope not," the voice whispered. "I hope not."

5.

Aiden

Alli walked into my room without bothering to knock. "Mom told me that you're planning on going to school Monday. Do you really think you should? You almost died, you know, Ad."

"Yeah, I know, but Thanksgiving break will be over and…I don't know. I just have to," I told her. "I can't stay in this house for one more day. It's driving me insane. And I'm fine. It won't be long before I'm completely healed. One of the perks of being half wolf, I guess."

I didn't look up. I'd been trying to read the same book for the past few hours, but with my wandering mind and a helicopter mom, I hadn't made it very far. Actually, it wasn't even just her who was helicoptering. I'd come home from the infirmary two days ago and now all three of my parents were hovering. That sounded so weird. All *three* parents? Well, four if you counted Noel. Did she count?

What was I thinking? Marcus didn't even really count. Technically he was just the sperm donor. And it was bad enough having my mom and dad constantly checking on me. Having Marcus come by several times had made all of this way more uncomfortable than it needed to be.

"What are you going to tell the throngs of females waiting in line to kiss your boo-boos?" Alli asked. "Obviously, you can't say that you were randomly attacked by a wolf."

I knew she was messing with me, but she did bring up a good point. What was I going to tell people? Obviously, the full truth was out of the question. People outside of our enclave didn't know what we were. And the full truth was totally humiliating, even if humans did know of our existence. I mean, I'd gotten my ass handed to me. I'd gotten beaten up by a guy because he could shift and I still couldn't.

She was right, though. My pride aside, there would be plenty of questions asked, especially looking the way I did. "I haven't thought about it. Why? What do you think I should I tell them?"

Alli sat down beside me. "It has to be something believable. And, we need to tell everyone the same thing so that our stories match. There will be questions, you know. Marcus said we had to sync our stories."

"Why not a car accident?" I offered, thinking that would be the easiest excuse, and it was kind of true, even though I wasn't actually in the car that crashed.

"Whose car? There isn't a single scratch on ours or mom and dad's, so that won't work. Wait... What about a snowboarding accident? We can say that a bunch of us went snowboarding during break and you were...I don't know, trying some stupid trick or another. That would work. It kind of fits your injuries. It would explain why your arm is in a sling and the cuts on your face," she added.

"Yeah, that would work, I guess," I admitted. "But let's leave out the part about me attempting to be an X-treme snowboarder."

"What, Ad? Do you have a better idea? Something a little more glamorous to keep your fans all hot and bothered?"

I didn't want to admit it, but I was just hoping for something that didn't make me look like a complete klutz.

We were both silent. After a few moments, Allison moved a bit closer, put her hand on my good shoulder and asked, "So, how are you taking the whole Marcus thing? *Really*. I meant to ask you before but...well, you know."

What the hell was I supposed to say? Mom had been lying to me my entire life. How could she have been pregnant with another man's baby when she hooked up with Dad, and how could Dad just accept it? It kind of made Mom look like a tramp. I didn't think she was, though. Everything seemed one big confusing mess.

"I'm okay, I guess," I said.

Alli didn't buy it. "You are *so* not okay, Aiden. You don't think I can tell? How can you just pretend like everything is fine?"

Instinctively I jerked away, which hurt my damn shoulder, but I didn't need her trying to be all sisterly right now. She had no idea what I was going through. How could she? Before I could stop the words from coming out of my mouth I blurted, "Why do you care, anyway? This is my problem, not yours, and I'll handle it in my own way, on my own time. Just back off, okay? I don't need you suffocating me too."

My sister stood up, furious. "You're an ass," she said. Then she stormed out of my room without turning back, practically shaking the house by slamming the door.

I lay back on my bed and closed my eyes. Everything was so screwed up.

I must have dozed off, because the next thing I knew Mom was waking me up for dinner and to take my crappy pain meds. I swear, the only proof I'd ever had that I might actually one day become a werewolf was that the damn pain medication didn't work. It was like taking freaking baby aspirin for a massive migraine. What was the point?

I guess I was healing faster than a normal human would, too.

Mom handed me a pill and cup of water. I tried, I honestly tried to smile and thank her, but I couldn't. The only thing I saw when I looked at her was betrayal. It was hard to smile at someone who'd been lying to you for your entire life.

"Why don't you come downstairs and visit with us for a while?" Mom asked.

"Nah, I'm good here."

"Aiden, we miss you. You haven't come out of this room since we got back. Not really. It will do you some good to get out of this bed," she pleaded.

"Mom, I know you're trying to make this all okay, but I need you to back off. I need some time. Everyone just needs to leave me alone for a while."

She put the cup of water on my nightstand and backed toward my door. Just before she left she looked down and said, "When you're ready to talk... Aiden, I really thought I was protecting you from everything I ran away from. I didn't know it would all turn out like this."

Then she turned and headed outside and down the hallway. I didn't have time to respond. Not that I would have known what to say.

6.

Teagan

"Hey, Teagan, wait up!"

It was Alli Wright. She was yelling from across the school parking lot, headed my way with Cade Walker. Close behind were a few other choice members of The Beautiful People: Cami Moore, Becca Sumner, Shari Jones, Luke Stanton, Sammy Cook. All people I could definitely live without. They could usually do without me, too.

Against my better judgment I stopped and waited. I mean, I love Alli, I really do. Even though we only met a month or so ago, she's been a great friend, always nice, never intrusive, but the crowd that she hangs with now is, well…they're hateful-ass douche bags, and that's putting it nicely. I especially didn't want the day ruined by Cade, a.k.a. the Evil One's boy toy. What was Alli doing walking with him anyway? At least Kendall was nowhere to be seen. Last year, Kendall Stuart and her crew had made my first week at Red Ridge High a nightmare, and all I'd done was introduce myself to her in class. I had to endure a week of horror simply because I said, "Hi, my name is Teagan."

Yes, I would have expected Kendall on Cade's arm, ruling the school as Queen Bitch of Red Ridge's cultish group of beautiful people, but instead it was Alli hurrying my way with Kendall's man. Weird.

While Alli and Cade stopped to chat, the rest of their crew thankfully continued into the school. "Hey, Alli. How was your Thanksgiving?" I asked, giving her an awkward hug.

She glanced at Cade before answering. "Interesting, to say the least. What about yours?"

"It was okay." I didn't want to discuss the home situation, and there wasn't much else to say. Also, I might not have known Alli for long, but I could read her face and knew that I was going to hear a really juicy story in first period. There was no point in competing.

Cade slipped his hand into Alli's. Then, before my brain could register what my eyes were seeing, Alli said it, the absolute last thing I expected to hear, not to mention the absolute last thing I *wanted* to hear.

"Teagan, this is my boyfriend Cade."

This couldn't be happening. The douche bags had taken over the only nice person in their strange, exclusive little clique?

I took a short breath before I said anything I'd regret, planted a friendly smile on my face and said, "Hi, Cade. I think we might have met before."

He held out his hand to shake mine. "Well, it's nice to meet you again, Teagan." Then he turned to Alli, gave her a sweet peck on the cheek and politely left us to catch up. Either that, or he could only stand to be around someone like me for short bursts of time. As if my boring normalness might rub off on him.

I knew I was being a jerk about it, but Cade was one of *them,* a freakishly beautiful, freakishly exclusive asshole, and it kind of pissed me off that the one person I actually liked in this hellhole of a school was now the girlfriend of its King Jackass. I wondered what the hell had happened with Kendall, anyway. I had a feeling I would soon find out.

Alli and I chatted on the way to first period, but it was nothing more than small talk: the weather, the dreaded upcoming semester exams, and Christmas shopping. Both of us seemed to be skirting what had happened over holiday break. I was dodging because I knew Alli didn't want to hear that my dad was a drunken bastard who found a way to ruin anything and everything around him. She didn't want to hear how the day we're supposed to give thanks had ended with him ranting again about my mother's mysterious disappearance, how my mother would have never left us. How he liked to use me as a punching bag because he was so drunk and angry that he didn't know what else to do. How he would finally pass out and then act like nothing had happened the next morning—that was, until he drank his fill and it started all over again. No, that wasn't really the usual how-was-your-holiday conversation, and I figured Alli could give it a miss. But I was growing more and more curious to hear how and why Alli had ended up with Cade Walker as her boyfriend.

As she and I took our seats she finally said, "Okay, Teagan. I can totally tell you're weirded out about the whole Cade thing."

Thank heavens! I'd started to think that she wasn't going to spill the story.

"No, not at all," I said. Damn. Sarcasm was dripping from my lips. Though I'd known I had to choose my words carefully, I hadn't been able to help myself.

Alli just smiled and sighed. "I knew you would react this way." She didn't say it like she was mad, though; more like she was trying to comfort me. I almost expected her to reach out and grab my hand like we were in a counseling session. Thankfully, she didn't. That would have been kind of creeper-esque.

"Okay, here's the deal. Cade was the mystery guy I've been talking about for the last few weeks. I know you think I'm crazy, Teagan, but he is really great and Kendall is totally out of the picture now. In fact, she left town and we never have to see her again."

What? Kendall left town? That was awesome.

About the rest, though...well, I wasn't sure what to think. I mean, it wasn't like Alli and I were lifelong friends or that who she dated was any of my business at all. My opinion shouldn't have even mattered. So, why was Alli sitting there looking at me like she needed my approval?

I wasn't getting any answers by sitting silent, so I finally responded with, "Well, that's the first good news I've heard in a long time. No more Kendall Stuart? Hallelujah! Praise the good Lord above."

Alli laughed, and the tension in the air seemed to lessen. A bit.

Okay, I decided, so what if my friend was dating Cade Walker, head jackass of the school and the king of Red Ridge's Beautiful People clique? A true friend would think something like, As long as she is happy, I am happy. And she was clearly trying to be a true friend to me. I tried my hand at being the same.

"I think it's great, Alli. You and Cade, I mean. You seem really happy."

She seemed to sense my wariness. "They aren't all bad, Teagan. Really, they aren't. I know how it seems, but some of them are really nice and normal."

I just gave her a doubting look. I couldn't help it.

"Seriously, Teagan! I mean it. Just sit with us at lunch today. You'll see. Things are different now. Promise."

Did she really expect me to sit with those people? Kendall might be gone, but Becca, Shari, and Cami were still around. I'd seen them gathered at Shari's locker earlier, so it was only a matter of time until one of them took over Kendall's reign as Queen Bitch. Kendall might have been the lead mean-girl, but they'd all had a hand in treating me like a worthless piece of shit when I moved here and the only thing I knew for sure was that I wasn't going to get involved with them. Ever. My dad might be crap, but he taught me one thing: A tiger can't change its stripes. That means people are who they are, and those people—Cade's people—were assholes.

Ms. Wallace came in to start class, which was something of a reprieve for me. I leaned over and whispered, "Thanks for the invite, but I have some work to do in the library during lunch. I promised my friend Sean that I would tutor him in French. Maybe some other time."

But I think we both knew that it would never happen.

*****

At lunchtime, I hurried down the crowded hall toward the library, as I really was supposed to meet Sean outside. He and I had been friends since the day I moved to Red Ridge, but only school friends, nothing more. He's one of the only guys I know who is capable of being just-friends with a girl. It's not that he's not boyfriend material or anything; I'd just never had those kinds of feelings for him. Plus, if he was the least bit interested in being more than a friend, he'd never done anything to show it. Which was just fine with me. That would only make things awkward.

Maybe he's gay. Either way, I count myself lucky to have a guy like him around.

He was standing outside the library, eyeing me with his typical thank-God-you're-here-to-save-me smile. As I walked up, he reinforced the sentiment.

"So, I'm flunking French. Like, really, *really* flunking."

Poor Sean. He'd never been the brightest crayon in the box, but he played football and soccer, and he was the lead in almost all the school's musicals so he could usually squeak by with a passing grade in his classes; it was kind of an unspoken rule to take it easy on the top athletes. Unfortunately for him, Ms. Jones our French teacher was relentless. She wouldn't hesitate to fail you by one measly point and smirk while she did it. Students lovingly referred to her as the devil incarnate.

I supposed I would have to try to pry him out of her grasp.

7.

Aiden

My fears of humiliation were unfounded. With all the attention I was getting, you would have thought I'd just saved the world from alien invaders who wanted to jab giant straws up our noses and suck out our brains. The attention didn't stop when I told everyone that I hadn't gotten hurt saving the world but skiing, either.

I was used to attention from the ladies, to be honest. Back in Houston, I pretty much had my choice of any girl I wanted, and trust me, I took full advantage. But since I got here, it's been different. Maybe this whole werewolf thing has thrown me off my game. But this level of attention was crazy.

It started as soon as I got out of the car that morning, and it hadn't stopped since. On the way to school I'd been feeling a little self-conscious because the bruises and cuts on my face hadn't healed completely. I was healing faster than a regular human, but I still looked like shit. Interestingly enough, the girls didn't seem to mind. Especially Becca, one of Kendall Stuart's old friends and one of the hotter, more popular girls from the werewolf enclave.

"Omigod! Aiden, your poor face!" she exclaimed as she walked up, interrupting Ashley, who was just about to give me her number—you know, just in case I needed anything. With Nurse Ashley brushed aside, Becca hugged me gently, careful not to hurt my shoulder.

"It's not as bad as it looks," I said.

"You can't lie to me, sweetie," she whispered. "I have a sixth sense about these things."

"No, really. I'm doing better. The doc gave me some painkillers, but they aren't too helpful. So, yeah, I guess it still hurts a little."

Becca smiled and took my arm. I didn't remember offering it, but what the hell, I just went along with her, not sure what else to do. But as we made our way down the school hallway I noticed scowls on the faces of the girls who had flirted with me earlier that morning. Not that I was interested in anyone at the moment, but I didn't want to hurt anyone's feelings. I'm not a total asshole.

I tried breaking free of Becca, but she wouldn't have it; the girl literally had a death grip on my arm. Which was strange. Up until this morning she'd just been a friend. I'd been fine with that, and from what I'd been able to tell, so was she. So, I couldn't help but wonder what had changed her mind. What had she heard or decided over break?

"This is me," she said, slowing to a stop and nodding to a science classroom. Then she stood on her toes and whispered in my ear, "Meet me after?" She didn't wait for a response, either. Turning, she walked into class like what she'd done was the most normal thing in the world, like I was hers for the taking.

I fought back annoyance. Was this all a way of marking her territory? Becca might as well have peed on my leg. For that matter, all the pack girls were acting strange. Why? What had they heard? The additional attention from them that had previously been kind of cool was now just annoying.

I didn't need Becca using me as arm candy, so I decided not to meet her after class and pretty much hid from her for the rest of the morning. She needed to realize that I didn't belong to anyone, especially not her.

Just before lunch, Alli tracked me down. "Hey, Ad, how you holding up?" Of course Cade was with her. Like always.

I was happy for my sister, really. It was just a bit weird. She didn't date anyone for almost a year, and then at seventeen years old she finds herself the happy victim of a werewolf thing and suddenly "mated for life" to my newly discovered biological half-brother? All of those things just sounded…wrong. Their relationship really messed with my head. I was trying to be supportive and— Well, I was trying at least not to vomit. Alli and Cade weren't blood-related in any way, but still. No matter how you spun the whole my-sister-is-dating-my-half-brother situation, it still sounded disgustingly incestuous.

"I hate to admit it," I told Alli, careful not to draw the attention of any students passing by, "but maybe you and Mom were right. I really want to be at home in bed."

Cade kind of chuckled and pulled me aside. He leaned in, making sure no one else could hear as he whispered, "A little overwhelming, isn't it?"

"What do you mean?" I asked.

"The attention," he said, looking around. He was trying not to laugh. "Sorry, man, I should have had Allison warn you that it would be like this. There's just something about girls and wounded animals. Females—wolf or human—they just can't seem to help themselves. It's like they can smell it on you." Then Cade did chuckle.

Really? They could smell it, or was he just screwing with me? Surely, that couldn't be true, but I didn't want to ask and sound like even more of a dumbass. God, I totally sucked at being a werewolf. If only I could run outside and go roll around in some mud, just in case. Maybe then I'd get some peace.

"Look, why don't you go find a quiet spot in the library to hide out for a while?" Cade offered. "Alli and I will bring you something to eat."

"Nah, I'm not hungry," I said. "But I think I will go hang in the library for a while. None of the girls will be in there. Thanks, man."

From where she stood, just a few feet away, my sister gave a weak little smile like she felt sorry for me then turned to leave with Cade. I started to walk away, myself, but stopped and made sure they wouldn't mind keeping my location a *complete* secret. The last thing I needed was to have them think Becca or any of the other girls had special clearance or anything. Nothing sounded better than being alone.

Walking to the library, I kept my head down and tried really hard not to bring any attention to myself. I could feel the girls' searing eyes on me as I passed, but I refused to look up, hoping they would all just keep going. Most did, but a few said hi. Some even touched my arm as they passed. I gave them each a small smile, just so as not to be a total ass, but otherwise I kept going, hoping none of them would actually follow me. I ducked into the bathroom to lose any who considered it.

I could feel myself relax as soon as I entered the library, turned and saw that I was still alone. The tension in my neck and back dissipated, and even my shoulder felt a bit better. The space here was warm, quiet, and nearly empty. All I needed now was a comfy couch and it would be lights out.

I walked over to a large old recliner and all but collapsed into it. Instead of taking my much needed nap, however, I reached into my backpack for my copy of *Their Eyes Were Watching God* that I needed to finish for Ms. Watson's class. While I usually enjoy reading, this book was work, and I hadn't gotten a chance over break so now I was way behind. I forced myself to stay awake and at least try to get some of it read, but only one chapter later my head popped up and I looked around, searching for…I wasn't quite sure what.

Suddenly, time seemed to freeze. Something overcame me, something so beautiful, so oddly familiar and overwhelming at the same time. It was a scent like no other, and it was pouring off of the girl who'd just sat down at one of the tables across from me.

8.

Teagan

Sean was making his way toward the comfy couch and chairs when I stopped him.

"Uh, I don't think so, Sean. Let's sit over here so we can actually get something done," I suggested as I led him to a nearby table. As we settled in I assured him, "No worries. We'll get you caught up. We always do. Did you go by your locker and get all of your missing assignments?"

Sean pulled a stack of papers from his binder and grinned.

"Nice," I said. "You do realize that in order to pass a class you have to turn *in* your work, don't you? No wonder you're 'like, really, really flunking.'"

His face fell. "I know. I just hate Ms. Jones. And I don't get her instructions, especially since she's speaking French the whole time. How the hell am I supposed to know what to do when I don't speak French?"

Suppressing a laugh, I said, *"L'immersion est la seule manière d'apprendre vraiment une langue."* In response, Sean made a huge production of huffing and shooting me dirty looks, so I reminded him, in English this time, that Ms. Jones firmly believed that immersion was the only way to truly learn a new language. Of course, her methodology didn't take into account those who might completely drown during the process. Like Sean. Poor Sean.

As I began separating his work and figuring out a battle plan, my peripheral vision caught someone looking my way. To my surprise, I glanced over to find one of Red Ridge's beautiful people staring at me. Aiden Wright, Alli's older brother.

I'd seen him before, actually. He was hard to miss, with his flawless, olive-toned complexion, his shiny (not purposely shiny, either, *naturally* shiny) almost-black hair, and those bright green eyes that a girl could so easily get lost in. We'd never talked, though. I'd always figured he thought himself better than me. All of that group did, with the exception of his sister.

He caught my eye and gave me a brazenly crooked smile that could make a girl weak in the knees. Unfortunately for him, it just looked cocky to me. He kind of reminded me of a peacock spreading out its feathers to attract a mate. Ha!

I quickly looked away, not wanting to give him the satisfaction of thinking he could make me fall in love with him, especially not with just one glance. He was beautiful and I was normal, but I was also smarter than the average bear. Ignoring the gawking eyes of Mr. Creeper, I went back to helping Sean organize his assignments. "So, which of these is the most important? Are any of these major grades?"

Sean scooted his chair a bit closer and leaned over to whisper in my ear. "Not to freak you out or anything, but that guy over there is staring at you. Isn't that Aiden Wright?"

I resisted the urge to look over again and hissed at Sean to just to ignore him. I wasn't interested in whatever game this guy was playing; I hadn't ever been part of his paparazzi and certainly didn't plan to join now, even if he was the sexiest guy to ever walk the halls of Red Ridge High. Not even if he was *People* magazine's Sexiest Man Alive.

Sean and I were just about to get down to business when Alli and Cade popped into the library carrying a tray of food. They were clearly on their way to Aiden, but Alli stopped at my table. "Hey, Teagan. How's the studying going?"

"We were just about to get started," I replied. Flipping through Sean's incomplete work again, I asked, "Hey, Sean, you know Alli and Cade, right?" I was noncommittal, though. The proximity of both Aiden and Cade was weirding me out. Too many beautiful people in one small area.

Sean shook his head and replied with a polite, "Hey."

"What's up with you guys?" I asked before Sean invited them to sit with us. I was praying they'd just go away.

They didn't. Instead, Alli waved Aiden over and said, "Hey, before you get to work, I want you to meet my brother. I don't think you two were ever introduced. Teagan, this is Aiden. Aiden, this is my friend Teagan."

As Alli made the introductions, her brother sauntered the short distance to our table. With a smug smile he reached out his hand to shake mine and said, "Hi, Teagan. It's nice to finally meet the girl my sister is always talking about."

His sister was always talking about me?

Our hands came together, and warmth spread throughout my entire body. I silently cussed at myself for letting him get to me; I was NOT going to be one of those girls. It didn't help matters that Aiden held on to my hand for a bit longer than a normal handshake should last. And as his eyes bored into mine, I felt a bit light-headed. Damn him!

Thankfully, Sean interrupted the moment. "I'm Sean. Nice to finally meet you, man. I've seen you around school."

Aiden let go of my hand to shake Sean's. Then he turned to thank Cade and Alli for his lunch before heading back to the recliner in which he'd been sitting. Alli and Cade followed and sat down on one of the nearby couches. They quietly chatted amongst themselves.

Relieved to have introductions over with, I went back to helping Sean. I could still feel Aiden glancing my way from time to time, though. What was he trying to accomplish? He had every girl in the school hanging all over him, especially today, so why did he seem so hell-bent on getting my attention?

Whatever the reason, it was making it quite difficult to stay focused. Sean and I didn't get all that much accomplished before the bell rang and lunch was over. Sean and I gathered our things, and I promised to help him some more after school. I silently reminded myself to walk straight toward the exit without looking back, but for some reason I couldn't explain if I tried, my body refused to listen to my brain. My head turned in Aiden's direction despite my best intentions, and yes, he was staring straight at me. Worse, it looked like he'd been waiting for me to turn his way.

9.

Peter

"Red Ridge, New Mexico. Hmmm...pretty," Peter said to himself as he drove through the small picturesque town. On the drive, he and his uncle had decided on a plan. Peter was to drive to Albuquerque. There he would set up a base. Albuquerque was central enough for him to investigate the missing persons and animal attacks without being noticed, and the last thing either he or Raymond wanted was to warn any no-good, murdering werewolves that anyone was on to them. At least, they didn't want it known until they were ready to act.

Peter pulled off the main road and into the parking lot of the local coffee shop, needing to stop and regroup his thoughts. It was beginning to snow again, and truth be told he didn't much like the idea of driving through the mountains in this kind of weather. In the nearly empty restaurant he placed an order and grabbed a copy of the local paper.

"Sir...you had the cream cheese Danish and the large coffee. Cream and sugar?" the waitress asked a short time later. Peter just smiled politely and took his order.

He'd just taken a bite from his Danish when he saw the headline in the paper: **LARGE BLACK WOLF FOUND MUTILATED**. It nearly caused him to choke. He dropped his snack and quickly read the article. The local authorities were looking for the feral animal that was responsible, but until they could locate and gain custody of the beast, they were urging residents to keep a watchful eye on their pets and small children. They were also asking residents to stay out of the woods at all costs, because whatever animal was responsible for the attack was most likely incredibly large, and by the looks of what it had done to the wolf, extremely hostile.

"Bingo," Peter said to himself. To the waitress he said, "Um…excuse me, miss. Could you recommend a hotel?"

Plans had changed. This was a good place to stick around and see what might show its ugly, furry face.

10.

Aiden

Teagan Rhodes.

Wow, just thinking her name sent chills down my arms. How was it possible I'd been going to this school for over a month and I'd just met this girl? Our high school wasn't even that big. How in the world had I missed her?

And that scent. Was it perfume? Body spray? Whatever it was, it was all-consuming, amazing, mind-blowing. I'd never smelled anything like it, and if I could have, I would have stripped down naked and rolled around in it. Creepy? Yes. I know it was, but I couldn't help myself. I hoped to God that the guy in the library wasn't her boyfriend. Sean, wasn't that his name? He looked nice enough. I would hate to have to break them up, and I would *have* to break them up if this connection was as strong as it seemed. I'd never felt anything like it.

"Earth to Aiden. The bell rang. You coming?" my sister asked.

What? Lost in my Teagan-filled thoughts, I hadn't even heard. I grabbed my backpack and the rest of my leftover lunch and prepared to follow Alli and Cade out of the library, but Teagan was leaving, too, so I stood there waiting, wanting her to look my way. *Willing* her to look my way. And…she did.

Yeah, sorry, Sean. There's definitely something there.

"So, that's the Teagan you're always talking about?" I asked Alli as we left the library. I hurried to catch up.

"Yeah, she's great," my sister replied. "She was like the only person that was nice to me when we first moved here, and she's sweet and really smart."

She kissed Cade goodbye, then, and I stood there waiting with my head turned, trying to ignore them. It was still too weird.

"Later, Aiden," Cade called with a wave.

"Yeah, thanks for the sandwich," I called out in return. I still didn't look at him. Then I got back to the subject I was most interested in: "How come you never told me Teagan was so hot, Alli?"

"Oh. So, you think she's hot?"

Please. The girl was definitely hot; there was no doubt about it. I gave my sister a look that said just that, even if Teagan was different from the girls I usually hung with, definitely unlike any of the pack girls. She was the complete opposite, actually. She had hair so light blonde that I'd bet it looked white in the sun. It was long and messy-looking, but in a sexy way. Her eyes were a dark blue—or maybe they only looked dark because her skin was so fair—and she was tiny, probably a foot shorter than me, but something about that tiny frame just made her even hotter. Alli looked like an Amazon standing next to her.

"Aiden? Damn, you've got it bad, huh?" my sister said, stopping in front of me and crossing her arms.

I guess I did have it bad, but I didn't know what to say. I didn't answer.

"Well, maybe I can put in a good word for you. I'll tell you what, let me think about it," she said.

I mimicked her stance, and with one raised eyebrow I stared her down. She'd *think* about it?

"All right, all right, you win!" She laughed.

"Alli, have I ever needed your help with the ladies?" I asked. "Come on, look at me."

But, something told me this time I would. Teagan had eyed me like I was crazy. Not only had I practically drooled all over her in the library, but my face was a mess. I could barely move my shoulder, and when I'd smiled at her I think my lip split back open. *Real smooth, Ad.*

Alli clearly felt the same. "You might actually need my help this time," she said. "Teagan is…not fond of the pack. She refers to them as 'The Beautiful People' and I think you're included in that. She's not really a fan. She's…had a run-in."

"What do you mean?" I asked.

"Teagan was new to the school last year, and let's just say Kendall didn't exactly roll out the welcome mat. Kendall's friends weren't any nicer, them or any of the people you hang with. Since then, Teagan's avoided that group like the plague."

"She's friends with you," I pointed out.

"True, but up until last week I really didn't hang with y'all much. Just carpooling to and from school with the pack," she reminded me.

I could feel that my cheeks were flushed, and I ground my teeth. "If that bitch Kendall ruined any chance I might have with Teagan, I swear to God I will hunt her down," I growled.

Alli's face fell. "Chill, Aiden. You okay? Maybe you should just skip the rest of the day and get some rest."

Only an idiot would fail to realize Kendall was still a touchy subject, and maybe Alli could tell I wasn't kidding about hunting her down; the look on my sister's face was truly worried. Truth be told, I wasn't sure what had come over me. Hearing that I might not have a chance with Teagan just because of some crazy-ass girl that didn't even go to the school anymore had made me see red. I wasn't usually so quick to get angry. I clearly wasn't acting myself.

Just as I'd decided that Alli was right and it would really be best for me to go home, I smelled her again. *Teagan.* She was close. Just down the hallway? I turned in time to see Sean give her a hug, and the two began an animated conversation just outside a classroom.

He saw me watching, and I swear he glared. Good, I thought. Be worried. Because there was no way I was leaving school now.

"I'm fine. Sorry, just got a little carried away," I assured Alli, not taking my eyes off Teagan. "I won't do anything crazy."

"Okay," she said. "Well, I'm glad you like her or think she's hot or whatever. She is pretty cool." A sudden notion seemed to occur. "Hey, maybe we can go on a double date! That would be so much fun."

"Now who's getting carried away?" I asked. But Alli had already started making plans. I could tell by her goofy grin.

"Come on," she said. "We're going to be late to class."

*****

Everything kind of went downhill after that. I'd thought I was in the clear, as I'd made it all the way through lunch without seeing Becca, but just as I was about to walk into my next class she grabbed me.

"Hey, baby, I missed you at lunch," she said, making a pouty little face. "Is someone not feeling good?"

"I'm fine," I told her, taking a step back. "Just a little tired. Nothing to worry about."

She took a step forward. "Do you want me to give you a ride home? Maybe we could stop for pizza or something."

"That's okay, really. I should probably go straight home. Besides, Alli drove today. Maybe another time?"

I said the last bit just to be nice, but Becca was really starting to piss me off. I'm sure every other guy in the school would have loved to have her so interested in them, but not me. She was just way too aggressive; I was seeing that more and more. What irritated me even more was that she hadn't paid me any mind before today. The only thing that made sense was if she'd found out that Marcus was my real father. She was probably hoping to slide into Kendall's place now that Kendall was gone, Queen of the Populars.

Becca didn't skip a beat. "Anytime," she squeaked. Then she gave me a hug that lasted way too long. I tried to pull away, but she just held on tighter. Her scent flooded my senses, and I knew right then that Teagan was the only one for me. It was her that I wanted, not Becca or anyone else. She just smelled…perfect.

Becca finally let me go, and I left so fast you would've thought the school was on fire. I didn't see her for the rest of the day, which was good, but I didn't see Teagan either.

Damn. I was going to have to find a way to get to know that girl.

11.

Teagan

I managed to avoid Aiden for the rest of the day, though to be honest I couldn't stop thinking about him. And I really *needed* to stop thinking about him. To help, I thought back to my first week of school here at Red Ridge, remembered that Aiden was now part of the clan that spent their days making everyone else feel inferior in every way. I reminded myself of the strange cultish behavior of the Beautiful People here and how the rest of us were mere mortals.

Of course, now that Kendall had mysteriously disappeared, things did seem a bit different. Alli didn't elaborate on where Kendall had gone, but I didn't care as long as she wasn't here. It had only been one day, but already it seemed the climate of the school had changed. The "common" people seemed more relaxed; happier even. I could be imagining it, but maybe, just maybe, things would be better now for good. Maybe she'd been the driving force behind the awfulness at this school. Or maybe I was just making excuses for having Aiden still on my mind.

I couldn't fall for a guy like Aiden. Not again. I'd made that mistake once before and I wouldn't be stupid enough to do it again. Alex Foster, AKA Asshole of the Universe, walked these halls like he could have any girl he wanted, and the fact was that he could. He was hot, a senior, and for some reason he set his sights on me when I first moved here. I fell right under his spell, like an idiot. He'd made all sorts of promises and talked sweet, and my mom had just run off...and as soon as he got what he wanted, he dumped me like yesterday's garbage. To make matters worse, he let the whole school know how he managed to get the new girl into bed and then broke up with me in the cafeteria the next day. No, I wouldn't fall for a guy like that again. Aiden Wright would have to find someone else to bat his eyes at.

*****

I rushed home after school to grab a quick bite before work. I walked in the door to find Dad holding pasta.

"Hey, hon. I'm making dinner so you can eat something good before work," he said, as if this were a completely normal occurrence.

Not that he'd never before attempted to play father of the year. Unfortunately, it usually ended with a drunken brawl at the local tavern or a drunken rage at home where he'd once again blame me for everything wrong in his life, especially Mom's disappearance. James, the good Dad, never lasted longer than a few days tops. Still, this felt different. Something was up.

Part of me wanted to tell him never to bother trying to make up for being a shitty father, but it was easier just to play along and ride it out. I put my purse and school bag down and went over to check out dinner. There wasn't much to say about it.

"Looks pretty good, huh?" Dad asked.

"Sure, it looks great. Thanks," I replied then pasted a fake smile on my face as I took a seat at the kitchen table. "I only have about twenty minutes before I need to leave, though."

Dad started making up our plates. "Well, about that. I had to put the Subaru in the shop, so I need to borrow your car. Before you say anything, I can drive you to work and then pick you up when you get off."

I'd known there was a catch. "Seriously, Dad? Where do you need to go?"

"Actually, to an AA meeting. I know I've been horrible lately, and I just want to make things better. Really, Teagan."

Asshole! Now I couldn't even be mad or say no, even though I knew his AA ventures never lasted. If I told him he couldn't borrow my car, I would look like the jerk. I'd look like I didn't want him to get sober.

I tried to keep the bitterness out of my voice. "Fine, but make sure you pick me up at nine o'clock. I have homework to do when I get home."

He put our plates on the table, and the little-boy-lost look on his face immediately made me feel guilty. How could he still manage to do that after all these years? But I knew exactly what he wanted to hear, so like a good little daughter I said, "And Dad, I'm really glad you are going to AA. I hope it helps."

"I'm really going to try this time. You'll see, Teagan. Things will be different from now on."

I wish I'd kept count of how many times I'd heard that.

I didn't reply. I was pretty sure that anything that came out of my mouth would be sarcasm-filled, which would only fuel the fire. Better to just let it go and eat. So, that's what we did. With only a few minutes to spare, Dad and I made our way out to the car and headed to the mall. Not much was said on the way besides small-talk and the usual parent-child pleasantries. Dad needed me to be nice, so I was, even though I knew how this brand-new-man thing would soon end. Been there, done that.

Dad pulled up to the entrance nearest Sephora and promised once more, "I'll be here at nine p.m. sharp."

I got out and said, "Okay, Dad. Be careful." Then I watched him drive away. I prayed his sobriety would at least last through the night.

12.

Peter

Peter grabbed a map from the lobby of the Red Ridge Motel. He'd been hoping for nicer accommodations, but his choices were limited in this cozy little town and he now knew he needed to be here. He was determined to learn every inch of the place before he left. Maybe he'd never hit Albuquerque after all. Something about this town was calling him. Uncle Raymond seemed to agree.

His room was small and dark, but at least it looked clean and Peter wasted no time. He unpacked and set up his bulletin board with all of the newspaper articles that he'd collected over the last few months. Once he was finished, he grabbed his coat, the town map and his laptop bag, and he headed to the diner down the street. He'd seen a sign bragging that they provided free Wi-Fi.

Within minutes, he was connected to the Internet and searching for anything new on werewolves: facts, sightings, fictions. He had done this so many times that finding new material was almost impossible, but he wasn't about to give up. His uncle wouldn't let him even if he wanted. Ray was always in Peter's head, encouraging him to continue the search, pushing him to avenge his death.

The diner turned out to be a great place to people-watch, too. It seemed a hotspot for the locals, and before long Peter had a good understanding of the Red Ridge population. Still, no one came in that fit the werewolf profile that he and his uncle had put together. Not perfectly at least.

Given their research, they'd decided werewolves in human form would all be well-built and athletic-looking. They'd imagined the bastards all stood on the taller side, too, even the women. Uncle Raymond was sure the wolves would have dark features, dark skin and hair, though Peter wasn't quite sure why. However, the most important part of the werewolf "profile" wouldn't be a guess for Peter. It was the eyes. Peter couldn't describe verbally what he was looking for, but he knew with absolute certainty that he'd know when he found it. He remembered that inhuman look as well as he remembered any other moment of his life. He remembered his uncle's killer, and he remembered those eyes.

Peter had a good feeling about this town. All he had to do was keep his wits about him and be ready to find what he was looking for. And he was always ready for that.

13.

Aiden

I tried to pry more information about Teagan out of Alli on the way home from school, but it turned out she didn't know that much. Not really. So much for them being really good friends. When I mentioned this, that she must be a pretty shitty friend if she didn't even know where Teagan lived, Alli stopped speaking to me completely. Of course, with the way I felt right then, that was probably a good thing. My shoulder was throbbing, and I needed sleep in the worst way.

I suddenly realized that I was being an ass and that I should probably apologize.

"Listen, Alli, I'm sorry," I said as we walked into the house. "You're not a shitty friend. I'm just tired and achy and taking it out on you. Forgive me?" I asked, giving her my best puppy dog eyes.

She turned and said, "I forgive you, Aiden. Actually, I think you're right. I must be a pretty crappy friend. I don't even know if she has a boyfriend or not. That's going change starting with this text." She started for the stairs with her phone in her hand. Glancing back she asked, "Hey, anything else you want to know about her?"

"Plenty. But I plan on finding it all out on my own," I said with a wink.

"Eww…you're a pig." But Alli laughed as she went upstairs.

"Who do you plan on getting to know?" my mom asked, appearing from the kitchen and scaring the hell out of me.

"Oh, hey, Mom. Just a girl," I answered.

She smiled encouragingly. I knew she wanted me to elaborate, but things were still weird between us. I didn't know what to say or how to act around her. I just needed space and time. Time away from her and Dad. And from Marcus. Definitely from Marcus.

"I'm going to go lie down before dinner, all right?" I asked.

The smile faded from her face. She just nodded and went back into the kitchen.

*****

I must have been really tired, because I fell asleep as soon as my head hit the pillow.

I hadn't been sleeping well because of the nightmares. I was still dreaming of the night Alli was kidnapped and Dylan nearly killed me. What bothered me most about it was how defenseless I'd been. If I wasn't such a weretard and could shift like any other teenage wolf, at least I could have tried to fight, but I'd just stood there stunned. That dream, that whole night, made me feel like such a loser. Like I wasn't the man I thought I was—which led to the second part of the nightmare, with me waking up not knowing who I am. This part was almost worse than nearly dying. I think that's why I was so angry with my parents. That they'd kept from me the secret of my biological father's identity made me feel the same way: like I don't know who I am anymore.

I wasn't in the best mood when I woke up for dinner, so the fact that my parents and I got into it wasn't a surprise. It was my fault, I know it was, but I just couldn't seem to control my temper. The situation was new to my parents. They'd always known what to say and do when Alli lost it, but not me. Before this week, I don't think I'd ever even raised my voice at the dinner table. It was a silly argument, too. They'd wanted to talk about our feelings, about how I was handling things, about what I really thought of my new father and brother, and…well, I didn't want to talk about it. Hell, I didn't even want to think about it. I just wanted to let it all go.

I walked out on dinner and went to my room, but I couldn't stay in the house so instead I changed and quickly headed back downstairs. Grabbing the keys to our car, I put them in my pocket.

"Where are you going?" my mom asked, and I could tell that she was worried.

I didn't want to make her any more upset, so I walked over and kissed her cheek. "Mom, I'm sorry. I just can't, okay?"

She nodded.

"I need some retail therapy," I said, using one of her favorite phrases. "I'm going shopping. I could use some new jeans anyway." Then I smiled, which clearly made her a little happier.

"Be careful and don't drive too fast," she said.

"I won't."

"I love you. You know that, don't you?"

"Of course I do," I said. And I did. "I won't be long, Mom," I promised.

Shopping had always been my thing. It calmed me down and helped me think. The guys back home used to make fun of me for it. They said I was a metrosexual, but my response was always the same. "I've got to look good for the ladies." And they couldn't argue because, well…I *had* done pretty well with the ladies because of it.

The local mall was nice and had some good stores, probably because Red Ridge was a ski town that got a lot of visitors during the season, but it wasn't all *that* big. Back in Houston I might have wandered around longer, but here I was able to get all my shopping done by eight forty-five, fifteen minutes to spare before closing— and that included stopping to chat with Luke, who was there buying his father a birthday present. I liked Luke, though he rarely hung out with anyone from the pack besides Gage, who'd apparently taken a leave of absence after the incident with Dylan and Kendall. I guessed Luke was kind of a loner. Lately, I could relate.

I was almost to the exit when I saw her. She was sitting on a bench by the exit, obviously waiting for her ride.

"Hey, Teagan," I said, walking up. She smelled so good, it was hard to keep my distance, but I didn't want to come off as a creeper.

"Oh. Hey, Aiden. How are you?" she asked.

She looked surprised to see me. A little unsettled, even. I cursed Kendall again and sat down on the bench next to her. "Did you just get off work?"

"Yeah," she said. "I'm just waiting for my dad. His car is in the shop, so he borrowed mine."

I became acutely aware of how close her leg was to mine. So close that if I moved even one little inch, we would be touching. "I can give you a lift if you want."

She was quiet for a while, and I hoped that she was considering. Finally she looked down at her watch and sighed, and I made up my mind.

"It's getting late. Let me give you a ride."

"Thanks," she said. "I don't know where he is. He isn't answering his phone. Maybe he just forgot."

Well, the reason didn't matter. All I knew was that I'd been extremely lucky.

"Come on," I said, "it will give us a chance to get to know each other a little better. My sister and you are good friends, so I guess I've got some catching up to do."

14.

Teagan

Most people would be worried if their dad didn't show up when he was supposed to, would be worried that something bad had happened, like a car accident or something. I just knew he'd fallen off the wagon. Already. His break hadn't even lasted a day this time. It hadn't even lasted beyond the meeting! I guess he'd decided to stop off at the local bar afterward—that was, if he'd even made it to AA in the first place. So typical. I wasn't even sure why I was surprised, let alone disappointed. I might tell myself over and over again how nothing would ever change, but I'd be lying if I didn't admit that a tiny part of me always hoped I was wrong. I suppose I'm kind of stupid that way.

I tried to hide my disappointment as I got into Aiden's car. I didn't want him thinking that my sour mood had anything to do with him, but I also couldn't help but wonder what the hell I was doing letting him take me home. I'd told myself to stay far, far away from him. He might be Alli's brother, but that didn't mean he was any better than the rest of the group he ran with.

He was being nice, though. Quite the opposite of the other beautiful people with whom I'd had dealings. Maybe he was more like Alli than the others.

He slid into the driver's seat of his Jetta and asked, "Where to?"

"Over by the elementary school on Almond Point. Just drive that way, and I'll show you where from there." I paused for a moment, trying to come up with something to add but finally decided on simply thanking him for the ride.

He looked in my direction. "My pleasure. I just hope your dad is okay."

What was I supposed to say to that? Oh, *him*? No worries. Dear ol' Dad's probably drunk as a skunk by now. Yeah, he likes to swing by Alcoholics Anonymous and then head out for a beer or twelve.

I settled for, "I'm sure he's fine. He probably just forgot. I should have reminded him."

We drove in silence for a few minutes. For some reason, I had the feeling that I was making Aiden uncomfortable. He kept shifting in his seat and fidgeting. The tension continued to grow. Finally I asked, "Are you feeling okay? Does your shoulder still hurt?"

"Actually, it hurts like a mother-fu—" He stopped mid-word, probably trying to be a gentleman and not to offend my virgin ears. When I smiled and assured him that I had heard worse, much worse, he just laughed and said, "Sorry. Just didn't want to sound like a jerk with a potty-mouth."

That, in turn, made me laugh. Potty-mouth? Really? That sounded like something a mother would say.

He seemed to sense my train of thought. "You're laughing at me for saying 'potty-mouth,' aren't you? Yeah, I said it. And I'll say it again. *Potty-mouth!*"

Giggling, I suddenly found myself unable to stop. Jeez, I probably sounded like one of his many ditzy female admires, but I couldn't help it. It had been far too long since I'd laughed like this. Something about Aiden just made me happy. Maybe it was that he was so gorgeous and had gone out of his way to take me home. Maybe it was—

No. I was going to ignore him, right? That's what I'd decided. Or did I not need to?

I caught my breath and said, "Yes, I'm most definitely laughing at you for saying 'potty-mouth.' Really? Is that what you call it?"

Aiden elbowed me in the arm, and the brief contact sent tingles through me. "As a matter of fact, that's exactly what I call it. You got a gosh-darn problem with that? Potty-mouth?"

I just started laughing again. How easily he seemed to take my mind off what I was sure to find at home.

"Stop laughing at me. I was trying to be polite," Aiden pointed out. But there was a glint of humor in his eye. "I didn't want you to think I had a—"

"A what? A potty-mouth?" I repeated, trying in vain to hold in my laughter.

Aiden took those gorgeous green eyes off the road and looked at me, I mean really *looked* at me. I became a quivering blob of melty goo, and right then I realized how dangerous this guy really was. I'd had no sense of it before when he was just a gorgeous heartthrob. This guy could easily steal my heart, no questions asked, and with my luck he'd crush it into a million pieces. I could not let that happen. As a matter of fact, I would not let that happen.

Suddenly, nothing seemed funny anymore. I looked away, and his eyes returned to the road. We were almost to my house, so I started calling out directions to get him the rest of the way there. I didn't speak other than to tell him to turn or stop, though, and at last we pulled onto my block.

"So." He turned and looked at me again, slowing the car as he did. His crooked smile let loose a rabble of butterflies in my stomach. "You never said. Do you have a problem with my potty-mouth?"

Trying to act as if his flirting had no effect, I replied, "Not one fucking bit."

His face registered surprise and then delight. It was his turn to laugh, and the sound infected me. We were soon both howling with laughter. It made no sense, but it felt great.

Aiden regained his composure first. "Well, good. I'm glad that's out of the way."

I pointed, knowing this had to end. His car was approaching the end of the street. "It's that house."

Aiden slowed, and my smile immediately faded. Right there on my front porch was my worst nightmare. It was my father, and his company was a case of beer. From the looks of it, he'd been out there awhile. Empty beer bottles littered the surrounding area. Guess he never made it to AA.

Before I could stop myself, I looked down at my lap and muttered, "Shit."

Aiden stopped the car. "Is everything okay?"

I turned toward the window, not wanting him to see my face. "Yeah. My house is up here on the right. Just pull up to the curb." I hadn't wanted him to see this, but it appeared as if I had no choice. The best I could hope for was that I could thank Aiden, hop out of the car and breeze through the front door without my dad giving me any trouble.

Unfortunately, that was exactly the opposite of what happened.

I turned to Aiden and said, "Thanks again for the ride. I'll see you at school." But before I made it out of the car, Aiden placed his hand over my arm.

"You sure you're okay?"

I could feel my face turning red and tears threatened my eyes. "Yeah, I'm okay, really." I knew he didn't believe me, but he let my arm go so I could get out of the car. I opened the door, got out, and shut it without looking back.

I hadn't made it to the sidewalk before my father started shouting. "What the hell do you think you're doing? Don't you know better than taking rides from strangers?" He tried to get out of his chair but stumbled a bit before he finally grabbed hold of a little side table for support.

"He's not a stranger, Dad, so settle down," I said, loud enough for him to hear me but quietly enough that Aiden couldn't. Aiden's car didn't pull away from the curb, though, which only meant one thing. He was watching.

Dad swayed and grabbed the porch rail. "I'm not going to settle down. Not when my slut daughter is showing up after being who knows where for hours doing who knows what!"

I made it to the porch before he had the chance to fall down the stairs. "Dad, I was at work. Remember? You were supposed to pick me up. Guess you got sidetracked, huh?" I pushed past him, anxious to get in the house. Aiden was still parked at the curb.

Dad staggered back to his chair instead of following me inside, but not before he yelled, "Just get your ass inside and clean up the kitchen. You left a huge mess in there, you stupid little tramp."

The door slammed behind me. I waited a few moments, sure I hadn't heard Aiden pull away from the curb. He was still out there, and all I could do was pray that he'd drive away. Before my father made things worse than they already were.

Was that even possible?

15.

Aiden

I sat, fists clenched around the steering wheel while I listened to every word her sorry excuse for a father said. It was one of those situations where there was no good outcome. If I just left and pretended that I hadn't heard anything, I would be up all night worrying, but if I charged in there, guns blazing, I got the definite feeling things would probably be worse for Teagan. I mean, she had to live with him, right? What I really wanted to do was find her and make sure she was okay.

Of course, the way the scene went down on the porch told me that this wasn't anything new. I could tell by her body language she wasn't shocked to see him sitting out there. Obviously things weren't right in the Rhodes home, but she'd seemed angry not afraid.

I had just put the car in reverse when he called her a tramp, which instantly made my vision narrow. All I could see was his hand on her arm, all I could hear was my blood pulsing in my ears. The decision was made. Something needed to be done.

Just as I opened the car door, I felt the first cramp. It was so bad I couldn't move. The pain was completely unbearable, like my insides were trying to fight their way out of me. I tried to breathe evenly to make the pain manageable, but that was useless so I closed my eyes and tried to imagine something else. Something calm, something pleasant. *Teagan.* She was the first thing that came to mind.

Teagan. She was sitting next to me in the car laughing at something I'd said. It was a big laugh, the kind of laugh that makes you join in and ends with everyone in happy tears. Slowly my breathing evened out, and then as quickly as it came, the pain was gone.

It killed me, but I had to leave. I was in no shape to play hero. Not only was I very close to keeling over from the pain, but if I shifted for my first time in front of Teagan, I'm guessing it wouldn't go over so well. As much as I wanted to shift, this wasn't the time or the place. I needed to get out of there.

Anyway, Teagan looked like she knew how to handle her father. But I swore to God right then and there that if I ever saw him lay a hand on her I would rip that arm off and beat him over the head with it.

I was barely back out on the highway before it happened again; searing pain coursed through my body and I was instantly drenched in sweat. This time it was worse. The cramp seemed to spread like wildfire. It started in my stomach just like before, but it quickly traveled to my chest, through my limbs and down to my fingers and toes. I thought I was dying for sure. Luckily, I was able to pull the car over before I crashed.

No matter how much air I sucked in, I still couldn't catch my breath. My lungs felt like they were on fire, but it didn't stop there. Before I knew it, my head was throbbing; being stabbed in the brain over and over with a fork would have hurt less.

I was just on the verge of passing out when the pain stopped, and what followed was painless but very freaking weird. I felt tingles deep under my skin like tiny hairs brushing up and out of me from the inside. Was this finally it? Would I finally be able to shift?

It all stopped as suddenly as it had begun, and though I waited for a few minutes, nothing else happened. I didn't know what the hell was wrong with me. Had it not been the werewolf thing? I'd been so sure it was, especially with the sensation of tiny hairs, but then why had it stopped?

Finally, I decided nothing more was going to happen and continued home. By the time I pulled into my driveway, everything was back to normal. At least, as normal as it ever was in my life after we moved to Red Ridge.

16.

Teagan

Unbelievable! I'm not sure I could have imagined a more embarrassing moment than the scene on my front porch. Things could have only been more humiliating if the whole neighborhood had been out to watch. Why couldn't Aiden have just driven off? No, he'd had to sit and watch the drama unfold. I was just glad he hadn't stuck around long enough to see my dad follow me inside.

Guess he got lonely out there on the porch, Dad, and when he came in I had the pleasure of witnessing his verbal abuse at its best. I think he managed to call me every name in the book before I safely escaped to my bedroom. Thank God for doors that lock.

I'd refused to give him the satisfaction of tears, but as soon as my door slammed the flash flood began. I cried about everything: my loser dad, my missing mother, my screwed-up existence. I also cried because I felt like such a fool. What would Aiden think of me now? Who would want to get involved with someone like this? Then I cried some more for having had those thoughts. Aiden wasn't even in my realm of boyfriend possibilities, anyway. Not for keeps. His kind didn't mix with mine. And even if they did, I'd most certainly seen my fate sealed with the night's little escapade.

It didn't matter. If Aiden Wright wouldn't want to be with someone like me, what did I care? I didn't want to be with someone like him—someone who judged everyone by their social standing, by their place in the pecking order, by their physical beauty. Someone who only worried about popularity, about the Who's Who of Red Ridge High. Tonight had been just a coincidence.

Happenstance. He'd just been acting nice by driving me home, but he probably wouldn't even look my way at school tomorrow.

Damn it! I hated myself for giving two shits whether he liked me or not. But I did. I also couldn't stand not knowing if he'd told Alli what had happened. She was one of the very best people at Red Ridge, and I hated the idea of having to be embarrassed around her.

It took me ten minutes just to figure out what to say, but finally I decided on playing it safe and texting her:

Teagan: Hey, Alli. Got ur text earlier. Was at work. Sorry I couldn't text back. But ur brother gave me a ride home tonight from work. Will you thank him for me?

Seconds later, she replied:

Alli: Sure will. BTW, that's what I texted u about. I get the feeling he likes you. Just in case...

Before I could stop myself, a smile spread across my face. My finger trembled as I tried to type a response. He liked me? Seriously, he liked me enough that his sister was commenting on it? I didn't know what to say, so I put the ball back in her court:

Teagan: Just in case what?

No answer. I sat on my bed, staring at my phone and willing it to chime. What was taking so damn long? Finally, her text came through, and I suddenly couldn't decide if I wanted to read it or not. What if she got my hopes up and was wrong? But a second later I decided that I couldn't possibly not look.

Alli: In case you're interested. Trust me. I know when Aiden's smitten. And his face practically lit up the room when he told me he got to drive you home. He just got back.

I had to ask. I had to know. It was really bothering me.

Teagan: Did he mention anything else?

Closing my eyes, I prayed that he hadn't told Alli about my dad.

My phone chimed again, and with my heart pounding and my fingers fumbling with the stupid little buttons, I rushed to read her response.

Alli: No, why? What happened?

Thankful, I replied quickly.

Teagan: Nothing. Just wondering. I'll see you at school tomorrow.

Unable to control myself, I felt another smile creep across my tear-and-mascara streaked face. I must have looked like I belonged in a loony bin. Was I crazy? I was certainly walking the line to think that someone like Aiden would be interested in someone like me, even if his super-nice sister thought it was a possibility. There were lines of girls waiting to steal his heart, and each of them was hotter, richer, and way less dysfunctional than me.

I again reminded myself that it was wrong to like someone like him; he wasn't the type I'd ever dreamed of. Aiden was part of a crowd that made others feel less than human, as if his clique was better than the rest of us. He'd fallen right into that crowd even though he was new to the school. That right there showed what kind of person he was. At least Alli had tried to keep her distance from them at first. Now it seemed we'd lost her to the pod people as well.

No, a little voice in my head promised, I didn't want to be with someone like him. But even as I heard the words, I knew I was lying to myself.

*****

The next morning I found myself carefully applying just the right amount of makeup, fixing my hair, and picking out one of my favorite outfits. No matter what excuse I gave, the truth was that I wanted to look good. I wanted Aiden to notice me. I'd have been kidding myself to think otherwise.

Luckily, Dad was passed out on the couch. I didn't want to wake up Sleeping Boozy, so I carefully stepped over the empty beer bottles on my way to the door. I made it safely without notice, but when I stealthily turned the knob, the door screeched. I went out cursing and praying he wouldn't wake up. With the door closed and locked, I hurried to the car for my grand escape. Too bad if I was leaving Dad without transportation. He deserved it. He'd just have to find another way to get to work.

I reached school a short time later. Walking into the commons, I looked around for someone—anyone—to talk to, not wanting to stand alone like a leper, especially not all fancied up. I especially didn't want to be alone if Aiden happened to pass by.

Just as I was about to casually meander over to a group of girls from my French class, Alli appeared. "Hey, Teagan. Don't you look amazing! Any reason in particular?" She gave me a knowing look.

With an awkward grin I glanced down at my outfit. "What? I don't look this amazing every day?"

Before Alli could grill me any further, *he* appeared as if from nowhere: Aiden. My pulse quickened, and I silently reminded myself not to fidget. I reminded myself of every reason why he and I were wrong for each other.

"Hey, Teagan. What's up?" He walked over and propped his elbow on Alli's shoulder. She gave him a glance that said she was humoring him.

Every synapse in my brain was firing off warnings for me to stay away from him, and Aiden's smug smirk made me want to turn and run the opposite direction. But my body was tingling with his nearness. Instead of taking off, I ignored my fears and said, "Not much. Oh, and thanks again for the ride."

Then there was silence. Aiden, Alli and I all just stood there. It was extremely awkward.

Aiden's eyes left mine and drifted to the floor. His smug look had vanished. "So…uh, I was wondering if—"

Before he could finish, a familiar voice rang out. "Hey, Aiden!"

I cringed inside, knowing Becca, the next in line for queen of the beautiful people, was headed our way. She sauntered up and hooked her arm through Aiden's as if claiming a prize. Just the sight of her made me want to gouge my eyes out.

Completely ignoring the rest of us, Becca announced, "So, Aiden. I was thinking I'd let you take me to the movies this weekend." Aiden just stood there, so she proceeded to paw all over him while waiting for a response. Finally she asked, "Well, what do you think?"

That stupid little voice in my head answered first. It screamed, *"Forget him, Teagan. He's out of your league. Forget he even exists!"*

Well, there was no way in Hades I was going to stand there and watch Aiden hook up with that hooch. I waved at Alli and made my escape.

17.

Aiden

No, no, no, no, no.

Why did this keep happening? There was no way in the world Teagan would ever go out with me if she thought I was also seeing Becca. Teagan wasn't like the other girls at this school, even the other human ones. Hell, I could barely get her to look at me. Most human girls stared longingly at our pack males or followed us around. It was kind of sad actually, but what could you do? Pheromones were pheromones, and wolves have those to spare.

As Alli excused herself for class, I removed Becca's arm from mine, looked her straight in her eye and said as gently as possible, "Listen, Becca, I thought we were just friends. I like being your friend, okay?"

"Sure, Ad, but there's nothing wrong with us being *really* friendly. Right? We don't need anything official to enjoy ourselves."

She must have learned that coyness from Kendall, but I knew exactly what she meant. Apparently, the girl had no pride. I was all for having a good time, but she moved a little too fast for even me. Besides, I had my sights set on someone else.

"Sorry, Becs. I'm not that kind of guy," I said with a small smile. "I kind of like 'official.'" Then, not sure what else to do and still save our pride, I walked away.

"We'll see about that Aiden Wright," she called as I made my escape. I wanted to turn and say, "Becca, you're acting like a tramp. I'm not now, nor will I ever be, interested." But I couldn't. It just wasn't in me—though I was seriously considering channeling my inner asshole if she did that shit in front of Teagan again. She clearly wasn't taking a hint.

Alli was waiting near my locker. "What the hell was that about?" she asked. She'd apparently witnessed Becca's offer.

I shrugged. "She's been weird since we got back."

"Well, you better set her straight, Aiden. At least, you should if you're interested in Teagan. You can't be acting like the man-whore we both know you are."

"Man-whore? Really?"

"Yes, man-whore. It's no secret, you know. And Teagan looked repulsed by the sight of you and Becca. You know she has issues with the people we hang with, anyway."

"No kidding," I said. "And, I'm trying. Avoiding Becca doesn't seem to be working. I don't know what else to do...short of just telling her to get lost."

"Well, I don't know Becca very well, but considering who her best friend was, you're probably going to have to do just that. I'd give it to her straight."

Alli was right. If I really wanted any chance with Teagan—and I did—I was going to have to make it clear to Becca that I was off-limits. It's not like I'd have been interested in her even if Teagan wasn't in the picture. She was way too overbearing. More and more she reminded me of Kendall.

I glanced up and down the hall, hoping to find Teagan and explain there was nothing going on between Becca and me, but I decided it was probably for the best when I didn't see her. Maybe I was being a bit premature. I mean, I didn't even know if she was interested.

Still, I wasn't going to take no for an answer.

*****

I didn't see either Teagan or Becca the rest of the day, but I was feeling a lot better by the time school let out. My shoulder was stronger, the cut on my face had gone from stinging to itching, which I suppose was only slightly better, and my mood was almost normal. The super quick healing confirmed I was a werewolf after all, despite my slow development, and that made me feel better, too.

I rode home from school with Alli and Cade, which looked to become a norm. This time, however, Alli started in on me about Teagan.

"Did you find her and explain? Are you going to ask her out? Can we go on a double date?"

I replied with the reasons Teagan should avoid me. Like, my inability to shoo away pretty girls, the new scar on my otherwise perfect face, and of course my incredible humility. Thankfully, Alli and Cade got me. Sarcasm has always been my way of dealing with things, but sometimes it backfires.

Regardless of my concerns, before we made it home Alli made me promise to ask Teagan out. Just as we pulled onto the estate I assured Alli I'd talk to her as soon as I had the opportunity.

"Well, you better be quick about it," my sister said, "or I might take matters into my own hands."

Strangely, Cade didn't weigh in. Normally he would have been super chatty and opinionated, but he didn't make a sound. I wanted to ask him if that was because Teagan was human and his father was outspokenly against human-werewolf relations, but before I could, the vehicle sitting in our driveway stole my attention. Speak of the devil.

To say that seeing Marcus's car at our house put a damper on my good mood was an understatement. It seemed to have an effect on all of us. I knew that Cade and Marcus were still on bad terms, and I didn't blame Cade for being angry with his father; knowing what Marcus originally said about my family and my little sister made him an ass in my book as well. I wondered what he would think of me wanting to date a human. For a moment I was nervous, but then I decided it didn't matter. Sooner or later I'd have to have a real conversation with my sperm donor, but I'd deal with that day when it came. In the meantime, Mom had been doing a good job running interference. She'd been telling Marcus that I was always sleeping.

He was on the porch before Alli even turned off the car. "Hey, kids, how was school?"

We all just kind of looked at each other. Who was going to speak first?

"It was good," Cade said, grabbing Alli's hand. It was hard to tell if he was doing it just to rub his relationship in his dad's face or because he and my sister could rarely keep their hands off each other these days. That "true mates" thing supposedly made you all crazy for one another, but still…when it's your sister, it's just gross.

Alli and Cade walked straight past Marcus and into our house, leaving me alone to face him. It's not that I was afraid of Marcus; I just wasn't sure what to say or how to act around him. There wasn't a rulebook lying around to inform me how someone is supposed to behave when he finds out his dad for the past seventeen years is not his real father—or how to behave around the new biological father. And was I *really* supposed to think of Marcus as my father now?

We stood there in silence for a moment as Alli and Cade made their escape. When the front door shut, Marcus finally spoke. "How are you healing, son?"

My first instinct was to tell him, "I'm not your son," and go inside, but considering I am his son and he is the pack's alpha, I figured that might be a bad idea.

"I'm feeling a little better, sir," I said, trying to keep it formal.

I could tell by his deflated expression that he'd been hoping for something a little less uptight. Instead of correcting me he said, "Come on, Aiden. Take a walk with me."

"Now?"

"Unless you'd rather go inside and have your mother lie to me again about you being asleep."

"Oh. Yeah. Sorry about that," I said.

So, I guess he knew I'd been avoiding him. That probably made me the biggest coward alive.

"Come on, just a short walk," he said, and he turned down our path to the sidewalk.

I put my backpack on the porch and zipped up my coat. The only thing I hated more than the cold weather here was having to walk through it. I really missed warm Houston winters.

"I know you haven't had much time to think about things like this, but have you considered the fact that you are my eldest son?" Marcus asked after we'd walked a short distance. I must have looked puzzled, because he continued without awaiting my reply. "You are my heir, which makes you the next alpha of this pack."

WTF! And I went from *Huh?* to *No fucking way!* in about two seconds.

"You're kidding, right?" I said with a laugh.

It apparently wasn't the reaction he was looking for, because irritation spread across his face. "This is no joke, Aiden. I hope you realize that I don't take this lightly."

"I don't either. But...really? Me, the alpha? I haven't even changed yet. I'm eighteen and have never turned. I just got my ass handed to me by a rogue werewolf and there was nothing I could do about it. No, Mr. Walker, Cade is your next Alpha. You've been prepping him for it his whole life."

"Cade disobeyed me," Marcus growled. "He put his wants and needs before the pack, Aiden. A true alpha wouldn't do that. The pack must always come first."

"Mr. Walker—" I started.

He stopped in mid-stride and turned. "Damn it, Aiden, I'm your father. At least call me Marcus," he snapped.

At that point, I was getting pissed. I didn't tolerate being yelled at by anyone. I tried to keep in mind that: 1) he was my alpha, 2) he was technically my father, and 3) I'm supposed to respect my elders, but it was really, really hard not to say what was really on my mind.

I took a few short breaths before I replied. "Okay, Marcus. Even if I wanted to be the alpha, I don't think the pack would ever allow it. They know Cade. They consider him family. We're still new here. Do you really believe that everyone will just accept me because I'm yours?"

My words seemed make him think. He paced back and forth a few times before asking me to simply give the possibility some thought. I told him I would, but deep down inside I knew that me running this pack was a joke. I was eighteen and therefore technically should have been making the transition to alpha already, if I was going to take over. No one here would accept me as a leader when I hadn't even figured out how to shift.

18.

Peter

As the pair walked into the coffee shop, Peter almost dropped his drink in his lap. Breathtaking beauties, they had just the right builds, the right faces, and the right haughty mannerisms. He could hardly believe his eyes. They were only a few years younger than himself, but the girls met ten out of ten points on his were-points system. For the second time since arriving in Red Ridge, Peter felt absolutely positive that he was in the right place.

The two girls were soon ready to leave with their lattes, so Peter gathered his things. He couldn't let them out of his sight. He had a lot to learn, and it all started with finding out where they were going. He had to find the network.

He followed the girls out of the coffee shop and stayed close behind them as they walked through the town center. He waited as they went into a small boutique store, and he watched through the front windows as they tried on hats, sunglasses and frilly scarves. While they played around, giggling at how silly they looked, he took the opportunity to snap a few pictures of them with his phone.

"I'm sure *they* don't have any trouble luring in prey," Peter said to himself as he viewed the photos. The pair would have been gorgeous if he didn't know they were bloodthirsty animals. But he did know, and Peter immediately chastised himself. Their attractive facades would not blind him.

"Remember Peter, they're not human." The voice of his uncle rang in his head. His uncle's voice kept him strong. Motivated. It was Raymond's voice that had helped him survive all those years in

isolation, survive the abuse of the doctors and guards who'd made his life a living hell, and the voice was a constant reminder of why he'd dedicated his life to exposing werewolves. Because they were evil. Because they could hide in plain sight and still do great harm.

Lost in the memory of his uncle and the night Raymond was murdered, Peter almost missed the two were-girls as they walked out of the boutique. But it was obvious the pair was in no hurry. Just out window-shopping, they continued popping into store after store. Peter soon began to feel he was wasting his time. He wanted to know their leaders, he wanted to know their base of operations. He didn't care if they preferred beanies or berets. He didn't have time for this nonsense.

Giving it one last hour, Peter followed them into the local bookstore. He pretended to read a book on the same shelf that they were scanning, and surprisingly, one of the girls smiled seductively at him and said, "Hey, there."

Peter's blood ran cold. He plastered his best smile across his face and countered with, "Hey, yourself."

The second girl giggled, grabbed her friend's arm and said, "Come on, Becca. Let's get out of here."

Becca smiled at Peter again, and then they were walking away. He knew they were talking about him as they did.

Peter went back to fake reading for a moment, just long enough for the girls to head toward the door. They exited, and Peter followed. Just as he opened the door, though, he saw the talkative one toss her latte into the trashcan just outside. A light bulb went off. *DNA.* He could get a DNA sample from her cup.

Hurrying to the trashcan, he found the girl's cup, light pink lip gloss marking the rim. Excitement boiled through him.

"I would give anything for a Ziploc bag right now," he said to his uncle. His uncle didn't respond, and at that point it occurred to Peter he had no idea what to do next. It wasn't like he carried a DNA kit around. He didn't even know how to get his hands on something like that. So he headed back to his motel room feeling like a kid at Christmas waiting to play with a new toy that didn't have any batteries.

Just as he arrived, he had another thought—or maybe it was his uncle whispering in his ear. He opened his laptop, double-clicked on the Internet icon and Googled "home DNA kits."

Score!

19.

Teagan

After the incident with Becca, I managed to successfully dodge Aiden and his harem for a few days. Alli didn't mention him in class, so I wasn't sure what to think about what had happened, but that was fine with me upon later reflection. Then, just as I was leaving school on Friday afternoon she stopped me. Her brother stood a few feet away.

I refused to look his way. I knew if I did, all my efforts to convince myself to stay away from him would be lost. He had that effect on me, just like he had that effect on a lot of other girls. I didn't want to be one in a long line of admirers. I had to keep my distance or I had a desperate feeling I might become another one of his mindless, love-struck groupies.

"Hey, Teagan. I was thinking we could get some work done on our economics project at my house tonight," Alli said.

Her house? I was caught completely off guard. "Uh, I thought we were going to meet at the library or something. Tomorrow."

Alli paused, and I could swear she glanced over at Aiden. "Yeah, well, uh…don't you think we'd be more comfortable at my house? I don't want to get stuck in that stuffy old library for hours. Besides, we'll have snacks and stuff, and you've never been to my house. It will be fun."

Something told me there was no way out of this, and we certainly couldn't meet at my house for "snacks and stuff," so I reluctantly agreed. I would most likely regret the decision, but who knew, maybe Aiden wouldn't even be home. We did have to get the project done.

"Great! How about six o'clock? I'll text you directions," Alli said.

She walked off toward Cade, then, and Aiden did too. But he caught my eye and smiled before he went.

Damn him for smiling. This would be so much easier if he would just ignore me in return.

*****

It was six on the dot as I drove down the winding dirt road that supposedly led to Alli's house. For a moment I thought that I'd been the butt of some practical joke. Who the hell would live way out here in the woods? But I continued down the path convinced that Alli was not Kendall. She wasn't like the rest of the Beautiful People; she wouldn't lead me out to no-man's land if she didn't actually live there. Then the road narrowed, and I was literally driving on a dirt path with gigantic trees and brush on each side. Shit. Maybe this was a prank. I was going to get lost and die out here.

I pressed my foot down on the brake and brought the car to a stop. Searching for my cell phone, I prayed that I could actually get a signal. Surprisingly enough, I had four solid bars. What were the odds of that out here in the boonies? But I wasn't going any further until I was sure there was a house on the other end of the path, so I texted Alli:

Teagan: Hey, I'm hoping u forgot to mention that u live in the woods. On a dirt path. Worried I'm lost.

Seconds later, my phone chimed.

Alli: Ur going the right way. I told u it was kinda out of the way. No worries. Keep driving.

Still unsure if I was crazy for believing Alli, I put my car in drive and kept going.

Only a minute or so down the path I breathed a sigh of relief. The whole area opened up, and right in front of me lay the most picturesque scene imaginable. I stopped my car and stared. In the middle of a vast open area was a small lake, and lining its banks, a ring of massive houses. It was like a hidden neighborhood in the middle of nowhere. Totally off the grid.

A hidden compound, eh? Again I was reminded of a cult. A beautiful people cult.

As I contemplated turning around, my cell chimed again.

Alli: R u coming? I see you. Drive around to the left. I'll meet u outside.

Too late to turn back now. Hesitantly pressing the gas, I turned my car to the left and drove slowly down the curved road.

Alli's house could've had its own zip code, it was that huge. Her life was *so* different from mine. She stood outside and waved her arm over her head to get my attention. I pulled my car into her long driveway and got out.

She led me to the front door and said, "So...whatcha think? A little weird, right?" She almost sounded embarrassed.

Oh, thank God. She knew this was strange.

Relieved, I replied, "Well, a little. Shocking is more like it." Then I laughed to soften my words. "What *is* this place?"

"The estate. All of the adults here work at a pretty profitable company together, so the company built this for their families. Kinda like a perk, I guess. That's why Cade and all of his friends seem so tight. They all grew up together, though they don't broadcast the fact. Aiden and me are the new kids on the block, but it's not so bad."

So, the beautiful people all came from their own little community that didn't discuss itself. Yeah, that was definitely odd, but I supposed royalty has always had a way of protecting itself. And I didn't have much more time to think about it, because Alli opened her front door and my jaw immediately hit the floor.

My God. This wasn't a house. It was a mansion. Something you'd expect to see on *MTV Cribs*.

Alli shut the door behind us and laughed. "I know it's a bit much, but it comes with the job when you work for the company."

"It's beautiful, Alli," I whispered. "I can't believe you live here."

Alli showed me through a kitchen built for a top-tier chef and then up the stairs to the second floor. There didn't appear to be anyone else home. I started to ask where Aiden was but decided against it. I didn't want her asking any questions in return that I wasn't ready to answer.

We walked into her bedroom, and again I was in awe. It was literally as big as my whole house. *Thank God I didn't bring her home with me,* I found myself thinking. This place was unbelievable.

Alli plopped down on some comfy chairs by her window. "So...where should we start?"

The econ assignment was to make a PowerPoint presentation or a video, and also to make a poster. I made my way over to the chairs, trying to pretend like being in this monstrosity of a bedroom was no big deal and said, "How about an outline?"

*****

It was soon after seven. Alli and I were working hard on our project, but the end was nowhere in sight. She stood up and stretched, looked at her watch and said, "We need to eat."

She was right. I hadn't realized I was even hungry, but I was.

Together we made our way downstairs, and I could hear someone rustling around in the kitchen. Part of me hoped it wasn't Aiden. The other part of me prayed it was.

Just before we entered the kitchen a gorgeous woman popped her head around the corner. She looked like she belonged on a commercial for some expensive facial cleanser. She was absolutely flawless, just like Alli but older.

"Oh, Alli, you didn't mention you had a friend over. I was wondering whose car that was."

"Sorry, Mom. This is Teagan. We're working on a project for school. Is there anything to eat? We're starved."

As if on cue, the back door swung open. In walked a man holding several pizzas. "Dinner is served," he announced. His eyes reached me. A look of uncertainty washed across his face; then, just like that it disappeared. He smiled brightly and asked, "Alli? Who's your friend?"

Her father, I assumed. He reached out his hand and introduced himself to me as Paul. Alli's mother was equally polite, but as we grabbed a box of pizza and some Cokes to take upstairs, Alli's mom stopped her.

"Alli, can we talk to you for a minute?"

Alli turned to me and said, "I'll meet you upstairs in just a minute, 'kay?"

I nodded my head. Balancing the pizza box, I made my way toward the stairs but couldn't help pausing when I heard my name. Before I knew what I was doing, I'd moved back closer to the kitchen to listen.

"I'm not sure that's a good idea, hon." Mrs. Wright was speaking.

"What's the big deal? It's just one night. And we're doing homework."

Mr. Wright: "I know, honey, but what if Marcus finds out?"

Marcus? Who the hell was Marcus?

"Exactly," Alli's mom said. "I'm not sure how he'd feel about her being here."

"Come on, this is stupid." Alli again. "Are you really saying I can't have any other friends besides the pack?

The pack?

"Of course not. But let's keep their visits to a minimum. Just tonight, okay? Let's not risk drawing attention to—"

I thought I heard Alli coming my way, so I scurried up the stairs and prayed I'd successfully turned the corner before she saw me. I grabbed a piece of pizza and pretended I'd been up in her room all along.

If she was suspicious, it didn't show. Alli grabbed a slice, too, and after swallowing a massive bite announced, "So, my mom said you can stay overnight if you want. Then we can get more done."

I wasn't sure what to think. It didn't sound like her parents wanted me here. In fact, it kind of sounded like they were worried they'd get in trouble. Red flags were flying high, but I nonetheless found myself saying, "Sure, why not?" What was I thinking? I guess that it was nice to have a friend and feel normal.

We finished off most of the pizza and went back to work. With our PowerPoint presentation well on its way, I started on the poster. Alli and I chatted as we worked, and I wanted desperately to ask about Marcus and "the pack" but finally decided I shouldn't. I also wanted to ask about Aiden. I needed to keep my mind on the task at hand. Honestly, though, I couldn't have cared less about stupid supply and demand.

After an hour and a half of more work, we still had quite a bit to do but we agreed that it was time to take another break. It was after nine. Alli ran downstairs to grab something to drink, but I stayed upstairs, not wanting to see her parents again. Once was enough. Instead I took the opportunity to stretch my legs and wandered over to take a closer look at the framed pictures on Alli's bookcase. They were all of her family, mostly snaps from when she and Aiden were young. The two kids had been both perfect; it almost looked as if the photos had come with the frames. Even when they were ten, they'd both been adorable. What had happened to their awkward stage? It was like they'd come out of the womb ready to pose for a camera.

I was just about to grab a framed picture of Aiden in a baseball uniform for a closer look when there came a loud knock at the door. Before I could say anything, the door swung open and there was he was. Aiden.

Shirtless.

"Hey, Alli, would you—" He stopped mid-sentence.

Holy mother of God. My hands of their own volition flew up to my mouth to cover my gasp. Bright red scars covered his shoulder and part of his chest. They looked horribly painful but...well, the rest of him was perfect. His sweat pants hung loosely on his hips, and it only took a moment for my eyes to drift down those wonderfully chiseled abs.

My God, could he be any more gorgeous? It was like looking at Adonis himself.

He noticed me staring—gawking was more like it—and he covered the scars with the t-shirt in his hand. "Oh, sorry. It's not as bad as it looks, really."

I didn't know what to say, not that my mouth was cooperating. Neither were my eyes, since I couldn't take them off him. Aiden. Unbelievably hot Aiden. Shirtless. This was so not good.

I must have looked like a complete fool just standing there speechless, and he finally broke the silence. For a moment he got a weird look in his eye and I was afraid he was going to mention what had happened when he dropped me off, but then the look changed. He said, "Sorry to barge in on you, Teagan. I thought you'd gone home already. I was looking for Alli."

He stood there, half in, half out of the room, half-naked, waiting for me to respond, but my brain was betraying me.

Say something, you idiot!

"Uh…Alli went downstairs to get some Cokes," I finally managed.

"Oh." Aiden looked down at the tube of ointment in his hand. His eyes wandered around the room as if still waiting for me to say something, but I didn't know what, so I just continued to stand there, completely wordless. Oddly enough, he just stood there too.

Maybe he didn't know what to say, either. Strange, him being such a ladies' man, but he kind of seemed nervous. He shifted his weight from foot to foot, and I couldn't figure out if he was about to take off in the other direction or come further inside the bedroom.

Get a grip, Rhodes. You can handle this. He's just a guy. A guy that happens to be extremely hot and shirtless. Chill out and speak.

Trying my best to act as if his half-naked presence was having no effect, I said, "Do you need some help with that?" I pointed to the medicine in his hand.

Shit. What had I just asked? *Do you need some help with that?* Really? I could barely look at him without turning to mush, and I was offering to rub ointment on him?

He looked down at the tube. "Sure—if you don't mind. I'd do it myself, but I can't reach my back."

I could have sworn he blushed as he walked forward, but surely it was my imagination. Guys like Aiden Wright didn't blush. Not at girls like me. Did they?

He sat down on the bed. As I walked over to him, it was suddenly me that was blushing; that I was sure of. Out of nowhere I felt flushed all over, as if the temperature in the room had skyrocketed. Damn it. Where the hell was Alli?

With shaking hands I took the ointment and prayed he couldn't feel the panic welling up inside me. When his fingers grazed mine, I was overcome by Aiden's nearness, and my legs felt as though they might give out at any moment. What the hell was wrong with me? *Get it together, Rhodes,* I told myself.

Doing my best to ignore my racing pulse and trembling hands, I squeezed out some of the medicine. It appeared to be antibiotic cream, though I'd never seen anything exactly like it. Spreading it over my fingers, I took a deep breath and gently placed my hand on his back.

When he shuddered, I swiftly tore my hand away. "Omigod, I'm sorry! Did I hurt you?" I was feeling a bit lightheaded.

Aiden inhaled sharply, and I watched his entire torso rise and fall. Then he replied, "Uh, no. It's okay. Just cold, I guess. Go ahead. I'm fine, really."

But he didn't sound fine. There was a hitch in his voice, and he was breathing funny. Even so, I tried again, even more gently. I placed my hand on his back and began to spread the ointment over the red and puckered areas, all while trying to slow my racing pulse before my heart gave out.

I rubbed the medicine over his shoulder. Aiden's breathing slowed, and he closed his eyes. Suddenly, though, he jumped up off the bed, knocking the ointment right out of my hand, and when we both leaned down to grab it, my cheek brushed his lips. For a moment, everything moved in slow motion.

All too soon, time sped up and there we stood, face to face, eye to eye. I opened my mouth to say something, but once again I couldn't find the words. Aiden just backed up a bit.

"Thanks, Teagan," he said. His voice was husky. "I can get the rest."

He rushed out of the room before I could respond.

20.

Aiden

Breathe, goddammit.

What in the world was wrong with me? This was so embarrassing. I stood outside of Alli's room with my forehead resting on the closed door trying to calm myself down. First I'd been embarrassed to be shirtless, then I'd remembered that terrible scene with her father, then I'd been completely swept away by Teagan's offer to rub the medicine on me. The feel of her hands had been—

Alli came around the corner smiling. "Were you just in there with Teagan?"

I took a deep breath and glared. "I walked in there to get you to help me and nearly gave her a heart attack." I pointed to my shoulder.

I knew she still blamed herself for what had happened to me, and Alli's smile faded as she saw my scars. "It actually looks way better, Ad. Did you need me to put that on your back?"

I looked down at the medicine in my hand and felt flushed all over again. The residual memory of Teagan's soft hands on my skin was torture. Sweet torture.

"No thanks," I managed. "Teagan helped me out."

Alli smiled again. "I bet she did. You know, I think you're blushing." She opened the door and walked into her room.

I fought to breathe. This was crazy. I'd never met a girl that made me act like such an ass. I couldn't even put a sentence together when I was alone with her. I mean, the last few minutes should have been the perfect opportunity. I liked her. I'd been alone in a bedroom with her. I was already half naked, and she'd obviously noticed. I'd had so many opportunities to make a move, but no. I'd frozen, stumbled over my words and then bolted like the room was on fire.

One more humiliating encounter with Teagan and I knew I'd have to hand in my man card, so I decided to avoid the ladies for the rest of the evening. Instead I tried to distract myself with video games and movies, but not even a Godfather marathon took my mind off the girl in the next room. When had I become so pathetic? Oh yeah, it was as soon as her hands touched my skin.

I could still feel them. She'd been so careful, so tentative—and I was glad she had been, because with the way her touch warmed my skin I would have caught on fire if she hadn't.

It was probably a bad idea to date her. I knew that, given Marcus's recent comments and the way the pack felt about humans, so I stayed awake most of the night trying to figure out how to get her out of my mind. I considered avoiding her for the rest of the year or going one step better, giving in and going out with Becca or one of the other pack girls at school, but I just couldn't bring myself to consider anyone else. Finally I decided the only way out of this obsession was to give in to it completely. I was going to have to find a way to get Teagan to go out with me—and to keep it from Marcus if that became necessary.

Of course, to have any chance with Teagan I first had to have another conversation with her.

I shook my head, confused. The day I'd driven her home from the mall I'd been my cool, calm self. I'd smiled. She'd smiled. I'd made her laugh. I'd been comfortable around her then, but now I was a fucking mess. What had happened to me?

Another thought suddenly took me: If I couldn't even deal with her hands on my back, what was going to happen when I got to touch her the way I really wanted?

*****

The next morning I knew what I needed to do. It was now or never. I was going to find a way to ask her out.

I was feeling like my old self as I made my way downstairs. I was charming to the point of irresistible, or at least that was the way it had always seemed with girls. Teagan would have no choice but to gleefully accept when I asked her out. Well, that was what I kept telling myself. I'd been acting like a wuss.

My ego deflated as soon as I walked into the kitchen. Teagan, Mom, Dad, and Alli were all sitting around the breakfast bar eating pancakes and laughing, and as soon as I saw her there, so comfortable with my family, all the confidence I'd built up flew out the window. Was it wrong that I found her so sexy sitting there in my sister's pajamas? She didn't have any makeup on. Her hair was pulled back in a ponytail, and still she was the most beautiful girl I had ever seen.

Shit. This was bad. I looked like an idiot just standing there staring at her.

Thankfully, Dad snapped me out of my trance. "Look who's up!" he called out. Then he glanced from me to Teagan and said, "And on a Saturday. We should have you over more often if it's going to get this lazybones out of bed before noon."

Completely mortified, I faked a smile at my dad, who gave Teagan an exaggerated wink. She smiled at my dad and then me, but I could tell the expression wasn't genuine. Still, there was a glint in her eye that told me what I needed to know: What had happened last night between us, whatever it was, definitely changed things. Better, this attraction wasn't just one-sided. She felt it too.

I made myself a plate of pancakes and went to the only barstool available, which was directly across from Teagan. Eating became impossible. From time to time our eyes would accidently meet; I would attempt to smile at her and she would look away. But it was there. The chemistry between us was undeniable, and I wouldn't have been surprised if everyone in the room felt it.

We sat there a little while after breakfast, talking and laughing with the folks, but before I could find a way to get her alone, Teagan said she needed to get home. A few minutes later I found myself standing on the porch watching her drive away.

"Why didn't you ask her out?" Alli demanded when Teagan was gone.

I didn't want to admit I couldn't work up the nerve. I mean, she'd been there all night. All I'd needed to do was knock on Alli's door. I'd asked out tons of girls, and never once had I been nervous. Not like with Teagan. She just…did something to me.

The truth spilled out despite my resolve. "I don't know. I just get so nervous around her."

As soon as the words left my lips I regretted saying them. My sister shot me a you're-such-a-wimp look, and I knew I'd never live it down.

Ugh. Why did I freak out every time I'm around this girl? I'd never had this problem before.

21.

Peter

It was revolting how long it took to get DNA results, and nothing else he'd done had proven as productive as the day following those two teenage girls. Depressed, Peter wandered over to Red Ridge's main watering hole.

It was obvious as he entered that this was an establishment that catered to the locals and not ski enthusiasts. All conversation ceased as he shut the door and approached the bar. He really wanted a frozen margarita, but after a quick look around he settled on a beer.

"Don't be discouraged, Peter. I still have a good feeling about this town. You saw them. They are here," his uncle said.

Peter hated when Ray spoke to him in public. It was hard to ignore his uncle and not answer back, and the last thing he needed right now was for everyone in the bar to think him crazy. Peter did listen, though. His uncle always gave him good advice.

Once again the door opened, and this time Peter joined the locals in turning to see who it was. The man must have been a regular, because the patrons just nodded and went back to their conversations.

"Mind if I sit here?" the man asked Peter.

"Sure, go ahead," Peter said.

Uncle Raymond wasted no time in making a suggestion. "Now's our chance. Get to know him, Peter. See what you can find out."

Always obedient, Peter did as he was told. He introduced himself to man next to him, and soon the two were deep in conversation. The man's name was James Rhodes, and he had lived in Red Ridge for a little over a year.

"So, you didn't tell me what brings you here, Pete. The skiing?"

Peter thought first about lying, but after a moment he decided the man might just be the ally he so desperately needed. "Actually, James, I'm investigating some missing-persons cases and animal attacks that have been reported in the area."

The man grew quiet. He looked lost in thought, so Peter decided to wait. They sat in silence for awhile. Finally the man said, "I told my daughter that I would go to an AA meeting today."

The admission had come out of nowhere, so Peter just sat, unsure of what to say. After a few more seconds of silence, James confessed to having been a disappointment to his daughter ever since his wife disappeared.

A disappeared wife? Peter's heart beat faster. This just might be his in.

He was figuring out how best to broach his topic when James spoke once more. "Peter...I would like to help you with your cases, if you will allow me. Maybe by helping you I can find out what happened to my Janie."

Peter smiled. Finding believers might turn out easier than he'd expected.

Without hesitation he replied, "I tell you what, James. I'll go to AA with you tomorrow and then we'll get started with my case. How does *that* sound? Then we can make your daughter happy and your Janie happy too."

A few hours later, as Peter walked back to his motel room, he gave himself a big pat on the back. He'd accomplished more today than he'd expected. Everything was falling into place. It had definitely been a good day.

22.

Teagan

Waking up Monday morning, I found my mind on one thing and one thing only: Aiden. And while I wished more than anything to put him out of my thoughts, time and time again he sneaked back in.

I couldn't stop thinking about our moment together in Alli's room. It was all so confusing. What had happened in there? No matter how many times I replayed the scene in my head, I still couldn't decide if it was just me or if Aiden had felt something too. But, I needed to stay away from him. For my own sake. There was only one way things would end, and that was with complete and utter heartbreak.

I tried to convince myself that I didn't want him to want me. I didn't want to be with him, didn't want to kiss his perfect lips, didn't want to run my fingers through his shiny, dark hair. But I couldn't stop imagining what might have happened that night had he not run off. It's not like I hadn't been alone in a bedroom with a guy before, but with Aiden it felt different.

To make things even more confusing, I'd had to sit in the same room with him during breakfast the next morning. He'd looked like he wanted to say something, but there hadn't been a chance with everyone around. Now it was Monday. I knew I'd see him at school.

I decided on a fitted t-shirt, jeans, and Converse as I was getting ready. Then, with just a touch of makeup and a messy ponytail I was out the door. I was going for understated. I didn't want Aiden to think I'd gotten all dolled up for him. I was supposed to not want him. Supposed to not care.

My damn brain just needed to inform my pathetic heart of that fact.

*****

I noticed him right away as I walked into school. He stood on the stairs at the main entrance, completely surrounded by a mob of eligible and even a few supposedly not-so-eligible girls. The scene made me want to throw up. How could I even be on his radar when half the junior and senior classes were vying for his attention?

I pretended not to see him, walking right past like I had somewhere to go. I didn't, of course, but thankfully the library was always open.

Just as I got the door open I heard, "Teagan, wait up!" Aiden's voice was unmistakable, smooth like silk but with the slightest bit of a Texas twang. Door in hand, I turned to see him hurrying my way.

"How'd you manage to escape the paparazzi?" I asked, then immediately wished I hadn't. It only proved that I'd noticed, and where I had been meant to sound playful, my delivery was way bitchy.

Aiden stood there, only a few feet away, and he looked down at his feet. I glanced down as well to see if I was missing anything. No, nothing. What was he doing? What did he want from me?

His eyes rose to meet mine, and I instantly turned to mush—but I refused to give him the satisfaction of knowing it. Trying desperately to appear as if he had no effect, I shrewdly asked, "So, what's up? You chase me down for a reason?"

Unintentional hostility oozed from my words, and again I regretted it. I wanted desperately to know what he wanted, but now he looked like I'd kicked his puppy. His gaze returned to the floor then flashed off down the hallway.

"Never mind. Maybe I'll catch you later."

Nicely done, Rhodes. Run him off. Why had I been such a bitch?

He turned to walk away, and I couldn't help myself. My hand reached out to lightly grab his arm. "Hey, sorry. It's been a bad morning. I didn't mean to be rude," I said.

He didn't respond. With a small defeated smile, he turned and walked away.

Had I really just hurt his feelings? Aiden Wright was that fragile? Now I felt even worse. I wanted to scream, "I'm protecting myself from the inevitable. If I let you into my life, I'll end up gluing the pieces of heart back together until I'm thirty." I couldn't have been more certain of anything in my life. Still, the next time Aiden talked to me—if there was a next time—I wasn't going to screw things up. I was going to be bubbly and sweet. Well, maybe not bubbly, but I'd at least try my best not to be a total jerk.

I went inside the library and tried to work, but Aiden's expression haunted me. He'd actually wanted to talk to me instead of all the girls who seemed to follow him everywhere, and I'd totally given him the cold shoulder. What the hell was wrong with me?

Because I'd forgotten, my logical side reminded me: *He's not the one for you. He'll break your heart. He'll stomp on it, dance on the pieces then run off with some awful bitch like Becca. He's one of the Beautiful People. Remember who they are. Remember where they live. Remember how your mom ran off on your dad. How she ran off on you, too.*

At the same time, I couldn't stop my stupid heart from making excuses: *How can you be sure Aiden's like that? You don't even know him. Maybe he's not like those others, maybe his heart is good and kind and beautiful like the rest of him. How will you ever know if you don't give him a chance?*

I felt as if I needed an exorcism. Were my brain and my heart actually arguing? This couldn't be normal.

Teagan, it's completely normal!

Seriously? I so needed to clear my head.

I left the library and hurried to the restroom. Safely locked inside a stall, I stood and tried to reconcile my stupid feelings for this stupid guy I hardly knew, a guy who, for all I knew, didn't even like me the way I half wanted him to. I had run him off every time we were together. I supposed I had to find out how he felt or I'd drive myself insane. There just didn't seem to be any way around that.

How was I going to make it through the day, though? I couldn't even think straight.

The first period bell rang just as I slid into my seat, and I was getting out my class notes when Alli leaned over and whispered, "Hey, is everything okay? I saw you run off this morning. What did Aiden want?"

Great. Now I had Alli reminding me what an ass-tard I was. I flipped through my spiral and responded, "Nothing really."

"Nothing? *Really?*"

I didn't know what to say. I couldn't tell her the truth: Oh, I don't know what he wanted because I was a total bitch and he took off without telling me. I'm getting really good at avoiding him, though, don't ya think?

Alli just sat there waiting for me to say something. I silently cussed Ms. Wallace for choosing now to let the class sit and talk while she finished checking her email, put down my spiral and admitted, "Well…I'm not sure what he wanted. He didn't really say."

"What do you mean?" She obviously wasn't letting this go.

"Really, I don't know. He just caught up with me, and I asked him what he wanted, then he just said never mind."

Alli stared. I couldn't read her. Finally, I said, "What?"

"Teagan, just give the poor guy a chance."

I could barely wrap my brain around the fact that he even wanted a chance, which was what his sister's words seemed to confirm beyond all doubt, but before I could ask her to elaborate our teacher decided to start class.

Lovely. Perfect timing. School's always like that.

*****

After what seemed like an eternity and a half, the last bell of the day rang. I gathered my things and headed to my locker, and lo and behold Aiden Wright was standing there waiting for me. After the way I'd acted, it really seemed crazy that he was being so persistent.

I pasted a smile on my face, steeling myself to walk right up to him and be friendly. *Yes, friendly, Teagan,* I told myself. *I know it seems a foreign concept for you lately, but you can do this. Don't run him off again.*

As I approached, he smiled that perfect crooked smile and said, "Hi again."

"Hi," I replied. Lame. So lame. But how was I supposed to not melt like ice cream on a hot summer day around this guy? It was either that or bite off his head, and I'd sworn not to bite off his head this time.

He moved aside so that I could open my locker, and I welcomed the distraction of swapping out books. Then he leaned forward , and I was suddenly overwhelmed by his closeness. Trying not to swoon, I continued messing around in my locker and hoped he would speak before me and my stupid mouth blurted something I'd surely regret.

Shifting from foot to foot, he finally spoke. "So…I was thinking that maybe—"

Out of nowhere, Becca appeared at his side. "Hey, baby, I've been looking for you all over. Thought I could drive you home."

Aiden froze. Unable to control myself, I rolled my eyes and went back to fumbling inside my locker, even though there was nothing else that I needed. I wanted to see how he would handle this—assuming I could handle the way my heart was pounding. I wanted to take Becca and throw her out a window.

Before anything happened, Sean ambled our way. He stopped next to me, opposite of Aiden and Becca, and said, "Hey, Teagan. You busy this afternoon? Think you could help me study?"

Becca and Aiden were standing only inches away, and it was clear Sean was snubbing them. Great. He'd chosen that moment to start a war between the brave and the beautiful.

"Come on, Aiden. Let's get out of here," Becca said.

Sean asked again: "Well? Are you busy, Teagan?"

Holy Mother of God, this was awkward. I looked to Aiden, trying to gauge what he was thinking. Was I busy or not? I sure wanted to be.

Aiden turned to Becca. "Maybe another time. I was just about to see if Teagan wanted to hang out."

Becca shrugged and strolled away, and her face was purposefully blank. She was making it clear that she hadn't just got shot down, in case anyone was looking. A few people were.

Sean was still standing there. He lightly touched my arm and said, "Well…?"

Shit, shit, shit. Was I really going to go hang out with Aiden? Was I really going to put myself in that position, being alone with him, letting him make me all melty inside, when I didn't know what his ultimate intentions were? Been there, done that. I turned and said, "Maybe some other time. But, thanks."

My words sounded exactly like the ones he had used on Becca. Looking completely defeated Aiden echoed, "Sure. Some other time."

He turned and walked away without looking back.

23.

Aiden

"If they don't get a move on, we're going to be late," my dad complained as he plopped down next to me on the couch.

"Be patient, old man," I said. "Not everyone here is as naturally good-looking as we are. They have to get ready."

I leaned back and put my feet up on the coffee table. Things weren't tense between *us* for some reason. I didn't know exactly why. My mom wasn't alone in lying to me for all those years, but I knew that more than anything Dad wished he really *was* my biological father. I guess the pain in his eyes somehow made me less angry with him.

He didn't seem to heed my advice about my mom and sister, though. "All right, ladies," he called. "I'm going to warm up the car. Please be ready in the next five minutes."

A short time later he was saying, "Remind me why we're going to watch a musical starring that mean girl who left my baby at a pizza parlor penniless, phoneless, and twenty miles from home." We were on the way to the high school.

"Paul, we talked about this," my mom replied. "We have to try to get along and fit in now, and if one of the pack kids is in a play, that means we go and support them."

"Whatever," Dad muttered.

Even I had to admit Shari wasn't all bad. She'd been hanging with the wrong girl. She hadn't stood a chance going against someone like Kendall, and she had redeemed herself when Alli was kidnapped. If she hadn't shown us that text from Dylan, we would have never found my sister in time.

We pulled into the high school parking lot right behind the Walkers. Marcus, Noel, Cade. Awesome. Them and us, one big happy-ass family. Alli and Cade immediately took off together, so I was left walking in with my parents toward the auditorium. All four of them.

It was hard to believe, but I'd begun to appreciate the frigid weather here a little more. It calmed my nerves, actually, made that slight itchy feeling I'd been getting under my skin lately ease a bit, but I wanted to get away from the uncomfortable situation of walking with the two sets of parents so I faked that I was freezing and walked quicker into the school.

I knew Teagan was there the second I entered the lobby. I could sense her like I had radar—or really, I could smell her. After a quick, awkward smile to some waving girls, I set off to find the source of that delicious scent.

It didn't take long. She stood by the stage door with that guy friend of hers, Sean. When she smiled up at him, I felt this panic, this rage deep inside my gut, but I swallowed it down and listened instead. They weren't acting all lovey-dovey or anything, so hopefully that was a good sign that there wasn't anything romantic going on. Then I heard her tell him to break a leg.

Oh, he was in the show. Good. That meant he wouldn't be sitting with her during the performance. I definitely didn't need anyone else getting in the way of my asking her out. I'd had a hard enough time already.

As soon as he walked off, disappearing through the stage doors, I knew it was time to make my move. I forced myself to forget her refusal of the ride home from school and focused on nothing but her person: the shine of that long blonde hair, the curve of those hips in those jeans—

I was completely blindsided by my sister and Cade. They got to her just before I did, and at that moment I wanted to rip every single hair from Alli's head and shove them down Cade's throat. What was she doing? This was my chance!

"Teagan, come on. You're sitting with us. Right, Aiden?" my sister said, glancing over her shoulder at me.

Oh.

Alli took Teagan by the arm and led her into the auditorium. I just stood there with my mouth hanging open. She was pushing pretty hard for us to get together. I supposed I should thank her.

I caught up just as the lights dimmed. Shari had several rows of seats reserved, many of which were already filled, but thanks be to God we passed all of them and went down a little closer to the stage. There were three seats open, but we needed four now that we were with Teagan. It looked like Becca was saving a seat down at the other end of the row for me, but that was never going to happen.

Cade—being Cade, and the pack's original next-in-line alpha— acted. He just asked the people sitting there to move down. The giggling girls gladly scooted over, and suddenly the problem was solved. It made me both grateful and nervous. Now I had about an hour and a half to woo Teagan. If I could just figure out how.

The show started. I tried paying attention, but to be honest I'm not a fan of musicals and the intoxicating scent of Teagan didn't help. It seemed to pour off of her.

"Sean, right?" I leant in close and whispered into Teagan's ear when he came onstage, and as a small gasp escaped her perfectly shaped mouth I hoped it was me, not Sean, causing that reaction. Whatever caused it, the reaction was sexy as hell and made my pulse quicken.

Teagan nodded and gave me a small smile.

"He's good," I said, trying to act as if her mere proximity wasn't killing me.

This time, Teagan replied. "The best. He plans on moving to New York after he graduates."

The *best*? Her praise of Sean cut into me, but I figured it'd be best to wait until he finished his big first scene to ask if they were more than friends. This killed me to do, but I managed.

Teagan was still trying to act like my interest in her romantic life was no big deal, but even in the dark of the auditorium I could see a blush creep up her neck. She didn't answer right away when I did ask. Instead she said, "Well, what about you? Becca looks pretty upset, probably because you're not sitting with her. In fact, right now she's giving me a death stare."

I leaned forward to check it out. Sure as shit, Becca was watching me and Teagan—and she wasn't the only one. My flirting had caught Marcus's attention as well. He shook his head in a disapproving manner.

Seriously? I pretended not to notice.

"Becca is just a friend," I told Teagan.

"Bullshit," she pretended to cough.

I smiled then quickly set her straight. Turning in my seat, I looked Teagan square in her beautiful blue eyes and said, "I swear. She'd like us to be more, but I'm not interested."

Teagan seemed skeptical, but she nodded and let the subject drop. We didn't speak again until the show was over, and all the curtain calls.

The house lights came up. I knew this was my moment, as I hadn't managed during intermission. It was now or never. I had to ask her out, had to make my move. It was already crazy that it had taken this long, but I couldn't focus on the negative. Time to go all in.

The side theater door opened, so we were soon to be bombarded by overly excited actors. Like Sean. I gathered my courage, leaned over and whispered, "I'm interested in someone else."

Teagan looked stunned for a moment, like she was confused, but then I winked at her. She got it. Our eyes locked, and I held her gaze until it became too much. For both of us.

24.

Teagan

Aiden's green eyes bored into mine, and I had to look away. It was that or just take off and run the other direction.

Oh, what this guy did to me. I could hardly stand to be in his presence without turning to mush, and then he'd brazenly admitted he was interested in "someone else." Someone other than Becca. That someone had to be me, otherwise he wouldn't have said it, right?

Shit, it had better be me.

But did I really want him interested in me? He was one of them, part of a group to which I could never belong. Not only did Becca now look as if she wanted to rip my head off, the man I'd assumed to be Cade's dad hadn't taken his eyes off of Aiden and me all night. What the hell was up with that? *Creepy.* Aiden's own dad hadn't seemed to notice me, and here this stranger was getting all hot and bothered by us being in close proximity. They were definitely very cultish, that group.

I left the theater trying to shake off Aiden's spell. He was trailing behind, and I wasn't sure why or how to react, but before I could make up my mind, Alli grabbed my arm and said, "Hey, we're all going out for pizza. You should come."

I wanted to go. The more I thought about it, the more I wanted to spend time with Aiden—but not if Becca was going to be there. Not if Cade's dad would be there. I might not know how I felt about hanging out with this group, but I was pretty sure I didn't want to hang out with those two. I couldn't just ask if either was going, though.

Alli's persistence won out; she didn't let go of my arm until I agreed. We all walked together through the parking lot, but Aiden continued to keep his distance.

Soon we approached my car and I told Alli that I would meet her at the pizza place. As I did, Cade's dad turned and glared at me. He was getting into a car with his wife and Aiden's parents. Again, I wasn't so sure that this was a good idea. But they didn't seem to be joining us. That was something, I guess.

I got in my car and toyed with the idea of just driving home, but I knew Alli would be pissed. Pushing the desire aside, I followed Cade's car to the pizza joint down the street.

When I opened my car door, Aiden stood nearby. My insides flipped-flopped as I saw that dazzling smile. He didn't seem to be hanging back anymore. He must have decided on a course of action.

"Glad you decided to come."

I couldn't have stopped the girly grin that spread across my face if I tried. "Well, your sister wasn't going to take no for an answer," I admitted.

"Why would you have said no?"

And there it was: the question I needed to answer. Why would I have said no? Actually, it was easy. Because these people, Aiden's people, made me a panicky mess. His mere presence somehow made me feel like a bumbling disaster, reminded me that I had a mother who'd abandoned me and a drunk for a father and that I was the farthest thing from one of his beautiful people friends. So, there was no way I was answering truthfully.

"Well, I figured I'd do something with Sean. He's probably wondering where I went. I really should have stayed and at least congratulated him." There, I really was planning on seeing Sean afterward, so it wasn't a complete lie.

Aiden's smile slowly faded. Shit. Why had I mentioned Sean?

"Well, I guess his loss is my gain," he said after a moment. "I'm glad you're here."

My face flushed, and I couldn't help but wonder if he had this same effect on every girl. Unfortunately I knew the answer. Of course he had this effect on everyone, even if I wanted more than anything to be the exception. Why couldn't I just be the exception?

Trying to appear nonchalant, I strolled past him toward the entrance. Acting cool and casual had never been a strong suit, but I knew better than to let Aiden Wright think he could get in my pants by simply paying me a bit of attention. If that's what he was trying to do. Was that what he was trying to do?

Aiden sauntered after me. I had to convince my raging hormones to stop jumping up and down. The last thing he needed to know was how much I wanted to kiss him, to full on, no-holds-barred kiss him. I closed my eyes, attempting to clear my head, but his hand brushed the small of my back as he guided me through the door. Right then, at that small show of chivalry, a tiny piece of my heart was stolen. A piece I knew I'd never get back.

My previous fears returned. My subconscious was screaming again, *Wake up, Rhodes, he's bad news. Way too hot for you. Way too everything. Remember where you live. Remember where he lives. Remember who your father is. Aiden could never really care about you. He'll hurt you just like everyone else in your life has, you should get out now before it's too late.*

I stopped in midstride. Before I could stop the words tumbling out of my mouth, I asked, "What exactly are you doing?"

That caught him off guard to say the least, and it was Aiden's turn to blush. Standing in the doorway he asked, "What are you talking about?" There was true concern in those emerald green eyes.

"I just don't get it, that's all," I said. I resumed walking toward our table. It was filled with a group too beautiful to be real. They looked like they belonged on the set of *90210*, not at a small-town pizzeria. The adults were gone, so it was only Allison, Cade, Shari, Luke, Sammy, Cami, and five other kids whose names I didn't know. I'd never said more than five words total to any of them besides Allison. Thankfully, Becca wasn't there.

Aiden caught up. All eyes were on us as we took our seats. Surprisingly, the others smiled and greeted us. Maybe it was just for Aiden's sake, though. Who knew what any of them would have done if I had showed up alone.

As we sat, Aiden leaned over and whispered, "What don't you get?"

"Nothing. Forget I said anything," I replied, regretting I'd spoken up and hoping he'd let the subject drop. What had I been thinking? Why couldn't I just keep my big mouth shut for once?

We settled in, and everyone began to rave about how great Shari had performed. She beamed, and I hated to admit that she *had* been really good, and suddenly I felt guilty for not sticking around to tell Sean the same.

Drinks and several large pizzas were ordered. Aiden's leg brushed against mine, and I could tell he was looking my way. I did my best to ignore both him and the goose bumps that rose on every inch of my skin, taking a long swig of Coke and turning my attention to the conversation taking place at the table.

His leg gently grazed mine again, and he leaned over to whisper, "Are you going to tell me what you're talking about?"

His nearness sent chills through me, and I had to focus not to shudder. Damn, but I wished my body would behave around him.

Without looking his way I replied, "Didn't plan on it."

"Seriously, Teagan? You're kinda killin' my swag here."

I couldn't help but laugh. Then I wanted to kick myself for sounding like one of those giggling idiots who followed Aiden around every day. Aiden didn't seem to mind, though. He leaned my way and spoke again in a whisper. His breath tickled my ear.

"I like it when you laugh. You should do it more often. I can help you with that, you know. I'm kind of a funny guy—when I'm not a stammering fool."

This time I couldn't stop myself from looking. Those radiant green eyes burned into mine, and I reminded myself to speak. "A stammering fool? You?"

"You seem to have that effect on me," he said. A small smile played across his lips, and it took every ounce of self-control for me to not lean over and kiss him. I'd been dreaming about it non-stop.

Against my better judgment, I flirted back. "Why, Aiden Wright, I have no idea what you are talking about." And this time, there wasn't a speck of hostility in my voice. Not an ounce.

He noticed. Leaning in even closer, he let his lips almost graze my ear. "Oh, Teagan Rhodes, I think you know exactly what I'm talking about."

I suddenly caught Alli and Cade staring at us. Shit. I moved over a bit and smiled in embarrassment, but Aiden's sister was grinning ear-to-ear. I don't think I'd ever felt so uncomfortable.

"I'll be right back," I said.

I scooted out my chair and hurried toward the restroom. My head was down, so when I reached the door and moved to push it open I couldn't see whose hand gently grabbed my arm. I turned to find Aiden standing there. He'd followed.

"Are you okay?" he asked.

"Yeah, I'm fine. Just needed to go to the restroom," I lied.

"You sure?"

"Aiden, I just don't know what to think of all this," I finally admitted.

"What do you mean? Just tell me, Teagan," he pleaded.

I didn't know what to say. I was so unlike everyone else sitting at that table, so *average*—and that was being kind. And then there was Becca, the would-be new queen of the school who practically threw herself at him every chance she got. Why me? Why would he possibly want me?

"I just don't get you," I blurted. "Are you really interested in me, or is this all just a game? Because I'm not into games." There, I'd said it. I'd admitted that I thought he liked me and opened myself up for ridicule. Still, I felt a bit relieved.

Aiden stood there shell-shocked. "Really, a game? You think I'm playing some sort of *game* with you?"

"Isn't that what guys like you do? You have every girl in school eating out of your hand, so you want the one who isn't standing in line waiting her turn to hang on your arm. That's a game if I've ever seen one."

"It's not like that. Why would it be like that?" He eyed me, and a new expression crossed his face. "Why is it so hard to believe that I like you? I, Aiden Wright, like you, Teagan Rhodes."

"Because life doesn't work that way," I snapped. Then I marched into the restroom without turning back.

I hurried into a stall, locked it, and cussed the tears that filled my eyes. And I cursed Aiden. Damn him! Now what was I supposed to do, stay in here all night?

I hung out in the stall long enough to get my tear-reddened eyes under control. The last thing I wanted was to go back to the table and have everyone ask what was wrong. Would they even notice? Alli would.

As I made my way back to the table, I immediately noticed Aiden's chair was empty. *Way to run him off, Rhodes.* Alli shot me a look from across the room, but all I could do was shrug. Thank God the waiters were headed our way with the pizzas, and I took the opportunity to get the hell out of there.

Throwing my purse over my shoulder I announced, "Hey, I gotta go. My dad needs to borrow my car."

Alli frowned. "Okay. I'm glad you came. Be careful getting home. Call me tomorrow?"

I nodded as everyone else waved goodbye. No, I couldn't eat. Aiden's mysterious disappearing act had made my heart sink, but I also knew I'd done the right thing. Regret was better than disappointment. Much better than heartbreak. I just had to remember Alex Foster. Or I could just ask my dad.

25.

Aiden

"Are you *ever* going to ask her out?" Alli asked the next night.

We were sitting in the family room watching TV, and the expression on my face must have showed everything.

"She likes you," Alli rushed to say. "You two had some serious chemistry last night. It's obvious," she continued. "At least when you stay in the same place long enough."

"You think?" I wasn't so sure. "Last night at dinner she all but said she doesn't trust me. She thinks I'm playing some kind of game, chasing after the one girl that doesn't want to get caught."

Alli frowned. "Maybe she's just scared. Maybe she was burned before. But, trust me when I say that deep down she likes you."

Well, there was definitely something between us; I knew that. But possible attraction wasn't the only problem. The apprehension I'd been feeling wasn't just coming from Teagan or my pull to her; it was coming from everyone who had ever watched us interact. This was a complicated crush at best.

"Is it even smart?" I said. "I mean, Teagan and me getting together. I'm not sure anymore."

Alli looked pissed, really pissed. I'm-about-to-kick-the-living-shit-out-of-you pissed. Her hands flew to her hips as she scolded, "Why the hell not? I thought you liked her. The going gets rough and you fade into the background? Maybe she's right and you *did* just want a challenge. Maybe the challenge is too—"

"Calm down, calm down. I *do* like her. Why are you so hell-bent on us going out, anyway?"

Alli's hands dropped from her hips, and her face softened a bit. "I don't know. I like Teagan. She's my only normal friend here, and it would be cool if y'all got together. We could all hang out, you know? And I'd have to kill you if you ended up with someone like Becca!"

"Don't worry. That's sure as shit not going to happen. But, it's just…did you happen to notice the not-so-loving looks Teagan and I were getting from Marcus last night? I have a strong feeling that he doesn't approve," I said.

Alli's face fell. Then she set her jaw. "Since when do you care what Marcus thinks? Anyway, I don't think he would approve of anyone. He certainly didn't approve of me. He made that very clear." There was a hint of sadness in her voice.

"See? That's what I mean. It hurt you to hear those things. I don't want anyone making Teagan feel like that. And it's not just Marcus. I don't think anyone on the estate would approve, except maybe you and dad. Think about it. Teagan's a human. Mom had to run away and leave her family to be with Dad for that exact reason. Would ours be a doomed relationship before it even starts?"

Alli glanced pensively at her feet, but I could tell she wasn't convinced. She was probably trying to figure out what to say to make me to take a leap of faith.

She finally tucked her legs under her and reached for her Coke. "I don't think you should over-think this, Aiden. It's just a date. One date. Maybe the only chemistry you two have is physical. Maybe once you get to know each other, you'll realize you don't have anything in common after all and it'll fade. But you'll never know until you ask her out."

She actually made sense, my know-it-all sister. I mean, I wasn't pledging my eternal, undying love here. It was just a date, assuming I ever got up the nerve to ask. And maybe the way I asked could convince Teagan I was worth taking a chance on in return.

"You're right, Alli," I said. "Do you know what time she gets off work?"

"She's closing, so about nine thirty." My sister smiled. "If you leave now you can make it."

A short time later, I stood by my car in the almost empty mall parking lot. It was only a few minutes before I saw Teagan. She was with two other girls that I recognized from school.

I didn't want to scare them, so I called out her name as I walked forward. The other girls looked excited to see me, but not Teagan. She looked a little freaked out.

"Hey, Teagan. Ladies," I added.

"Hi, Aiden," cooed the girl with the big eyes from my physics class.

I smiled politely. "Teagan, I was hoping that we could talk. Maybe get some coffee or ice cream or sodas or something," I added nervously.

I could tell that Teagan was about to turn me down. Thank God the big-eyed girl spoke up. "She would love to. Actually, she was just saying how she skipped dinner, and now she's starving. Weren't you, Teagan? Maybe Aiden here can take you for a late dinner."

I could see Teagan's scarlet cheeks even in the semi-darkness of the parking lot. I held my hand out and said, "Come on. Let's get you some food. I'm always hungry." She hesitated for a moment, but with a sigh she took my outstretched hand.

Teagan knew of an all-night diner just on the other side of town. It wasn't where the pack kids usually hung out; the place was pretty empty except for a few truck drivers and some guy with a laptop. We took a booth by the window and opened our menus. The waitress came over and eyed me like I was some sort of science experiment.

"Teagan, honey, where have you been hiding this one?" she asked.

Teagan smiled. "Barb, this is Aiden. Aiden, Barb."

I was about to say something like, "Nice to meet you," or "A pleasure," but I wasn't given the chance.

"Oooh…he's a cute one, honey. I can see why you would keep him hidden." Then Barb gave a high-pitched giggle that made me feel a bit uncomfortable.

Teagan just smiled politely. "I'll have a grilled cheese with fries and a Coke please, Barb. Aiden?"

"I'll take the same."

As soon as creepy-ass waitress left, I reached across the table and took Teagan's hand. "About last night—"

"Aiden, please. Can we just forget it?" She took her hand back as Barb brought us our Cokes. "Thanks," we both mumbled.

I decided to lay it all out on the table: "I like you, Teagan. I really like you, and I want you to give me the chance to prove that to you."

I couldn't read her expression, so I had no idea what she was thinking. I decided not to say anything else until she did, and it was halfway through our sandwiches that she finally spoke.

"I just don't think it can work, Aiden. I'm sorry."

Rejected! It felt worse than being kicked in the balls. My emotions were all over the place. I was pissed that she didn't want me. I was hurt that she didn't want me. But more than anything, I was confused. I undoubtedly still wanted her.

"Why?" I asked, surely sounding pathetic. It was new for me.

"Come on, Aiden," she said. "You want me to say it again? I told you at the pizza shop. You're one the beautiful people at school. You could have any girl you want. I know that—"

I laughed. "You can't be serious. You won't go out with me because I'm good-looking? That's silly. You're far more beautiful than I am."

Her cheeks went red. I couldn't tell if it was because I was making her blush or she was pissed at me for laughing. It was clear she was still uncomfortable.

"Teagan," I said. I reached for her hand again, and surprisingly she let me take it. "Give me a chance. That's all I ask. I don't want all those other girls at school, I want you. One date?" I begged. I'd resorted to groveling, which I'd never done before, but didn't care. "Let me prove to you who I am."

She looked up and met my eyes. I could tell she was teetering on the edge.

"Okay," I offered, pulling back a bit. "How about one double date with Alli and Cade? Come on, Teagan. Just one date, and you won't even have to be alone with me. Your friend will be there to protect you. You trust my *sister,* don't you?"

She dropped my hand, and my heart dropped into my stomach. Had I said the wrong thing? Had I pushed too hard?

Teagan picked up her sandwich and repeated, "One date with Alli and Cade?"

I nodded.

"Okay, Aiden. One date," she conceded, but the look on her face told me that she doubted my ability to change her mind about things.

I grinned. It seemed my work was cut out for me.

26.

Peter

"Well, well, what do we have here?" Peter muttered to himself. He sat with his laptop at the last booth in the Black Diamond diner. The perfect suspect had walked in with a human girl. Stupid, stupid girl!

The young man was *clearly* a wolf, or at least he had every characteristic on Peter's checklist. He had the customary dark features, dark hair and tanned skin—and there was also something extra about him, something that made him stand out from the other possible wolves Peter had been watching in this town. Quickly, Peter began to take notes, typing as fast as he could. But he needed to a closer look. It was dangerous but necessary.

Peter closed his laptop and decided to fake a restroom trip. Without being too obvious, he walked as slowly as he could. He listened to the two teenagers, who were talking about something said between them last night. From this direction, he could only see the back of the male, though, and nothing unique stood out. Peter walked quickly into the restroom and went over to the sink to wash his hands.

"He's one of them, Peter."

Peter looked up, and in the mirror was the face of his uncle. The shock of seeing him nearly caused Peter to scream. He had heard his uncle's voice for a long time, but never had he seen his face.

"Ray?" he said with a shaky voice.

"Yes, Peter. Calm down. I'm sorry to have scared you, but I couldn't risk you missing that wolf out there."

Peter shook his head. "There was no way to miss him. He fits the profile perfectly. But, Uncle Ray, there's something different about him, too. That's why I came to the restroom, so I could get a better look."

"Good, good," his uncle said. "Find out everything you can about him—and about the poor girl he's with. You never know what information will be important."

"I'll find out," Peter promised.

"You're doing a good job, Peter," his uncle said. Then the image vanished.

Peter splashed some water on his face. After a moment he walked out, and as he approached he began to compile final notes about everything he could: the exact color of the kid's hair, the clothing he was wearing, his frame and build...

Holy shit! As Peter neared the table, the young wolf raised his head and made eye contact. It was all Peter could do to hide his disbelief he felt. This wolf had bright green eyes. *They could have green eyes!*

It seemed such a small thing, but Peter hurried back to his booth and grabbed his laptop and coat. If he was right and this boy was a wolf—and he felt the same assurance as did his uncle—he needed to get back to his motel room and safety. Everything he knew about werewolves could be wrong, the entire profile! And if that was the case...who else in the world might be a wolf without him knowing?

27.

Teagan

One date. Jeez, what was I getting myself into? I couldn't believe I'd actually agreed to this. Aiden Wright and me? With just one look, anyone would agree that we didn't belong together. He was just so hot, and I'm…well, not. We're like Ross and Rachel, except he's Rachel and I'm Ross. I mean, seriously, in the real world guys who look like him don't get girls like Jennifer Aniston. Wait…that makes no sense. Yes, they do get girls like Jennifer Aniston. Exactly like Jennifer Aniston. And I was no Jennifer!

So, why on my drive home could I not stop smiling? Maybe he really liked me.

Or maybe he just wanted to screw me and then screw me over like Alex Foster. Or like everyone else in my life, really.

I pulled into my driveway to find my dad sitting on the porch, surprisingly without a beer in his hand. I got out of my car, but he stopped me before I made it to the front door. "Hey, sweetheart. I've been waiting for you. I wanted to tell you how sorry I am for how I've behaved. I really want to make things right, and I've decided to go back to AA and give it a try. A real try this time."

I stood there staring, at a loss for words again. He always did this. Why did he expect me to just give in and believe him when every other time he'd turned his back on me and ended up three sheets to the wind at the bar down the street. I wanted to hate him, wanted to hate my mom for making him this way. I wanted to throw my hands up and tell him to fuck off. But, as usual, the look in his eyes—that look of utter sadness and regret—stopped me from admitting what I really wanted.

"Come on, Teagan. Say something," he pleaded. "I know I've messed everything up and you have no reason to believe me, but I really want to change."

I pushed my hatred deep down inside and said, "Okay, Dad. I'm glad to hear it. I hope it works out this time."

He stood and slowly put his arm around my shoulder, probably to gauge my reaction. When I didn't shrink away, he pulled me in a bit tighter. "I mean it this time, honey. I really think I can do this. Please forgive me for…everything. I've put you through hell and back. I just hope you can learn to love your messed-up ol' dad again."

His voice cracked. When I looked up, there were tears in his eyes.

Don't fall for it, Teagan. He's full of shit and you know it.

Before I realized what I was doing, I turned him and gave him a hug. A real hug. I couldn't remember the last time we'd embraced. Tears stung my eyes as I said, "I do love you, Dad. I never stopped." And it was true. After all the shit he'd put me through, I did love him, even if part of me hated him too.

I pulled away and went inside. He followed and asked if I was hungry. I had just eaten, but I offered to make him a sandwich. There wasn't much in our house, but I tried to at least keep some bread and lunchmeat around. God knows my dad didn't do the whole grocery thing.

Together we sat in the living room, sharing the small coffee table in front of our couch. I picked at the sandwich I'd made myself as the TV blared an old episode of *Friends*—how fitting—but I could hardly concentrate on it. I had my own drama to dwell on now. Like, the stupid date I'd agreed to.

One date. I could handle one date. Couldn't I?

Alli wouldn't let her own brother screw with me, either. We hadn't known each other for long, but she was the closest thing I had to a best friend. I wanted to believe that she had my best interest at heart, but it was also hard to believe anyone really gave a damn about me. Pity party? Yes, maybe, but when you got screwed over time and time again pity parties became a natural part of the equation.

Dad shook me out of my haze. "Hey? You okay?"

I smiled. "I'm fine. Just tired. Think I'm going to head to bed."

"Okay. Well, see you in the morning."

I got up from the couch and headed to my room, silently repeating in my head, *One date.*

I could do this.

28.

Aiden

"Looking good, son. Where are you headed all dressed up, huh? Hot date?"

"Yep," I said, glancing over at Dad. "I'm taking Alli's friend Teagan out tonight to El Tiempo, that little Mexican joint near our school. Alli and Cade are coming too," I added, grabbing a bottle of water from the fridge. I noticed my dad smiling and figured he was glad to see me getting back to normal after the accident.

"I thought you might have a thing for her. She's cute."

"I know," I said, smiling. She was.

"I know it's the weekend, but don't stay out too late. Where's your sister, anyway?"

"Here I am," Alli said, coming down the stairs.

She wasn't ready, though. I'd been a nervous wreck all day, and the thought of being late made the muscle in my jaw twitch.

"Aiden, Cade had to do something with his dad, so why don't you go pick up Teagan and we'll meet you at the restaurant? I'm sure it won't be too much longer," she said.

I wanted to scream. What was Teagan going to think, me saying that Alli and Cade were going to meet us at the restaurant? But, maybe this was a good thing. This way I could be alone with her for a little while.

"Okay, but try to hurry. I only got Teagan to go out with me because you were going to be there," I admitted.

Dad raised his eyebrows, so I told him how Teagan didn't trust me because I was too good-looking. Dad laughed, and then Alli laughed. Finally, I joined in too. It was pretty funny. Teagan was absolutely gorgeous. It was her that shouldn't be trusted.

"All right, Pops, I'm off. Wish me luck. And you," I said, pointing to Alli, "Text me when you leave."

My sister nodded. "Go get her, tiger."

I rolled my eyes and grabbed my coat and keys.

On the way out, I heard Dad ask Alli if she ever remembered me being this worried over a date. I thought about that while I was getting into the car. I didn't remember ever being nervous about a girl. Ever. I'd heard about guys being nervous in middle school when they first asked a girl to dance, or being nervous to tell a girl that they liked her. I'd never felt that way until now. Not until Teagan.

The closer I got to Teagan's house, the more anxious I became. My palms started sweating, and I felt that weird itchiness on my skin again. By the time I reached her driveway, I felt like I might be sick.

I took a deep breath and walked up to the door. Before I even raised my hand to knock, however, the door opened. Teagan was standing there, looking amazing in jeans and a fitted sweater. I smiled, and all the tension I was feeling just disappeared.

"Hey, you look amazing," I told her.

She blushed. "Thanks. Not looking too bad, yourself. I just need to get my coat."

I didn't know whether to stay on the porch or go inside, but before I knew it she was back outside with her purse and coat. We soon were getting into my car, and Teagan was asking about Alli and Cade. I told her that Cade had been held up, but assured her that they would both meet us at the restaurant.

We slipped into an uncomfortable silence about two minutes from the house. I panicked. I needed this date to go well, and I couldn't think of anything funny or witty or intelligent to say. I turned the music up, just as something to do, but quickly regretted my decision. "Baby Got Back" pounded through the speakers.

Teagan giggled. "You like big butts, do you?"

"And I cannot lie," I agreed, smiling. The silence was broken.

She turned the music up a little louder and started to sing along with Sir Mix-a-Lot. By the time we got to the restaurant, we had slaughtered the song but were both visibly relaxed. Thank God for '90s hip-hop.

I checked my phone as we walked inside. Still no text from Alli. We got a table for four, then went ahead and ordered an appetizer for us all to share.

"Maybe you should text Alli and see if they're still coming," Teagan suggested.

Nodding, I sent a quick text:

Aiden: Are y'all on your way?

As I waited for a response from my sister I said, "Alli told me that you're from Texas, too. This is a big change, huh? New Mexico."

Teagan nodded. "I don't know if I'll ever get used to it. I knew it would be cold here, but I never imagined how cold. I mean, it's just one state over. Last winter, we had this big blizzard… I swear I nearly froze to death!"

I was just about to say I thought I was getting used to it when I got a reply.

Alli: Sorry, Bro! Not going to make it. Don't hate me. Tell Teagan I'm sorry.

Shit.

When I handed my phone to Teagan, she just looked at me and smiled. "Guess we're on our own."

I wasn't sure what that meant. Was she happy? Was she mad? Why had a double date been so important before when now it wasn't?

The waiter came and took our orders, saving me from too much more pondering. As soon as he left Teagan asked, "Did you like the musical the other night?"

Oddly, we hadn't talked about it. Things hadn't gone so well at the pizza place after the show, and then after she agreed to the date we'd spent the whole time talking about stuff like schoolwork and our old hometowns.

"Honestly?" I said. She nodded, so I admitted, "I'm not a fan of them. I only went because Shari was in it and we promised we would be there. What about you?"

"Honestly?" she repeated. I grinned. "I'm not a fan either, but I promised Sean."

She looked like she wanted to ask me something then but was afraid. I hurried to reassure her: "What? You can ask me anything, you know."

"Well, it's just that...did you happen to notice Cade's father staring at us during the show? I know it sounds weird, but I could have sworn he was," she said. "And then after the show..."

I guess I was a little surprised that Teagan didn't know who Marcus was, at least in regard to me. Alli really was a shitty friend. Or, maybe she just thought it wasn't her secret to tell. Marcus had been pretty obvious about his disapproval.

"You don't have to tell me," Teagan said, reading my face.

"No, it's okay. Hell, it will probably do me some good to tell someone." I paused and took a breath. "When I had my accident over Thanksgiving break, I needed a blood transfusion."

"Omigod, Aiden. I didn't realize it was that serious!"

"Yeah," I said, "but the worst part was when I woke up. I needed blood, and it turned out neither of my parents was a match because…well, my dad's not my biological father."

Teagan covered her mouth with her fingers and gasped.

"Wait," I said, "it gets worse. Cade's father is my mom's ex-boyfriend from like nineteen years ago. Apparently he's my father."

"That's absolutely crazy! Aiden, I don't know how you are managing any of this. I would be a total wreck." She sat back in her chair and took a deep breath. Then, out of nowhere, she giggled, "I'm sorry, Aiden, I'm not laughing at you. I promise. It's just… well, your brother is dating your sister."

We both made the same disgusted face, totally at the same time, which sent us together into hysterics. It was awesome. I think the entire restaurant was wondering what the hell we are laughing at, though, and at that moment, sitting in that little Mexican restaurant, I realized I could listen to Teagan laugh every day for the rest of my life. Not only that, I wanted to.

I was in big trouble. At least, I was if I wanted Marcus to approve of my girlfriend.

29.

Teagan

Aiden opened the car door to let me in. Our eyes met, and his smile could have lit up every dark street in Red Ridge. Unable to hide my contentment, I returned the smile and slid into the passenger seat.

I thanked him as I did. Our date had gone so well that I wasn't ready to go home, but I sure as hell wasn't going to admit it; I knew if we spent much more time together, I'd be hooked and there'd be no turning back.

I watched as Aiden walked around to the driver's side and got in. He started the car, and as he put it into reverse, he said, "I had a really great time tonight."

I wanted to scream, "Me too, me too!" but held back. I couldn't let him know just how much I'd enjoyed myself, so instead I simply nodded my head and we were off into the night.

We sat in silence for a few minutes before I couldn't stand it any longer. "I had a good time, too," I admitted.

He turned. "Really?"

"Yes, really. Maybe you're not such a bad guy after all. I just hope you don't make me regret saying so." I smiled so that he knew I was joking. Sort of.

"You won't regret it, Teagan, I can promise you that." With his eyes on the road, Aiden added, "I just wish you'd give me a chance to prove it to you."

How the hell was I supposed to respond to that? Maybe he really wasn't like the rest of them, and really, were the rest of them all that bad? Maybe it *was* just Kendall. And who was I to judge the entire group? Wasn't that exactly what Kendall did to me the day I tried to befriend her? Didn't this make me a hypocrite?

It was all too confusing. For that reason, I put on my big girl panties and said, "Well, I guess you'll have to prove it to me then."

Shock registered on his face. Then he looked my way again, and his eyes were alight.

He didn't say anything until he pulled up at my house; we had agreed that this date would be short and sweet, dinner at a restaurant and nothing else. I kind of regretted it now. Aiden put the car into park and turned his body toward mine, lifted his hand to brush the hair back from my face. He gently tucked the strand behind my ear and leaned my way, but only a bit.

"You are one confusing girl, you know that?"

I leaned toward him as well, almost unaware of what I did. I closed half of the distance between us. "I'm not trying to be. You're kinda confusing, yourself."

He leaned in a tad more and whispered, "I don't want you to be confused. I like you, Teagan. A lot. I wish you felt the same."

He brushed his fingertips along my cheek. Before I knew it, his lips met mine. Without thinking I reached up, grabbed him by the back of the head and pulled him closer, deepening the kiss. His lips consumed me. I couldn't be close enough. I didn't ever want this moment to end.

I could have stayed wrapped in his warm embrace forever, but as our lips parted for a much-needed breath I noticed my porch light come on. That meant Dad was watching.

I pulled away reluctantly. "I'd better go."

Aiden's eyes were blazing, and they burned into me. A sweet smile spread across his face, and as I opened the car door he asked, "Can we do this again?"

I wasn't sure if he meant the date or the kiss, but it didn't matter. Before I shut the door I said, "Of course."

To my surprise, Aiden got out of the car. He followed me to the front door, and as I stepped onto my doorstep I turned to face him, praying he would kiss me again. He didn't.

30.

Aiden

I didn't want to let Teagan go. Ever. Even if I didn't remember what had happened the last time I'd dropped her off.

"You going to be okay?" I asked, praying I wasn't overstepping my boundaries.

"Yes," she replied. "Don't worry."

I think she blushed. I wasn't sure if it was from embarrassment about her father or pleasure at my concern, but it made my blood burn. I wanted to take her back to my car and continue were we left off. Kissing Teagan was unbelievable. The way she'd looked at me, the way she'd grabbed the back of my neck, the way her lips had molded to mine... Nothing compared. No girl. I hadn't known a kiss could feel like that.

I was about to steal another delicious kiss when the door swung open, scaring the shit out of me. Teagan jumped, too. The man who stood in the doorway was a disaster. His clothes were wrinkled and dirty, and worst was the smell of cigarettes and beer that seemed to pour off of him.

"Who the fuck is this?" he slurred at Teagan. He stood there looking me up and down like he was trying to figure me out.

The memory of this guy belittling his daughter came rushing back. I could feel the tension in Teagan, and it made me sick. She tried to let go of my hand, but I wouldn't let her. There was no way I was going to let this guy come between us. I hated him already.

Teagan looked at me, and for a moment I thought about picking her up and taking her away from all of this; the sadness and embarrassment in her eyes all but killed me. Reluctantly, however, I let her hand fall.

But I'd never felt this angry before. I couldn't just let it go. He was a drunken bully used to pushing my girl around, and it wasn't going to happen tonight. I would see to that. With full-on fury coursing through my veins, my jaw tight, I turned and looked her father straight in the eye. I poured every ounce of contempt that I felt for him into that glare, and her father visibly tensed. It made me want to smile.

I turned to Teagan, who was looking at her feet, humiliated. I lifted her chin with my fingers and grinned. I leaned over and whispered in her ear, "I'm going to wait out here until I see your light come on, okay? Call me if you need me. Anytime. Ever. I miss you already."

Her smile made me bold. I grabbed her face in my hands and kissed her hard on the lips. I couldn't help myself; I needed her dad to know that she was mine. *Mine.* And before I turned to leave, I stood toe-to-toe with him and said, "Lay a finger on her, you will regret it."

Her father's eyes narrowed and his body stiffened, but I stared him down until he finally gave up and turned to go inside. Teagan followed, but she gave me a final glance. It was nearly ten o'clock. I stood on the porch until the door closed behind her.

I'd thought that standing tall against Teagan's father would calm me down and make me feel better, but it didn't. I reached out to open the door to my car, and I saw blood. My blood. My fists had been clenched so tight that my fingernails dug into my palms and both hands were bleeding. I'd been so full of hate that I didn't even feel the cuts on my palms.

Worse, seeing the blood triggered something deep inside me. My stomach cramped, my skin started crawling, and I was sweating like I had just run a 10K. I had to get out of there. Fast.

I jumped into my car. As soon as I saw Teagan's light, I drove as fast as I could away from her house. With both windows down and the air-conditioning on max, I was still burning up. I knew what was happening this time, I was sure of the end result and I didn't think it'd stop. Somehow, I just knew. I had to get home. I couldn't do this. Not by myself. Not in this car.

I floored it and saw the city limit sign just as the pain became too much. I had to pull over. My breathing was ragged and urgent, my vision tunneling. How the hell had Alli done this? I tried to focus on something else, but it was so hard to think about anything besides the pain. With every ounce of energy I could muster, I parked the car and staggered toward the woods.

I wasn't going to make it. I was going to change!

I remembered the kiss then: the soft feel of Teagan's skin, the warmth of her mouth on mine. That memory was the only thing that got me into the trees.

Once in the woods, I fell to my knees. I rested my forehead on the ground. This close to the earth I could smell the clean soil, and it filled me with a need I had never before felt. My fingers dug into the cold earth, and I tried to take a deep breath. The pain was horrible, the fear nearly unbearable, but there was something about this experience that…just felt right. Thinking of Teagan again, I decided to let go, to embrace the pain and see where it would take me. I filled my lungs with the frigid night air…

All at once, the pain coursing through my body stopped.

31.

Peter

Peter cautiously changed lanes, allowing the idiot in the Jetta to pass. The car had been weaving for the last several miles, speeding up and slowing down. If there was one thing Peter hated as much as werewolves, it was reckless drivers.

The Jetta sped past, but he couldn't see who was driving. No worries, though. Soon the taillights disappeared down the hill, and Peter went back to his thoughts. Something very big had to happen soon. He had been working so hard exploring every lead possible. He deserved a big break, and this town was it. He just hadn't been here long enough, hadn't found the proof he needed. He knew that werewolves could have green eyes now, though. And he was still waiting for the results of the DNA test he'd sent in, a test he was certain would prove *some*thing. Any day could be the big one.

As Peter reached the top of the hill, the same Jetta from before appeared on the side of the road. It was parked, and as he got closer Peter realized something was wrong. The car was still on, but no one was inside. Peter decided to stop and see if he could be of any assistance.

He pulled over and turned off his car. Walking over toward the Jetta he called, "Hello? Do you need any help?"

The driver was nowhere to be seen. The door was unlocked, the air conditioning on high, and something that looked like blood on the steering wheel.

"What the hell happened here?" he whispered to himself.

He went back to his car and returned with a flashlight. After looking in the Jetta again, next he began to look around it. He walked to the tree line and tentatively took a few steps in.

A giant brown wolf burst past, running away from the scene. Shock caused Peter to drop his flashlight. By the time he picked it up and shone it in the direction of the wolf, the beast was gone. But things weren't all bad.

"Holy shit!" he mouthed.

This car, this Jetta, was the big break he'd been looking for. Whoever came back for it was his key to finding his wolves, his key to leveraging them and drawing them out of the woodwork then eradicating them. All he had to do was hide and wait.

Hiding and waiting was what Peter did best.

32.

Aiden

The pain suddenly vanished, and I saw the world in a completely new way. My once tunneled vision was now sharp and clear; new scents invaded my nose from every direction. The need to follow them was extreme.

I looked down at my hands. That was the first time I noticed my paws. Huge, brown paws. I felt strong. I felt powerful. This was what had been missing from my life all this time; I just didn't know it until now. I had always felt confident in my skin, but a feeling of absolute certainty came over me and it was new—and I liked it. I really, really liked it.

A noise from my left grabbed my attention: A car had pulled to a stop nearby. I had to get out of there. I needed to get home, but I had no idea how to change back, and I didn't want to. Not yet anyway. So I started running. Home?

I was at least five miles from the estate. Even in my normal form I could make it, but in this new form it would be no problem. It felt only natural to run, and I was fast; really fast. The feel of my new legs was exhilarating, as if I'd unlocked a newfound freedom that had been screaming to get out.

Somehow I knew exactly how to get home through the woods. I stopped a couple of times when I heard noises or picked up on some interesting scent, but I never stopped for long. The whole werewolf thing was so new to me, to be honest I was kind of afraid that if I saw a rabbit or deer or some other poor defenseless animal I might try to eat it. I wasn't quite ready for that. Did we even do that?

Surely not. God, I wish I wasn't so pissed at Mom. I had a lot of questions. Like, for one, how the hell to turn back.

I slowed when I came near the highway turnoff for the estate. Flashbacks of my sister's unfortunate experience came back to me, and I did not want to end up like her, naked in front of the entire pack, so I stayed far off the main road as I made my way to our house. This took a little longer, but it gave me more time to check out my new home. I now understood why we lived way out here in the middle of nowhere. It was like a lupine playground, what with all the scents and sounds everywhere.

It wasn't long before I made it to our back patio. There I stopped. What the hell did I do now? I couldn't knock on the door. Couldn't even yell for someone to open up. Shit.

I just stood there, staring at the door for the longest time. Then it dawned on me. Animals couldn't use speech to get what they want, but they found other means. We used to have a little dog that would scratch and jump at the door when he wanted in or out. No matter how humiliating it felt, that's what I probably had to do. I was kind of low on options.

I went over to the sliding glass door and gave it a scratch then stood back and waited. Nothing. I jumped up at the door, making as much noise as I could. Nothing. Crap. I gave it the ol' scratch/jump combo. Also nothing.

Okay, come on, guys. Help a brother out, I found myself thinking. This whole situation was awful. One more try, and if it didn't work...well, back to the drawing board.

I jumped up and smacked my paws against the door. As I did, the curtains covering the window moved, and my dad let out the most ear-piercing scream I'd ever heard. It was worse than the time Alli saw a mouse in our old house. I'd never known my dad could be so girly, and I couldn't stop myself from cracking up. Not that what came out sounded like laughter, but it was. In fact, I laughed so hard that I instinctively rolled over. I couldn't help it, the look on my father's face was ridiculous! He *is* married to a werewolf, for Christ's sake. You would think he'd be used to seeing wolves.

I rolled back over in time to see my mom rush up to him. She glanced out the window and gasped.

"Aiden? Is that you, honey?" She flung the door open.

I walked in the house and, just for the fun of it, jumped up on the couch. My dad was now sitting in a chair with his head in his hands, trying to recover from his near heart attack, while Mom just stood there smiling at me. She seemed so proud. For a moment I forgot I was mad at her.

I heard giggling from the kitchen and turned to see Alli and Cade there. They were smiling, too. Big, fat, cheese-eating grins.

Since no one seemed to be saying a thing, and obviously I couldn't talk, I jumped off the couch and sat in front of Mom, giving her my best what-now expression, or at least I tried, and waited for her to understand.

"Are you stuck, baby?" she asked.

I nodded my head.

"Don't worry, Aiden. Changing back is the easy part," she said. Then her hands flew up to her mouth. "Oh God! I am the worst mother ever! Both of my babies had to change on their own. The first time is so horrible!"

Trying to make her feel better, I moved closer and rubbed my face lightly against her leg. She put her hand on my neck and rubbed. Then she leaned down and planted a kiss on my nose.

"What about Teagan?" Alli suddenly said. "This didn't happen in front of her, did it?"

I shook my head, But I was quickly growing impatient with the communication issues. The room grew quiet, and my family stood around looking at me like I was a painting in a museum. My dad actually circled me, taking in my new form like I was a new car he was considering buying. Just to freak him out, I licked his hand. He pulled it back and laughed.

Cade whispered something to Alli, and her eyes widened a bit. I growled, wanting to know what the hell they were saying.

Alli glanced at me. Shaking her head in disbelief she said, "You and Cade look nearly identical. I think your eyes are a bit lighter, but other than that… Wow."

I didn't know what to think about that. I guess it made sense, though; we are half-brothers.

"I think Aiden might want to change back," Cade suggested. "I could help—if you want," he added, eyeing me. I would have shrugged if I could, but these shoulders didn't really lend themselves to that. I nodded instead.

"Thanks, Cade, but please, honey, let *me* help you," Mom practically begged.

I really, *really* didn't want to change and end up butt-ass naked on all fours in front of her.

"Paul, go get your son some shorts or something. I'll turn around, okay?" she said, not giving me the chance to turn her down. Dad left, and after he came back everyone else went into the kitchen, leaving Mom and me alone in the family room.

"Okay, baby. Changing back is painless. I promise. Think about a happy, easy time. Then start visualizing your human body from the bottom to the top," she said. "Close your eyes and think."

I motioned with my muzzle, trying to get her to turn around, and when she complied I did as she suggested and tried to change. What happy, easy time did I remember? I thought back to sitting in my car with Teagan. I thought about how comfortable I'd felt with her hand in mine, how much I'd relaxed when she met my kiss with the same intensity, like she needed it as much as I did. And once I had hold of that memory, I tried to bring back my human form. I saw my legs, my stomach, my chest, my shoulders, and finally my face.

When I had my whole body visualized, I opened my eyes. And just like that I was back. I snatched my basketball shorts from the floor and quickly dressed.

"You can turn around now. I'm back," I told my mom.

She turned around and threw her arms around me. "You did it!"

Everyone else came back into the family room. They sat down, clearly waiting to hear all about my hectic night, but I didn't feel much like talking about it. I understood now why Alli kept her first change a secret. It felt like such a private experience.

"Oh, shit. The car," I suddenly realized. I told them how I'd had to pull over and leave the Jetta on the side of the highway. When Alli and Cade offered to go get it, I gratefully accepted. I asked them to grab my clothes too, and gave them a general idea of where I'd torn them off.

I had a strong need to get away from everyone, so I excused myself and went upstairs as soon as they were gone. I needed to call Teagan, too, but when I tried I realized that my phone was still in my car.

Damn. It would have to wait until Alli got back.

*****

Twenty minutes later I was lying in bed thinking about how weird my evening had turned out. I worried about leaving Teagan with her father in his obviously drunken state, worried that I had overstepped some kind of invisible boundary by kissing her like I had in front of him. Worried that maybe someone saw me changing in the woods.

I had just about completely freaked myself out when Mom knocked on my bedroom door. "Aiden, can we talk?" She came in and sat on the end of the bed. "We have to tell Marcus that you changed."

"I know. Tomorrow, though," I said. It was half a question.

"Okay," she said. "It will be okay. Marcus really isn't a bad guy. Hell, I used to think that he hung the moon. I almost married him."

Not that I wanted to hear about her and Marcus, but she'd really never explained things to me or Alli since her big confession. It seemed like just yesterday I was a normal guy in New Mexico and my biggest concern was what I'd wear to school the next day. Maybe I needed to know more.

"If he's so great, why did you keep me a secret from him?" I asked.

She thought about the answer so long that I told her to just forget it, but she told me no; she just wanted to get it right.

"You know, if I would've stayed home that night, not gone to the music fest with my friends, you would have had a very different life. But I did go. I met Paul, and I can't explain it, but I knew he was the one. He made me realize that what I felt for Marcus wasn't real love. Up until that night, I'd really thought it was."

She closed her eyes, like she was reliving the moment. "If I would have told Marcus about you, I would've had to tell Paul goodbye forever. Marcus would never have let me leave with you. Or, if I did somehow manage to leave, he would have found us and brought us back. I realize now how selfish this was on my part, but please try to understand. I needed your father. For the first time in my life I needed someone, and he accepted me, wolf nature and all. Another man's child and all. I hope that one day you meet someone who does the same, who makes you feel the same way. Someone you don't want to live without," she added, reaching for my hand.

That was when she noticed the fingernail cuts in my palm. They were already healing, but the evidence was still there.

"What the hell did you do to yourself?"

"It's nothing. I just got angry and had to find a way to control myself. This was the best I could manage," I admitted.

She raised her eyebrows. "Anything to do with your date tonight?"

"Yeah, but it's okay. Really," I said.

"Do you want to talk about it?"

"No, Mom. Not now. Everything's fine, really."

"Okay. Goodnight, baby. I...I'm so proud of you." Then she got up and left my room.

I started thinking about her and my dad. I couldn't even begin to imagine someone trying to keep me away from Teagan. Thinking of her again was driving me mad, actually. I really needed to call her, or at least send a text to make sure she was okay. What the hell was taking Alli so long?

I lay down, planning to wait for Allison and Cade to get back, but after all that had happened I struggled to keep my eyes open.

It was a losing battle.

33.

Teagan

My dad slammed the door behind us and shoved me into the wall. His eyes burned with rage.

"What the hell are you doing?" I screamed.

"What the hell are *you* doing? Making out with some random boy in our driveway? Right in front of my face? I should have killed that piece of shit for touching you."

"Get a freakin' grip," I sneered. "He would have ripped you to shreds, especially in your condition. Guess AA didn't work out after all, huh, Dad?"

My father stumbled back a bit, ran shaky fingers through his unwashed hair. "You don't know what you're talking about. I'm just fine. You're the one who thinks you can run all over town doing God knows what. You think he's going to save you, take you away from here and make everything better?"

He paused for a response, but I didn't give him one. I'd learned a long time ago that it wasn't worth it.

"He's just waiting for you to spread your legs. Then he'll be done with you. Just like that last boyfriend of yours, Adam whatever. You'll see. But I guess it won't matter to you. You'll just find another man, and another, just like that whore mother of yours—"

I slapped him so hard that he stumbled backwards. He reached up to touch his cheek, and something I'd never seen before registered on his face. Fear? Remorse? I didn't know what it was, but it wasn't the drunken rage to which I'd grown accustomed. Maybe it was simply guilt.

We just stood there, staring into one another's eyes. When tears threatened, I turned to walk away, not wanting to give him the satisfaction of seeing me hurt yet again. But before I could escape, Dad grabbed my arm. He was gentle this time.

"Teagan. I'm sorry, baby. Really, I am." Slowly he let go of my arm, and I didn't want to look at him but I couldn't stop myself. A single tear was rolling down his swollen cheek.

I was tired—tired of feeling bad for him, tired of his excuses, tired of it all, and the first of many tears made its way down my own face. "Keep your fucking hands off me. You're dead to me. Do you hear me, Dad? Dead. To. Me." Then, without looking back, I stormed off to my room and slammed the door.

I backed up against the wall and slowly slid to the ground, unable to stand any longer. I was done. Done trying to make it work. Done listening to excuse after excuse. I only had a few months until my eighteenth birthday, and after that I was out of here and would never look back.

It took what seemed like hours, but finally I had the energy to move. I lifted what was left of myself off the floor and crawled up into bed. My eyes were a mess from the buckets of tears I'd cried, and I needed sleep, needed this day to end.

Knowing I'd look like hell in the morning, I curled up in a ball and closed my eyes. I tried to relax, pushing all thoughts of my screwed up father aside. That was when memories of Aiden's lips filled my mind, and for the first time since I'd gotten home I smiled. The way he'd stared down my father, grabbed my hand as if he couldn't bear to let it go, kissed me hard right there in front of the world…

Heaven help me. This boy was trouble. He'd been like an alpha dog claiming his territory, but it sent chills up my spine. Good chills. And with Aiden planted firmly in my thoughts, I drifted off to sleep, praying that I'd see him soon.

What was that he'd said? Oh, yeah. I missed him already.

34.

Peter

Peter circled his car around to park deep in the shadows where no one would see him. He felt like a real detective on a stakeout, which added to his excitement. This was the most conclusive evidence he'd ever found. Today was the day, and his quest was nearing its conclusion. At the very least the path was becoming clear.

He knew he wouldn't have to wait long, because the driver had left the car running. Someone would have to come for it soon, or it would run out of gas, or worse, it would be stolen.

Raymond's voice echoed from the car's back seat. "This is it, Peter. I can feel it in my bones."

Peter adjusted his rear view mirror, and there his uncle was. "You're a ghost. You don't have bones," said he said with a smile. But he was glad to have his uncle's company. He was a little nervous about what might take place here. He wasn't yet ready for a direct assault. He was still working on that drunk from the bar to be his second in command, and he had yet to begin recruiting his werewolf attack team.

"If we get what we're hoping for tonight, you'll need to work faster," Uncle Raymond commanded.

"I will. I promise."

"You'll need more than the town drunk. Weres are strong, dangerous, and don't forget they have teams of their own. Packs. Weres are as deadly as they come," Raymond said.

"This is it! Look!" Peter pointed to a motorcycle that was slowing down near the Jetta. "Who the hell drives a motorcycle in the winter, in the mountains no less? He's *got* to be one of them. Any normal person would freeze to death."

Both Peter and Raymond sat in the car and watched as the motorcycle stopped. Someone got off the back, a second rider that Peter hadn't seen. And when the bike helmets came off, confusion sat in. It was a beautiful blonde teenager. He quickly grabbed his camera from the glove compartment and shot a few photos. She walked over to the Jetta and took a look inside before walking into the woods, came back out with something in her hands. Getting into the car, she closed the door.

"A blonde? They can have blonde hair, too? Damn. Do we really know anything about them at all?" Peter yelled. He slammed his hands down on the steering wheel and turned to his uncle in confusion.

"We're learning more and more every day. Now, stop being a baby and follow them," Raymond commanded.

The motorcycle had pulled away from the side of the road, following closely behind the blonde. Peter rolled his eyes at his uncle's insult and eased his car from the shadows. He tried to stay far enough behind so he would not be seen, but he didn't want to lose the wolves, either. He would never hear the end of it if he did.

"They're slowing," his uncle whispered. "There! They're turning right."

Peter slowed his car and watched. Both the Jetta and the motorcycle turned off the interstate and onto a dirt road. They disappeared in the darkness.

Should he follow? He didn't think so. He would come back another time, when it wasn't so dark, when he could see where he was headed. The road looked little-traveled, and he didn't want anyone asking what he was doing there. Also, these were dangerous creatures and he didn't want to be caught unprepared in their territory.

"I'll start building a team tomorrow," Peter said to Raymond, but there was no response.

When he looked in the back seat, his uncle was gone.

35.

Aiden

"Aiden, wake up."

Alli tapped on my door before letting herself in. I opened one eye then the other and looked at the alarm clock on my bedside table. "Jesus, Alli, it's Saturday and only nine. I want to sleep." I covered my face with my pillow and listened for her to leave, but she didn't. I growled, "What?"

She walked into the room and leaned down like she didn't want anyone else to hear. "You better get up. Everyone is here."

"Who's everyone?" I asked.

"Marcus, Noel, our grandparents, your other grandparents, nearly the whole freaking pack. I swear Dad is about to lose his mind. You have to come down before it gets to be too much," she said.

WTF.

"News travel fast around here, huh?" I sat up and rubbed my hands over my face. I didn't want to do this today. I wanted to get my phone and make sure Teagan was okay; I'd fallen asleep before they got back with it. But I relented. "Give me five minutes and I'll be down."

Alli gave me a little smile and started walking out, but before she made it through the door she turned to me and said, "Hey, Ad, you do what *you* want to do, okay? I've always loved that about you, you don't care what people think as long as you're good with it. I wish I had that quality myself."

A chill went down my spine. "What are you not telling me, baby sis?"

"Just hurry, okay?"

As soon as I walked down the stairs, I knew what was happening. All conversation stopped, and the gathered people stared at me like I was from another planet.

"There he is! Son, we are so proud of you," Marcus announced, liked I'd just won an Oscar.

"Umm…thanks, sir," I said. But, what the hell? Had he just called me son in front of my dad?

I glanced around the room at my new family, though only three of them counted. My dad was sitting in the kitchen staring at his coffee cup, my mom was placing store-bought muffins on a plate for her impromptu guests, and my sister was sitting by the fireplace with Cade. No one else in the room was really family. None of them even knew me.

"None of that 'sir' stuff anymore, Aiden. Call me Dad," Marcus said, smiling at everyone in the room except me. I was about to tell him that maybe I should start with "Marcus" when he introduced me to his parents. They were very nice, but it still felt like they were putting on a show. I looked to Mom for help but she just shrugged. Marcus was incredibly overbearing, and I got a glimpse of what life might have been like living with him. I was thankful that Mom got us the hell out.

"Aiden," Marcus said, "we're having a meeting this morning so that I can formally introduce you to everyone as my son. Go get dressed. The meeting starts at ten sharp."

My dad stood up, looked around the room full of strangers and left. I wanted to run after him. I wanted to tell him that Marcus wasn't not my dad, that he was, but I wasn't given a chance. I was hurried up to my room.

Was this what Alli had been talking about?

It was almost time to leave for the meeting when I came back down from my room. My dad had emerged from his, and he was dressed for the meeting.

"You're coming with us, aren't you?" I asked.

"Yes. I won't hide. I'm part of this family too."

"Dad, it doesn't matter what he says, you know. We both know who my real dad is, right?"

He stood up and gave me a quick hug. When he pulled back, I saw tears threatening to spill from his eyes, but he shrugged them off and said, "Car's rolling out in five minutes. We better get going."

I turned to get a bottle of water from the kitchen and saw my mom standing there. She must have been watching the whole time. Walking up to me, she rose onto her tiptoes and kissed my cheek. "You are the best kid, you know that?" she said.

"Yeah, I know," I said. But it was feigned cheerfulness as I walked out of the house.

*****

The lodge was packed. As the meeting hall and the main gathering space for all members of the pack, it was decorated like a high-end ski resort lounge, complete with a huge fireplace and a few comfy-looking sofas toward the back. All that was missing were some dead animal heads displayed on the wall. At the front stood an imposing podium on a raised stage. The rows and rows of chairs facing that podium were filling up quickly as Marcus made his way to the stage.

As soon as I entered, I was ushered to the front by Phillip, Marcus's right-hand man, and given a seat next to Cade and Noel in the first row. It felt weird to be sitting up here again. The last time had been with Cade, Alli missing. It was hard to believe that so much had happened so fast.

"Ladies and gentlemen, please take your seats," Phillip said to the assembled pack. "Marcus has some exciting news to share with you today."

Cade looked over at me and said, "Are you ready for this?"

"Dude, if I could disappear right now, I would," I admitted. He smiled, but I got the feeling that he was just as nervous about this announcement as I.

The pack waited patiently for Marcus to speak.

"I have just come to learn that Cade is not my only child," he announced. The entire room gasped simultaneously. Marcus motioned for Cade to come up and join him, waited for the excitement to die down a little before he continued: "You know Cade, but I have another son. Aiden, come up here. Ladies and gentlemen, my firstborn son."

The pack went crazy. Not in a good way. There was a lot of anxious discussion, and I looked around the room and thought I might be sick. Mom had her head in her hands. My dad was sitting tall, but the look on his face was one of pure torture. The only person enjoying himself was Marcus.

"All right, all right. Calm down, people. Long story short, Lily didn't know that she was pregnant when she left us all those years ago. We just recently found out that Aiden was my son when he needed a blood transfusion," Marcus set out to explain.

It was nice of him to cover for Mom, but somehow I knew this was not going to end well.

"I called this meeting for two reasons," he continued. "Yes, I wanted everyone to know that Aiden is my son," he said as he patted me on the shoulder. "But I also wanted to discuss the future of the pack. I will not be alpha forever, so I wanted to officially introduce my son Aiden as my eventual successor, the next alpha of the Red Ridge pack."

This time there wasn't just excited discussion, there was outright shouting. The elders, with the exception of my grandparents, seemed downright outraged.

I myself was dubious, just like I'd told Marcus before. This was crazy. I couldn't be the next alpha. I'd just turned into a wolf yesterday, and I couldn't even control my shifting yet. Even if I could, the people here didn't know me that well.

I glanced at Cade, and he watched me in disbelief.

"Marcus, you can't be serious!" one of the elders shouted above the others.

"I am very serious. Aiden is my eldest son. Lily is an extremely strong woman. Aiden will make a great leader. And that is that," he said, like it was final.

The same brave elder spoke again. "This is unacceptable, Marcus. Cade is the next alpha. He has always been. We trust him, we will follow him. We cannot and will not support this other decision."

I had to get out of there. Part of me was furious. How dare Marcus give me no warning, not discuss his announcement with me? How dare he put me on the spot like this? The other part was embarrassed. And as I looked around at the pandemonium that he'd just caused, I knew that if I didn't get out of there I was going to say or do something to cause myself further humiliation.

I looked to my dad. Our eyes met, and I nodded in the direction of the closest exit. He smiled and nodded back. That was all I needed. I had his support.

As I hurried past, he handed me the car keys.

36.

Teagan

I woke the next morning and checked my phone before I even managed to sit up in bed, hoping that Aiden might have texted. No such luck. Only a text from Sean, letting me know that he was finally passing French. As I held the phone in my hand, willing it to ring, my heart sank. It didn't. Maybe I'd officially freaked him out with the whole psycho dad thing. After last night, there was a good chance he'd never call again.

Begrudgingly, I tore myself from the safety of my bed and made way to the restroom. There I stood, staring at my mascara-stained face and examining my puffy eyes. After splashing some water on my cheeks, I rubbed away the evidence of last night's nightmarish encounter and brushed my teeth.

I needed food. Badly. I grabbed a bowl from the dishwasher, filled it with Frosted Flakes and milk and headed back to my room. The last thing I wanted was a run-in with my father. A murder in our sleepy little town would not be good for the ski and tourism business.

I finished my cereal and stuck the bowl on my nightstand, knowing I'd have to leave my room again at some point but that it wasn't going to be anytime soon. After checking my phone one last time, I curled back up in bed and closed my eyes. Maybe I could fall back asleep.

I did.

*****

When I woke again, there was still no word from Aiden. Weird, especially after how we'd connected. Maybe I should call him. Or text him. Or send an email. But, no. I needed to know if he was still interested in me after his encounter with my bat-shit crazy father. I needed to wait and see. That was the only way I'd get an honest answer.

Moving to my bedroom door, I stood there and strained my ears, listening for any sign of my dad. I needed my history book so I could study for an upcoming test but I wasn't ready to face the inevitable just yet. Silence filled the air.

With no sign of my father's presence, I tip-toed into the living room to grab my book. Dad wasn't home. I breathed a sigh of relief and felt my body relax.

Quickly I made a peanut butter and jelly sandwich and sat down at the table to eat. I opened my history book and scanned the chapters that would be covered on the upcoming test, but my mind continued to drift back to Aiden. His eyes, his lips, his …everything. I couldn't help but remember he could have any girl he wanted. Why on God's green earth had he chosen me? Obviously I was damaged goods. My dad had proven that twice now; I was a screwed-up chick with daddy issues. When I glanced over at my phone once more, my subconscious huffed, *Fat chance.*

If I had any chance of acing this test, I had a lot more work to do. Pushing all thought of Aiden aside, I dived into my study guide.

After about an hour or so, I'd gotten up to stretch my legs and grab a soda when the front door swung open. With the refrigerator wide and my stuff spread all over the kitchen table, there was no escape.

I turned around to find my dad standing a few feet away. He was flanked by a man I'd never seen before, a tall and thin, gangly-looking soul whose limbs were almost too long for his body. His hair was long and unwashed, and his clothes hung on his body as if they didn't belong to him. But he was young, surely only a few years older than me.

Something about him weirded me out, and his creep factor skyrocketed as he flashed me a wicked grin.

"Teagan, this is Peter," my father announced. "He's new to town."

The stranger reached out his hand. "Teagan? It's nice to finally meet you."

Finally? My gut screamed to get the hell out of there, but my southern hospitality forced my hand out. I smiled weakly and shook. "Nice to meet you, Peter, but I was just leaving."

When I turned to gather my things, Dad leaned over and whispered, "No, hon. Don't leave on our account. We're just going to sit and chat on the back porch. Stay. Finish your studying."

Hon? Seriously? One minute he was a drunken maniac throwing me around the room and the next he was calling me hon and hanging out with a creepy guy half his age? Would I ever stop being shocked by this man?

I glanced up to find Peter eyeing me like a piece of candy. Eww. I gave him my best in-your-dreams glare and started toward my bedroom, needing desperately to get away from both of them. Immediately.

One foot outside of the kitchen, Peter called, "Hey, Teagan, what are you studying? Maybe I can help."

I stopped mid-step, turned and replied, "Ummm, that's okay. Really, I got it covered." There was no point in being impolite.

As I continued through the living room, however, Peter followed. My dad had grabbed a beer and made his way back out onto the porch. He didn't seem to notice. It was unseasonably warm today, and apparently he'd decided to enjoy some time outside.

"I don't mean to pry," Peter said, "but your dad's really trying. I went with him to AA the other night. He spoke of you."

What? *Really?* This stranger was actually standing in my living room telling me that my dad was trying? Trying to what, completely ruin my life? And where did this dude get off, commenting on my family's personal affairs?

"That's really none of your business," I snapped. "But since we're being so open and all, he was drunk off his ass last night—and in case you haven't noticed, he's already drinking today. So, I guess all that trying isn't really working out."

I'd planned on heading to my room, but with Peter following me the last place I wanted to be was there, so I stopped in the living room and sat down in the recliner, worried he might join me on the couch if I had sat there. Thankfully, he didn't sit. Unfortunately, he didn't stop talking.

"Well, I hate to hear that. We're going to another meeting soon. It's a tough addiction, Teagan, one that others can't easily understand. But I know he's working at it, and he really wants to find your mother."

Oh, hell no. He did *not* just bring my mother into this.

Trying my best to wipe the shock off of my face, I smiled as politely as I could. "You know what, Peter? Maybe you should just go out there with my dad. I'm sure he's wondering where you wandered off to, and he may be a drunk and all but I'm quite sure he doesn't want you in here alone with his daughter. We wouldn't want him to get the wrong idea about you."

That must have been the trick. Without another word, Peter grinned and turned to leave. With him out of sight, I gathered up my things, grabbed my phone, and hurried to my room.

I made sure to lock the door behind me.

37.

Aiden

I didn't know where I was going, but I had to get out of there. I bolted from the lodge, and by the time I got to the car I could feel that eerie twitching all along the surface of my skin. I needed to get a hold of myself and calm down. If I didn't, today would surely be a repeat performance of yesterday. That didn't seem ideal.

I turned the radio up and put the air conditioning on max. Then I focused solely on Teagan. As I drove off the estate, I tried to remember how tempting she'd smelled in my arms last night, and that's when I suddenly knew where I was going. There was only one place I wanted to be.

I pulled my phone out of my pocket, and with shaky fingers typed out a short message:

Aiden: T, can U come outside?

Within seconds she'd responded:

Teagan: Be right there. :)

I no longer felt nervous. I only felt desperate to see her. To make sure she was okay. To feel the warmth of her body against mine. To hear the racing of her heart. That was what I needed. It was all I needed.

"Aiden, is everything okay?" she asked as I pulled up in her driveway and jumped out of my car. "Good timing. My dad and his weird friend just went ins—"

She headed toward me, but before she even made it all the way down the porch steps I grabbed her and wrapped her in my arms. I buried my face in her hair and took long, deep breaths. She smelled like heaven. Her intoxicating scent mixed with the violet fragrance of her shampoo, and it sent my desire into overdrive.

I could have stood there all day, but I needed to see her face. I needed to make sure that she was okay.

"How were things after I left last night?" I asked, pulling back and staring into her eyes.

Her cheeks reddened and she broke eye contact. I didn't like that. I didn't want her feeling embarrassed or ashamed of anything, certainly not anything her father did. It wasn't right. We were almost the same height with her standing above me on the porch steps, so I lifted her chin with my finger and made her look right at me.

"It was fine. I went to my room. He passed out," she confessed.

"I'm sorry if I made it worse," I said.

She gave me a sad little smile, and my heart broke. I reached for her hands and laced our fingers together. We were so close that I felt her entire body outlined against mine. Being this close to her was therapeutic, too. The anger, the tension, the stress of the day...all of it drained from my body.

"Are *you* okay?" she asked, pulling away from me.

"I am now," I said, and I trailed little kisses from her cheek down her neck. She giggled and the sound nearly drove me crazy.

"Want to talk about it?" she asked.

Reluctantly, I stopped kissing her. "It's just a little family drama."

"Well, you came to the right place. I'm the expert on that."

We sat outside on her porch. After a moment I began, "My biological father—"

"Mr. Walker?" Teagan interrupted.

"Yeah, him." I'd forgotten she'd caught him staring at her after the musical. She'd definitely remember him. "Well, today he kind of blindsided me. He announced that I would be taking over the...uh, family business. From the reaction of the…company and the look on Cade's face, no one knew about it," I added, trying to be honest without revealing too much. I wasn't sure how much she could handle.

"Is he, like, wanting you to take over the business now? You're only eighteen," Teagan pointed out. "Isn't that a little young to be running a company?" She laughed.

"Yeah," I agreed. "I don't know what he's thinking. But he expects me to start working with him as soon as I graduate. I'm not even sure if he expects me to go to college."

"And he didn't mention any of this beforehand?" Teagan asked.

"Well, kinda. But I thought he was crazy. I thought it would pass. I didn't know he was going to announce it to everyone! I can't imagine why he would want me to take over and not Cade. I don't even know him well enough to guess at his motives," I said, realizing that was true.

"Maybe you should get to know him better. You know, before you decide anything. Just a suggestion," she said.

"Yeah, maybe," I agreed. The problem was, I didn't know if I wanted to get to know him. From what I already knew, he was an ass. Anyone who'd put me on the spot like that didn't really care about *me*; that much was clear.

"Hey," Teagan said, scooting close. "You're a smart guy. You'll figure it out." Then she leaned over and kissed me.

As her lips covered mine, all other thoughts disappeared. All I could think was, *God, she tastes good.*

I wasted no time kissing her back. There was no hesitation, no doubt from either of us. Whatever this was, it was definitely right. It was the only thing that I was absolutely sure of anymore—which scared the hell out me. One day soon I'd have to tell her the truth about me.

But not now. What if she freaked out? I couldn't risk exposing the pack if she didn't understand, and I couldn't count on her being as accepting as my father Paul had been. We needed more time. When I was sure about her feelings, I'd tell her the truth. When I was sure she trusted and wanted me.

Was it truly possible she didn't feel the same way about me that I did for her? Given that kiss, I'd say no. Given the reactions of our bodies... She moved me in a way no other girl ever had. I might even lo—

No. I wasn't ready to think about that just yet.

38.

Peter

Peter watched through the window as Teagan Rhodes met her gentleman caller on the porch, more than a little curious to see if it was the same bloodthirsty animal he'd seen her with at the diner. Unfortunately, the blinds obscured an absolute identification.

"Soda, Peter?" her father asked, getting up from the sofa.

"Yes, please. That sounds great," Peter replied.

This was his opportunity. As soon as James was in the kitchen, Peter walked over and pulled the blinds aside. He pulled out his phone and discreetly took a picture to add to his research. In the picture were the two lovebirds, and what else he saw caused a grin he couldn't stop from spreading across his face. It was indeed the wolf-boy. And he recognized the Jetta.

Teagan laughed at something the demon wolf said. She, Peter realized, would be the key to getting to the rest of this pack. She was his plant, his "in." He desperately needed to recruit some believers.

He hurried from the window as he saw Teagan head back inside.

"Dad, I'm taking off for a bit," she called, poking her head in the door. Grabbing her coat, she left without waiting for a reply.

Peter wanted to stop her. He wanted to yell, "Don't go! He's a killer." But he couldn't. Not yet. Not until he had what he needed. What happened to the girl would remain to be seen. It couldn't really matter to him. She was just a pawn in the game, and he needed her.

"I don't like that guy Teagan is hanging out with," James confided as he returned with a couple of Cokes.

Peter smiled. It was time.

"Can I talk to you about something, James?"

"Sure, what's on your mind?" the older man replied.

"It's the reason I'm here in Red Ridge…." Peter took a deep breath and prepared to unveil his deepest secrets. It was now or never. "When I was young, I witnessed something unspeakable. In the years that followed, I was locked away, labeled insane, but now I have proof. I finally have all the evidence that I need. I can, finally, after all this time, avenge my uncle's death. You can avenge the disappearance of your wife. You can save your daughter from a similar fate!"

Confusion and concern filled James Rhodes's voice. "What the hell are you talking about? What about my wife and Teagan? Avenge them?"

"The guy your daughter is hanging out with, the man your wife left with, and the wolf that killed my uncle…well, they are all the same. The same breed of evil. They are *werewolves,*" Peter whispered. He'd argued with himself for some time before deciding on the lie about James's wife—he had no idea what happened to her after she split town—but he figured it was the best way to motivate him.

The look on James's face was familiar: Distrust. Disbelief. Not anger. Not rage. Had he misjudged the man after all?

"*What?* I don't know, Peter. You can't be serious. Werewolves? That just can't be."

"I understand your disbelief. But, James, I know what I'm talking about. I have dedicated my life to unveiling the existence of these beasts, and I have done all the work. I know where they live, what they look like, and unfortunately what they are capable of. James, did you know that your wife was seeing another man before she mysteriously vanished?" Peter felt bad about having to ask the question, but it was necessary. He wasn't certain what James had uncovered on his own, and this lent validity to the rest of the story.

"Of course I knew," James said through gritted teeth. He put his head in his hands.

"I did a little research. He was definitely one of them," Peter said. "And now your daughter is dating one of them. Do you want to lose them both?" He was becoming irritated by the man's lack of trust. What more did he need to say?

James sat back in his chair and reflected. After a moment: "You said you had proof?"

Peter felt a heavy weight lift off his shoulders. A small smile spread across his face and he said, "I do."

James released a large breath. "I'm not saying that I believe you, Peter, but I will want to see your proof."

"Next time we meet, you'll have all the answers you need," Peter replied. "Then you can help me destroy your daughter's boyfriend. We'll destroy all those goddamn monsters, every mutilating one."

As he was leaving, Peter felt better than he had in years. It was finally going to happen; he would finally have his chance. It didn't matter about collateral damage, the important thing was that he'd finally have revenge.

39.

Teagan

Just seeing Aiden filled my body with warmth despite the chill returning to the December air. He sat back with his hands stuffed in his coat pockets and a baseball cap on backwards, looking straight up like an Abercrombie & Fitch model, and I couldn't help but ask myself again what the hell he was doing with me. What did I care, though? I'd given in and abandoned my fears. So far it was worth it.

He pulled away from an all-too-brief kiss, gave me a knee-weakening grin and said, "Let's get out of here."

My God he was hot. Where was he planning on taking me?

He threw his arm around my shoulder and pulled me close. "It's not too cold for a walk, is it?" he asked.

There was no way I was going back inside my home, and I didn't want to go anywhere with people. I kind of just wanted Aiden all to myself, without every girl that passed checking him out; so, even though it seemed to be getting colder I said, "I can handle it if you can."

Aiden stopped in mid-step and put his other arm around me. "Oh, I think I can handle it. I'm sure we can find some way to keep warm."

Before I could respond, he leaned down and gently pressed his perfect lips to mine again. His hands moved up to my face and brushed the hair away from my cheeks, and I melted into his embrace, wishing this kiss would last forever. But all too soon he pulled away and said, "Come on. Let's get out of here. Don't want any more run-ins with your dad."

We made our way down the driveway. I ignored the urge to pout and instead cuddled back up under his arm. We continued down the street in silence.

My mind was running a mile a minute trying to think of something clever to say, trying also to disregard my he's-way-too-hot-for-me thoughts and fears.

Aiden broke the silence. "So, tell me something about yourself."

Shit. Really? Why did this suddenly make me nervous? "Well, let's see. My favorite color is orange."

Aiden smiled, but his eyes didn't quite meet mine when he glanced my way. "Seriously? That's what you got? Your favorite color is orange?"

"Yeah, orange," I said. "Your turn. Tell me something about *you.*" Turnabout was fair play.

"Okay," he said. "I don't really have a favorite color."

"How can you not have a favorite color?" I snapped. "Everyone has a favorite color. It's like the first major decision you make as a child."

Aiden laughed. "Huh. Well, I guess if I had to choose…I'd say silver."

"Silver?" I repeated with a smile. Was that even a color? I didn't know why I was grinning, considering I'd been nervous about playing this game, but I couldn't have contained my pleasure even if I wanted. Something about this guy made me grin like a giddy schoolgirl. It was the same thing that made the rest of me tingle in a very different way.

We made our way down the quiet street. Aiden squeezed my hand. "Tell me something else."

"Um, I don't know," I said. "There's not much to tell."

"Sure there is. Okay, I'll tell you three things about me, and then you have to do the same. Deal?" he asked.

"Deal," I agreed. There seemed no way out of it.

Aiden thought for a few seconds before he rambled off a list. "My favorite food is lasagna, I miss warm weather, and my family is absolutely nuts."

"Okay, let's see," I said. "I miss warm weather, too, as you know because we've discussed it. You're already well aware that my father is crazy, so I can relate to that, and my favorite food is macaroni and cheese."

"Hey, you can't just steal mine! You have to think up something else," Aiden complained.

"That wasn't in the rules. You'll need to be more specific next time," I teased.

Aiden laughed and shook his head. "Okay, fine. Tell me something else, though. One more thing and I'll let you off the hook."

I couldn't think of anything that was actually interesting. Not anything that I wanted to share with him, at least. Not yet. For that reason I responded, "I like animals."

Without a second thought he blatantly responded, "Well...I like *you.*"

"You hardly know me," I countered. I'd said it before I even thought, but it was true. I liked him, too, but I didn't necessarily think the feeling made any sense. Well, apart from it being natural to desire the hottest guy in the whole damn world. What I felt for him was irrationally powerful. More powerful than anything I'd felt for that douche bag Alex Foster, which made it even more dangerous.

Aiden stopped walking. He turned our bodies so that I was facing him. "Well, I know you better than I did five minutes ago, and I know enough to believe that these feelings are real. I liked you long before I knew anything about you, before you even said a word to me. I like you even more now."

I glanced away, unable to believe what this perfect specimen of a human being was saying to me. Danger, my mind screamed. The rest of me just tingled.

Aiden placed his fingertips against my chin and turned my face so that he could look into my eyes. "Really, Teagan, I feel so strongly about you that it hurts. I don't know if you feel the same way, though, and I really need to. Is it just me, or do you…like me too? Because I'm ready. I'm, like, bare-my-soul-and-offer-you-a-promise-ring, introduce-you-to-my-parents ready. I'm ready to call you mine forever. Am I crazy?"

Un-freakin'-believable. I didn't know what to do.

Jump his bones, kiss him until you can no longer breathe, make him yours too and never let go! That's what my body was begging for. I'd never felt anything like this. The burning in me was more intense than anything I'd ever felt, way more powerful than what I'd felt with Alex Foster. And it wasn't just Aiden's words that swayed me but something else, something primal.

Thank goodness my head kept my hormones in check. I managed to reply, "Are you seriously speaking in hyphenated modifiers right now?"

Hurt flashed across Aiden's face. He took my hand and said, "Are you seriously questioning my use of linguistic devices? That's what you have to say?"

"Aiden, this is just…all kind of sudden. I guess I'm shocked. That's it," I replied. I kept my voice low. My heart was screaming.

His eyes drifted to the ground, and then Aiden turned and started walking. As he dropped my hand, emptiness filled my body and a sudden chill ran up my spine. I just stood there, silently cussing myself for not saying the right thing. But what was a girl supposed to believe?

Aiden only took a few steps before he stopped, turned around, and walked slowly back. Without a word, he opened his coat, pulled me inside, and stood there silently holding me. Leaning down, he brushed his lips against my hair. "Guess, I'm crazy, huh?"

"No, you're not crazy," I said. "I am. For not telling you how I really feel."

He didn't move. I could feel his breath on my ear and wanted nothing more than to admit how much he scared me. I remembered Alex Foster, and I was terrified Aiden would hurt me in the same way. My dad's comments from the other night ran through my mind no matter how hard I tried to ignore them, too. How could I trust Aiden wouldn't love me then leave me?

Aiden interrupted my internal debate. "Well, tell me now. How do you really feel?"

"Honestly?" I asked.

"I would expect nothing less."

"Worried."

Aiden pulled away, but it was only so he could find my eyes. The look on his face told me everything I needed to know. He was scared too. He no longer looked like the womanizer that prowled our school hallways. He was just a guy—albeit a really hot guy—and he was worried just like me. When I looked into his soul, he was nothing like Alex. And yet...

"Why?" he asked.

"I'm worried that you'll break my heart."

No, I didn't ever want to feel that way again, the way I'd felt when Alex professed his love, screwed me then dumped my ass at school the next day. I'd been devastated, and the way I'd felt about Alex paled in comparison to how I felt about Aiden. If Aiden were to break my heart, I might not ever recover. But my feelings were too strong to deny, and I honestly didn't believe he was the same type of person. I couldn't say no to him. I *wouldn't*. I couldn't help but think again and again, "It's better to have loved and lost..." or whatever that damned saying was.

"But…I like you too, Aiden. More than I should. And I have for some time."

Without warning his lips covered mine. I didn't hesitate to deepen the kiss, either. I wanted this. I wanted to be Aiden's and for him to be mine. Scared or not, this was *right*.

My lips parted and our tongues met, dancing to the rhythm of our beating hearts. He breathed in and came back for more as if he couldn't stop if he wanted. But he didn't want to stop, and neither did I. My body became mush beneath his gentle hands, and he pulled me even closer. My fingers found minds of their own, and they ran up the back of his shirt, relishing the rippling muscles of his back and shoulders. A small moan escaped him.

All too soon he pulled away, resting his forehead against mine. Out of breath he whispered, "I won't hurt you, Teagan. Just give me a chance to prove it."

Before I knew, I'd whispered an answer.

Things would never be the same.

40.

Aiden

I was falling in love. Teagan was it: The One. So many things had changed in my life recently, and this was just another; but it was a very, very good change. I could only hope Teagan felt the same.

The ride back after returning her home was a strain. Her scent, still so strong on me in the tight confines of my Jetta, was overwhelming. Not that I was complaining. I freaking loved her scent. I just wished I hadn't had to get her back home. But it had been getting cold, and I'd been worried that if we stayed out there too much longer I would get carried away. We were finally making progress, and the last thing I wanted to do was scare her off.

All good times ended when I pulled into the driveway of our house. Marcus's car was there, and Dad was outside drinking a beer, which was never a good sign. I knew I was in trouble, too. He shot me a look that said I owed him big time. I wondered what happened after I left the meeting.

"Hey, big guy, what's all this about?" I asked.

"You better get in there," he said, pointing with his beer toward the door.

"I guess they noticed I left early, huh?"

"Oh yeah. They noticed," Dad confirmed.

I took a deep breath and walked in the door. The tension in the room was so thick you could actually smell it. Well, a wolf could.

"What's going on?" I asked, walking over to Mom and putting my arm around her shoulders.

"Marcus and Noel were just worried about you," she said. Her tone was sarcastic, a tone she reserved for people who were getting on her nerves.

Marcus, visibly irritated, ran his hand through his hair and turned to me. "The meeting was not over, Aiden. Why did you leave?"

"It was uncomfortable," I said.

Marcus's jaw clenched, and Mom took a step closer to me. I guess it was her wolfy instinct, to protect her young and all. I shot her a quick smile but took a step away. I didn't need her protection. I needed to handle this on my own.

"How are you supposed to lead this pack if you run away when things are uncomfortable?" Marcus asked.

I laughed, unintentionally, of course, but this whole situation was freaking ridiculous. "If I was leading this pack, I wouldn't have let my son go in there unaware and unprepared. But that's just my style. I guess yours is different."

Noel's hand flew to her mouth, like I'd just told her husband to go fuck himself—which I guess I had in a way. Marcus's eyes narrowed, and I could tell he wanted to punish me. He wanted total submission, and as alpha he was probably used to getting it; but he wasn't going to get it from me. Not after the stunt he'd pulled at that meeting.

"Listen, Marcus," I began.

"Dad," he interrupted.

"I'm not quite ready for that yet," I continued. Looking up to see if my other dad was in the room, I saw he was still outside but smiling through the window.

"I'm flattered that you want me to be the next alpha, but the decision is ultimately mine. Right?" I clarified.

"Of course it is," my mother said.

"Why the hell would you not want it?" came out of Marcus's mouth at the same time.

The truth was, I didn't know if I wanted a leadership role or not. Not yet anyway.

"I'm not saying that I don't want it," I told them. "I'm saying I need time to think about it. I need time to discuss it with my family. This is huge, and I only just turned yesterday. I just learned what it feels like to be a wolf. I need time to grow and develop if I'm going to lead a whole pack of them effectively."

"That sounds wise. Doesn't it, everyone?" Dad asked from the doorway.

Marcus probably wanted to tell him to shut his domestic-ass mouth, but thankfully Noel piped up. "It does, Paul. Come on, guys, let's go home."

"I'll meet you guys in a bit, okay?" Cade asked. He'd appeared out of nowhere. Noel just smiled at him and told him not to stay out too late. I was starting to like her. She really seemed to have it together, though I didn't know how she could stand by Marcus all the time. Agreeing with him constantly must get old.

"Alright, Aiden. But I want to discuss this further with you. In fact, I want you to take the day off from school tomorrow. Think about things; clear your head. And come see me when you're ready to really discuss this. Agreed?" Marcus asked, glancing at his wife.

"Sure," I said.

Once they were gone, Mom made some cinnamon rolls, and we all just sat around eating. We didn't talk about what had happened. Alli raised hell about me getting to skip school. Finally, she wore Mom down and somehow got her to agree to let both of us stay home. So, I wouldn't be lonely. I had a feeling everyone was waiting for me to bring up what had happened with Marcus, but it was a subject I wanted to ignore.

Eventually, Cade was ready to leave. As he put on his coat, he walked over and asked if I would mind giving him a ride home. I thought that strange, but I figured what the hell. Then it occurred to me he might have an ulterior motive. It hadn't just been my life turned upside down by Marcus's announcement.

"I was hoping we could talk about what happened today," Cade said as we got in the Jetta.

"Yeah, we probably should," I agreed.

He didn't speak for a moment. I started the car and we began heading toward his house.

"I understand that being the alpha is technically your birthright, since you're older, so if you decide that you want the job I won't fight you for it."

Holy shit. Fight me for it? The thought had never even crossed my mind. It got me wondering if anyone else would want to fight me for leadership. I'm a decent-sized guy, bigger than Cade, and if we fought as humans I could probably take him, but as a wolf…? Not a chance in hell.

"Okay," I muttered, unsure of how else to respond.

"But I need you to understand that this has always been my future. I have known all my life that I was going to replace my father. Until Alli showed up, I'd never disobeyed him. I have always put this pack first," he confided.

I pulled into his driveway. We sat there in silence for a while, then Cade continued, "I want this. I have always wanted this. So, please be one hundred percent sure before you decide to take it."

For some reason, I felt like he wanted—no, probably expected—me to step down and let him be the alpha. But I wasn't ready to just hand over the honor. I promised him that I would not take the decision lightly, and as Cade got out of the car I heard him say, "I can't believe my fucking dad."

That's when I really starting contemplating the situation. Why the hell would Marcus want me to be alpha and not Cade? Was this really about Cade choosing Al over Kendall? Was it because Cade hadn't done what he was told? Marcus was out of his mind if he thought that *I* was going to blindly do whatever he wanted. Cade would make a great alpha; but if he wanted it so bad, why would he just let me take the position away without a fight?

I drove back to my house. As I walked into my room and prepared for bed, all I wanted was to just go to sleep and make the day end; the only part I wanted to remember was the walk with Teagan. Which reminded me, before I fell asleep, I needed to text her and let her know that I wouldn't be at school the next day.

My phone buzzed just as I reached for it.

Teagan: Thanks for the visit today. :)

I grinned. Then I sent a quick text back before surrendering to sleep.

Aiden: My pleasure. I was about to text u. Not going to school tomorrow. Have some family stuff to deal with. Miss u. Night, beautiful. ;)

And I really did miss her. Like no other girl I'd ever been with.

41.

Peter

How to kill werewolves was typed into Peter's laptop search engine. He couldn't just expose this pack for what they were, they needed to be dead. All of them. And while he'd done research on eliminating the creatures before, he wanted to make sure he missed no new element that might give him an edge.

Finding a team of believers would be the hardest part of the plan. They were essential, though; he could not do this on his own. He knew firsthand just how powerful the beasts were. To try to kill an entire pack by himself would be nothing short of suicidal.

"I think we need a different strategy," James said as he took a seat across from Peter at the diner where they'd decided to meet. He'd been successfully convinced that werewolves existed and that his daughter was in grave danger. Peter had shown him all of his research last night after driving back with it: the newspaper articles about animal attacks, his official "werewolf profile," the photos of the local suspects that matched it. Soon he'd have DNA results, too. It was time to put a plan into action.

"Hey, James, glad you could make it," Peter said, quickly closing his laptop.

"So, I was thinking about this plan of yours all night. I'm sure there is no way that we will be able to convince enough locals that there are"—James looked around nervously before whispering—"werewolves living down by the lake."

Peter's eyes narrowed and his gut clenched. He resisted the urge to reach across the table and grab James by the throat. The only thing that stopped him was need. He didn't like the way this conversation had begun, though, and if James planned on backing out...well, Peter would just have to make sure that didn't happen.

"Listen, Peter, *I* believe you. I think. But to get that many grown men to believe in the unbelievable..." James let the sentence fall away. "Maybe we should just tell them it's something else."

"What are you suggesting?" Peter asked through clenched teeth. Telling people a lie wouldn't vindicate him or avenge his uncle. He wanted the truth to be known!

"A cult."

"What?" Peter said.

"We convince people that the lake-livers are all involved in some kind of weird cult. We could start some rumors about them brainwashing young women. Say they are convincing outsiders to marry their members or something like that, like those polygamists you see on TV. Have you been out there? It kind of looks like that already. All those huge houses surrounding the lake and woods like they're protecting something—or hiding something," James explained.

"When did you go out there?" Peter asked.

James looked ashamed. "I must have driven out there drunk one night a few months back. I passed out on the hood of my car with a bottle in my hand. A kid about Teagan's age woke me up and told me I was on private property. I got in my car and left."

"Did you get a good look around?" Peter asked, both surprised and excited.

"Not really. Like I said, I was drunk when I got there and hung over when I left," James answered.

Peter sat back in the booth and crossed his arms. He needed a minute to think about James's plan. Spreading rumors about a cult might work, he supposed. Based on his experience, crazed polygamist cults were more likely to be believed than werewolves.

And maybe the werewolves would shift back into wolf form when killed. That would prove he'd been telling the truth all these years.

"I like it! I think it will work. We need to get the rumors out there, and then we can let the grapevine take over," Peter said. Then they would fan the flames of revulsion and anger.

"Good," said James. "Let's meet at the bar tomorrow night after we draw up some actual rumors and figure out who to tell them to. The sooner I get Teagan away from that boy the better."

"Tomorrow? Yes, tomorrow. See you then, James," Peter told him.

As soon as James left the diner, Peter continued his search online. He would make one final scan and then he needed to get busy stockpiling weapons.

42.

Teagan

I walked in the door after school to the sound of my father banging around in the kitchen. What the hell was he doing now? I didn't have to wait long to find out, because before I made it two feet he was yelling.

"Teagan, get your ass in here. I need your damn help."

Seriously? I dropped my backpack and purse by the door and headed into the kitchen. His legs stuck out from underneath the sink, and I knew this wasn't going to be fun. My dad was no plumber, and he'd flood the entire house before he'd pay someone to fix anything.

"What's up, Dad. We got a leak?"

He lifted his head to give me his no-shit look. When apparently that glare wasn't enough, he muttered, "What do you think, dumbass? I'm just under here for the fun of it?"

Dumbass? Nice.

But, for some reason his insults didn't bother me like they used to. Maybe it was because I had Aiden. I did have Aiden, didn't I? I still tingled from yesterday's kisses.

I chuckled at the memory, which made my father angry. He cursed under his breath and scooted out from under the sink. Watching him struggle to his feet, I reached down to help him up.

"I don't need your goddamn help. Just get the hell out of here. You're no help to me anyway."

Without replying, I turned to walk out.

Apparently, that wasn't the right move either. Dad immediately started shouting obscenities so loud that the neighbors could hear.

Not that they hadn't heard it all before, but it was still as embarrassing now as when we first moved in. After hearing one of my father's infamous rants, someone came by to check if everything was okay. The meeting didn't go so well. Dad told them to mind their own damn business, and to stay the hell off our property unless there were gunshots or a fire. After that, the neighbors have just kept to themselves.

Figuring it was probably best to ignore him, I didn't stop. He could scream all he wanted; I didn't need to stay and listen to him call me every name in the book.

I slammed my bedroom door and began a search for my phone. It had been missing all day, and since Aiden wasn't at school, it was driving me crazy that I'd forgotten it at home. I finally found it between the wall and my bed, and I remembered that I'd fallen asleep holding it after reading Aiden's text.

There were no new missed calls or texts, so I resisted the urge to text him and wrote to Alli instead. Maybe she wanted to meet up at the mall. That seemed like a natural, girly thing to do this close to Christmas. Plus, for some reason she hadn't been at school either, and I kind of needed her to weigh in on what to do about Aiden. Truthfully, I wanted her to reassure me that he could be trusted.

My phone pinged. *Alli.* I was surprised to see that she'd invited me over to her house instead of meeting at the mall. I quickly texted back, let her know that I'd be there in a bit. After a long day at school I needed to freshen up. Aiden might be there, not to mention his parents.

Oh God, his parents! Things were different now, though. At least, I hoped they were.

I rushed to make myself presentable as quickly as possible. I tried to convince myself otherwise, but I knew it was because I was banking on Aiden being home. It might have only been a day since

I'd seen him, but butterflies had taken up permanent residence in my stomach after yesterday night and I couldn't wait to see him again.

The drive over was equally bizarre as the first time. It was definitely like these people were hiding from the outside world, but I shrugged off the weird and headed up to the Wrights' front door. Before I knocked, I took a deep breath, trying to contain my nervousness.

I had barely touched the door when it swung open. Alli ushered me in quick, like we were late for a movie. We bypassed the living room, with Alli shouting, "Going upstairs, guys."

Her parents, who seemed to be in the middle of an important conversation, looked up with surprise. I smiled and waved, trying not to be rude, but Alli grabbed my arm and all but dragged me up the stairs.

"Sorry, my parents have had kind of a weird day so far. We all have."

"Oh, is that why you weren't at school? Should I go?" I asked. Obviously something was going on.

Alli just smiled slightly and wandered to her bed. "No, it's okay. Really. Don't worry about it. Just family stuff. I'm glad you're here. How have you been?"

I wasn't sure what to say. How much had Aiden told her?

I walked over to the chair in the corner. "Good. I'm good. How about you?

Ignoring my question, Alli said, "So, you and Aiden, huh? I've hardly gotten the chance to talk to him alone, but I can tell something is up. So, what's going on with you two?"

Shit. How was I supposed to answer that? I'd been hoping to get information out of her. "We're good," I said.

"Good? What does that mean?"

"I mean, well…I like him, and I think he likes me too." There, I'd said it. No going back now. I'd set myself up for ridicule if it was going to come. Not that I really thought Alli was going to—

"You think he likes you too? Of course he does! I'd be surprised if he wasn't in his room right now writing love poetry and shit."

Alli never failed to make me laugh, and I loved her for it. "I didn't take Aiden for the love poetry type."

"Oh, no? Well, lately he's been all 'wherefore art thou Teagan,'" Alli said through laughter. Then, out of nowhere she banged on her wall. "Aiden!"

"Alli! Don't!" I begged, instinctively jumping out of my chair.

She didn't stop. "Calm down. Why do you think I invited you over? Figured I'd give y'all some time to chat."

Aiden's head poked through the door, and he smiled like he'd expected me to be standing there in the middle of his sister's room. He was wearing jeans and t-shirt, but his hair was wet and he was holding a towel by his side like he'd just gotten out of the shower. My heart all but leapt out of my chest.

"Hey. When'd you get here?"

"Just a few minutes ago. Alli invited me over," I answered, silently praying he was happy to see me. Walking over, he scooped me up in his arms. My body reacted as usual: complete and total meltdown.

"I'm glad you're here. I missed you today."

Alli chimed in. "Okay, you two. Get out of here and spend some time together. I got her here, Aiden, now it's up to you. But I'd take a walk or something. I have a feeling Mom will be up here any minute to offer Teagan a snack."

Aiden looked at me, nodded toward the door and asked, "You want to get out of here?"

Looking the way he did in that moment, I'd have followed him anywhere. I nodded and smiled at Alli, trying my best to thank her with my eyes. She just said, "Run out the door before Mom can stop you. Go! But don't forget your coats."

Aiden dragged me by the hand down the stairs. Out the front door we went, without a word to his parents, who both glanced up as we flew past the living room. Safely out the door, Aiden shrugged on his coat, and I noticed him looking around like he was checking to see if anyone was watching. Strange, but I tried to ignore the fact that he lived on what looked like some kind of freaky compound with people who seemed vaguely cultish. I thought it best to save that conversation for another time, a time in the distant future. The *very* distant future.

Aiden had yet to let go of my hand, and I welcomed the comfort of having him so near. Together we headed down toward the lake.

"You're going to get sick out here with wet hair, you know?" I said as we meandered alongside the water's edge.

"Nah, I'll be fine. You cold?"

"No, I'm fine. I wasn't inside long enough to take off my coat."

"Sorry about that. My parents are 'talking.'" Aiden air-quoted, which for some reason made me smile. Everything about him made me smile. I had officially turned into one of his giggling ding-bats.

"What's going on? I mean...you don't have to tell me if you don't want to. I just..." I stopped speaking and silently cussed myself for being so damn nosey.

"No, it's okay. Just stuff with Marcus. It's no big deal. Don't worry about it," Aiden said.

I quickly changed the subject. "So, how's your shoulder doing?"

"It's okay. The doc says my arm looks good. I'll be as good as new before I know it."

We walked a few feet in silence. Aiden let go of my hand and threw his arm around me, pulling me against him. Without thinking, I stopped moving and melted into his embrace. His lips found mine, and I snuck my arms into his coat and wrapped them around his perfectly sculpted body. Somehow, even in the frigid temps, his body was warm.

All too soon he pulled away. "I'm so glad you're here."

"Me too," I admitted as he held me tight, and for the first time I truly didn't doubt how he felt about me. With those strong arms engulfing my small frame, I knew he didn't want to ever let go.

Aiden's head perked up, and I turned to see a car pulling into the driveway a few houses down the street. He pulled away, and immediately the cold seeped into my bones. I shuddered.

"I should get back home," he said, "and you need to get out of this weather. Can I call you later?"

Oh. Trying to appear as though I was not completely bummed, I said, "Sure."

Aiden walked me to my car, and I told him to tell Alli that I'd call her later. I felt kind of bad since I was supposed to have come over to see her, but I was pretty sure she'd just been trying to get me and Aiden together. He gave me a soft kiss goodbye, and before I knew it I was on my way back home again.

43.

Aiden

"Man, it's getting cold out there," I said as I rubbed my hands together. I had just come back inside after Teagan left, and I was trying to be pleasant in attempt to hold on to my good mood. Mom and Dad were in the living room, so I hung up my coat and went in to thaw out by the fireplace.

I could almost feel my fingers again when my mom looked over and said, "Baby, it's probably not a good idea for Teagan to just show up here. We wouldn't want her to see something that she shouldn't. You know?"

What? Now *she* was telling me stupid things I could and couldn't do? I'd never had to ask permission for friends to come over before, not back in Texas. When I thought about it I saw Mom's point, but it wasn't like any of us wandered around here on all fours or sat on our haunches howling at the moon. What the hell would Teagan mistakenly see?

Just as I was about to start complaining, someone pounded on the front door.

"Who the hell could that be?" my dad asked, sounding extremely annoyed. "Of course," he muttered to himself after walking over and glancing through the door's peephole. He pulled the door open and made a grand gesture of ushering someone inside. "Come on in, Marcus. Obviously this is pretty important, but you don't have to punish our poor defenseless door."

Marcus stared at my dad like he was from another planet, clearly unamused. "I need to speak to Aiden."

"By all means," Dad said. He shut the door and followed Marcus back to the living room, leaned up against the wall next to the fireplace and crossed his arms.

Marcus looked pissed. I stood up and walked over. "What's up, Mr. W?" I asked, trying to stay cool.

"'What's up?' Aiden, are you serious? You had a domestic on the estate?"

I took a step back. Not because he was intimidating, but because I was extremely weirded out. I wasn't used to being yelled at. My parents rarely even raised their voices.

When I didn't say anything, Marcus continued his rant. "You can't go bringing random girls around here, Aiden. We can't have it. I can't have it. It is unacceptable."

"It's my fault, Mr. Walker," Alli interrupted, coming into the room. Everyone turned to stare at her. "She's my friend from school. I invited her. We were supposed to go shopping."

Alli looked at the ground then, like she was expecting to feel the wrath of Marcus firsthand. But there was no way in hell I was going to let her take the blame.

"No, Alli," I intervened. "Mr. Walker, Teagan is not some random domestic. She's my girlfriend, and I didn't realize having her at the house would be a problem. Now that I know that, it's fine. We can meet somewhere else," I added.

When I looked around, shock was written on my mom and Marcus's faces.

"Girlfriend, huh?" my dad said. He smiled. "Cool. I like that one."

"Well, I don't," Marcus growled. "Aiden, you cannot date a human. You are going to be the next alpha. You have to think about what is best for the pack. What's wrong with the girls on the estate? What would everyone think, you dating some weak domestic?"

"Now wait a minute. He can date whomever he wants," my dad said in return. He threw his hands in the air, and his voice was louder than I'd ever heard it.

Marcus completely ignored him, continued to glare at me.

"Mr. Walker—," I started.

"Quit calling me that! I am your father, damn it," he said. He turned to my mom and pointed his finger in her face. "This is your fault, Lily, and I expect you to fix it. He will not date a human, he will take my place as alpha of this pack, goddamn it, and he will start calling me father!"

Oh, hell no. This guy obviously knew nothing about parenting. Yelling at my mother in front Paul and my sister was beyond stupid. It certainly wasn't the best way to get me to do what he wanted.

My dad stepped up, took my mom's hand and pulled her to him. Alli walked over stand beside them, and she reached out to hold my mom's other hand. It was like they were building a wall, teaming up against Marcus. I walked over and took a position as well.

"I think we should talk about this another time, Mr. Walker," I said with disdain.

"Aiden, please," he begged.

"I will continue to consider your offer. I will make sure that Teagan does not come on the estate again, but she is my girlfriend, and I will not let anyone come between us. And I mean *anyone*," I growled. He wasn't going to bully me or my family ever again.

He stood there a moment longer, anger and frustration written all over his face, but finally he said, "Aiden, we will continue this conversation. I will not let you ruin your future or the future of this pack." And with that he walked out of the house.

"You okay, Ad?" Alli asked.

"Just great. But that guy is an ass, Mom," I said.

My dad chuckled. "I second that."

My mom didn't smile like she normally would have; she looked at me as if genuinely concerned for my well-being. She knew what Marcus was capable of, I suppose. She'd known for years, and that's why she left.

"Mom, is this how it's going to be from now on? He disapproves, so he runs over and jumps on my ass?" I asked.

She didn't argue. Instead, she whispered, "I'm so sorry, Aiden." Her voice cracked, and I thought she might start to cry right there in the middle of the living room.

"I don't know how Cade manages," Alli said under her breath. "Living under his roof."

This was all too much. I'd thought being a werewolf was going to be the shit, at least at first when I was told. Superhuman strength, speed, ultra awesome senses... But it's been nothing but stress and pain. First I got my ass kicked by Dylan because I couldn't shift; then I found out about Marcus; now all this crazy alpha drama? I'd only transformed once, and I had no idea how to even do it again.

Oh, man. I didn't even want to think about what Teagan was going to do when I told her the truth. I couldn't keep it from her forever.

I also couldn't tell her. Not just yet. She wasn't ready.

Or maybe the truth was, I wasn't.

44.

Teagan

I came home to find my father packing an overnight bag. He looked up and nodded, acknowledging my existence but not bothering to explain where he was headed. Nice. First he called me a dumbass, then he planned to just take off? Sometimes I wondered what would happen if he just left and didn't come back. Where would that leave me? There were times I worried that he would do just that. Mom had. Why not him too?

I stood in the doorway watching him. When it was clear he really wasn't going to divulge his little plan, I asked him straight out. "So, where are you off to?"

He cleared his throat: one of his infamous signs of deception. He's always been a shitty liar.

"Uh...just going on a little hunting trip with Peter. We should be back tomorrow."

"Hunting? Since when do you hunt?"

Avoiding eye contact Dad replied, "Well, I don't really. Just going along for the ride. No big deal. Like I said, I'll be back tomorrow."

I didn't bother with any more questions.

I'd only been home a few minutes and I already missed Aiden, so I wandered off to my room. Inside, I reached up and touched my lips. No matter how much I tried to fight it, I'd fallen for him. Hard. Fast. Just like I'd been afraid of. Damn it.

I sat down at my desk and shuffled through my schoolwork, hoping to catch up on some studying. As I did, I heard the front door close and the sound of my dad's car pulling out of the driveway. Relief washed over me. I was glad to have him out of my hair.

I'd almost made it to the halfway point of my math homework when my phone chimed. It was Aiden, so I couldn't help but smile. This was the distraction I needed.

Aiden: Gotta get out of my house. Want to meet somewhere?

As fast as my little fingers would move, I typed a response:

Teagan: My dad is gone for the night. Want to come here?

Wait, what was I doing? Was this a good idea? I sat and stared at my phone awaiting a reply. My pulse was racing just thinking about having Aiden here all to myself, in the house, and I wanted to kick myself for feeling excited but couldn't help it. Spending time alone with him was exactly what I wanted. Even if it was the worst idea in the world.

When my phone chimed again, a stupid schoolgirl giggle fled my lips. His response Inspired giddiness:

Aiden: Already on my way.

I rushed to the bathroom to reapply my makeup. A little blush and lip gloss would do; I didn't want to be too obvious. Then I hurried to the kitchen to see if there was anything to eat. I hadn't had dinner, and I thought it would be nice to make something. But of course our pantry and fridge were bare. The doorbell rang just as I started my search for the number to the pizza place down the street.

My heart pounded as I made my way to the door. I took a deep breath in an attempt to calm the swarm of butterflies in my stomach, then I opened the door and there he stood, looking as mouth-wateringly hot as always.

I moved aside to let him in. He entered without taking his eyes off of me, which only intensified the tension building inside. God, he could make me swoon with just a look. What was he going to do now that we were alone? Would my nervous energy ever subside? He was just too yummy for words.

He breezed past me, calm and cool, and I tried to ignore the urge to jump his bones right there in our tiny entryway. "So, you want to order pizza or something? Not much to eat around here."

Aiden turned on his heel and headed back. Wrapping his strong arm around my waist, he pulled me close and planted an all-too-chaste kiss on my lips. Damn him. Did he have any clue what he did to me? He always left me wanting more.

Seeming completely oblivious, he said, "I'm up for whatever you are."

My thoughts turned to everything but food. An evil little grin spread across his face, and suddenly I wondered if that had been his intent all along. Was he teasing me? Was he suggesting we do something other than eat? Hopefully his thoughts were more innocent than my own. At least, I thought I hoped that.

Much to my dismay, he left me standing there wanting again. Heading into the kitchen, he walked over to the landline and asked for the pizza menu. I reined in my raging hormones and found it, and after I ordered we sat at the kitchen table making small-talk.

In the back of my mind, all I could think about was the fact that we were alone. We'd only been seeing each other for a short time. If I took his hand and led him to my bedroom, which is what I really wanted to do, would he think I was a slut? The last time I was in this situation, it didn't turn out so well. But this was Aiden. It felt different this time. It *was* different with Aiden.

How long was the appropriate amount of time to wait before having sex, anyway? Was it right if you loved the guy? And he'd mentioned something about a ring during our walk earlier. Had he meant it?

Wait. What was I thinking? Did I love Aiden? I wondered. Was I ready for that kind of commitment?

Maybe I was.

The pizza arrived, and we had a carpet picnic in the living room and watched a *Jersey Shore* marathon. The show was completely ridiculous, to say the least, but we couldn't help watching. Then, on a commercial break, Aiden reached for my hand.

"So, can I ask you something?"

I looked at him, incredulous, worried what he might say, but finally I answered, "Sure."

"You think your dad will always hate me?"

It wasn't the question I'd been expecting. I wanted to say, "Who gives a shit what Dad thinks?" but I didn't figure that was the answer he was looking for. He wanted something real.

"I don't know." I gave a nervous laugh. "If you haven't noticed, he's not exactly mentally stable."

Aiden didn't laugh in return. Epic fail at my attempt to lighten the mood. A serious expression spread across his all-too-pretty face, and I felt my heart pounding again, this time with fear. Where was he going with this? Was he going to dump me because of my family, just like I'd figured all along? I wanted nothing more than to be able to read his mind.

He intertwined his fingers with mine and his eyes shifted to the floor. "So, what's up with him?"

I hadn't talked about this thing with anyone. No one. But for the first time ever, I wanted to. Aiden had already witnessed the bat-shit craziness of my father, and he hadn't run for the hills. Not yet. He'd actually stood up to him, which was the absolute last thing I'd expected. Even if he decided to run now, he deserved to have his questions answered honestly.

"I don't know, really. He's always been a drinker, but after my mom…well, after my mom took off everything just kinda fell apart.

It's not like he was ever the perfect dad, but he's…well, you've seen him. I think he's completely lost his mind."

"Your mom took off on you? That must have been hard, losing her. Hard on both of you." Aiden let his words just kind of hang there. It wasn't a question or a statement, exactly. More like something in between. Something sensitive and pensive.

He gave me a weak smile when I looked up at him. There wasn't pity in his eyes, either, just genuine concern. He did care about me. Did he *love* me? That I didn't know, but he did care, and that was enough for me. It was more than I'd ever imagined I'd get from him.

I laid my head on his shoulder and admitted, "I stopped hoping she'd come back a long time ago. The heartache turned into anger, and now if she did show back up, I'm not sure I'd even want to speak to her. I don't think I could handle the excuses, you know? There'd have to be excuses."

Aiden shook his head. "You're like the strongest person I know. You practically take care of yourself, and I'm all pissed off because I have too many people in my family worried about me. Kinda makes me feel like a jerk."

"You're not a jerk, Aiden," I said. "You're…perfect."

God, I was such an idiot. Why couldn't I just keep all my stupid thoughts in my head.

Aiden reached up and gently cupped my face in his hand. With his lips only millimeters away he whispered, "Can I tell you something?"

I just nodded my head. I couldn't find the strength to speak.

"You're absolutely nuts if you think I'm perfect. But I think *you're* kinda perfect. And, well…now you're going to think I'm nuts. Because…because I have to tell you something else. I've fallen in love with you, Teagan."

Holy shit, Batman. He *was* crazy. He'd freakin' lost his ever-loving mind. *Love* me? Seriously? You couldn't love someone after only a few weeks, could you?

Maybe you can.

Before I realized it, words were spilling out of my mouth, words that I meant whole-heartedly. Right there on my living room floor, I admitted for the first time how I truly felt about Aiden Wright. "I love you too."

Aiden launched himself forward. As his lips brushed mine, every ounce of need within me exploded. I wanted him. God, I wanted him. I pulled him closer and wrapped my arms around his neck, deepening our kiss and lying back with the hope he'd follow. He did, and his body covered mine, and I reveled in the feel of his weight on top of me. His lips never left mine.

Banishing all thoughts of where we were and whether or not what I was about to do made me a slut, I reached down and pulled his shirt up over his head. Aiden let me, but he drew back slightly and looked directly into my eyes.

"We don't have to do this. Not now. I'd wait a lifetime for you. I want you to be sure. No regrets."

I didn't respond with words. Instead, I grabbed the back of his neck and pulled him down until his lips covered mine once more.

45.

Peter

The plan was to meet James at Tucker's Icehouse tonight, the bar just down the street from the Red Ridge Motel. This was phase one of Recruitment. James had assured him that in order for their plan to work it needed to be done over a longer period than Peter originally intended; each night's story would grow more desperate. They'd both retired to their individual homes to consider the stories they'd tell. Peter agreed with the methodology, he supposed, but he was also anxious to get results.

He walked through the bar doors at exactly nine o'clock. James was already there, and if the number of empty beer bottles in front of him was any indication, the man was well on his way to belligerent.

"Shit," Peter muttered to himself. He hated drunks. He needed the man alert and focused tonight, not slurring his words. Peter faked a smile, though, as he walked over. "James, how's it going, man?"

"Peter, my friend, come sit!" the drunk called, waving down the joint's one cocktail waitress. She walked over and took Peter's order, and before he could say anything she was back with his beer.

Peter wasn't sure what James had in mind, so he just started in with what he hoped sounded like a normal question. "So, how's your daughter doing?" They had to establish themselves as normal, caring members of society. Fathers and such. Trustworthy.

James smiled like Peter had just asked the magic question. "I have to tell you, Pete. I'm worried about her," he said, a little too loudly. It was all part of the plan. "Why?" he asked.

"It's this new boyfriend of hers. He's one of those lakefront kids, and I don't know... I just don't trust them. Seems like those rich bastards are... Well, I dunno. They're just so cliquish. Secretive. *Elitist.*"

Peter looked around. A few of the barflies were already interested.

"Have you talked to Teagan about it?" he said, trying to appear genuinely concerned.

"Yeah, but she's smitten. She thinks he can do no wrong. He has her wrapped around his little finger," James complained.

"Does he seem like a decent kid?"

James leaned back in his chair and said, "No, he seems like a snake. Can I tell you something, Peter?" He leaned forward, like he was going to reveal a truly earth-shattering secret, but his voice didn't soften at all.

"Sure, James. Anything."

"I think he's *brainwashing* her. I think everyone out on that lake is crazy, and they're trying to take my daughter away from me. I think they're a bunch of brainwashing sex perverts!"

Peter sat back and pretended to contemplate what he'd just heard. Time passed. He was about to flag down the waitress for another beer when the man from the next table asked to join them.

William, his name was. James introduced them. William had been born and was raised in Red Ridge, James said, and Peter could tell that their suggestion had hit pay dirt.

"I heard you talking about the people down by the lake. I have always thought there was something weird going on there, James," William whispered. "It's too private, too secretive. Always has been. I think you need to get your Teagan away from that boy. She's too nice of a girl to get mixed up with them."

"Well, thanks, Bill. I just don't know what to do short of going over there guns blazing and grab her back from him," James complained.

"We do what we have to do for family," William said. "You know, there are a few of us around here that don't want their kind near our town. I bet the others would be willing to help you out. I know I would."

"I appreciate that, Will. I truly do. I might need to take you up on that offer sometime," James was quick to say.

Peter wanted to smile but refrained. This was a serious business. Recruiting had begun.

46.

Teagan

I awoke to my blaring alarm clock. It was already six thirty, and if I didn't hurry I was going to be late for school. I faintly remembered Aiden waking me with a kiss before he left to head home about an hour before.

Standing in front of the mirror, I starred at myself, wondering if I looked any different. I might not see any change, but I definitely was a new person. I might have had sex before, but this was the first time I'd ever made love. Memories of Aiden flooded my mind: his gentle touch, the way we'd melded together, how he'd held me afterward as though he never wanted to let go. Our night together had confirmed that our feelings were real. He did love me.

I quickly showered, put on a bit of makeup and threw on some clothes. As I left I had a damp ponytail, but I didn't want to be late. I couldn't wait to see Aiden. I loved him so much. There was no denying it now. There was no point, either.

I pulled into the parking lot with just enough time to rush to my locker and high-tail it to first period. Finding Aiden would have to wait, I supposed, as I got out of my car. But as I hurried through the main doors, my phone chimed.

Aiden: Running late, find u after 1st per.

I typed *OK* so he'd know I'd seen his text. I hoped he wasn't in trouble for staying out so late. My own dad probably wouldn't have noticed, but something told me Aiden's mom would. She probably didn't like her son staying out all night.

I made it to my locker with only a few minutes to spare, and as I fumbled with my locker combination someone practically pounced on me. There she stood, leaning her perfectly polished self against the locker next to mine. And before she said a single word, I knew it wasn't going to be good.

Without any pleasantries whatsoever, taking a page straight from Kendall Stuart's playbook, Becca attacked.

"So, I hate to be the one to tell you this, but you'd be better off ending whatever little fling you're having with Aiden. Now. Right now. Really, I'm just looking out for you. I don't know what he's even thinking. I mean, if his mother knew that your father was the town drunk—and trust me, she will find out—she'd never allow you within fifty feet of her son. Let's face it, Teagan. You're not good enough for him. But surely you already know that."

Becca finally decided to take a breath, so I cut in. "Thanks so much for your concern. Really, how kind of you to be looking out for my best interest...but do you really think this is any of your business?"

With a cruel smile, she continued. "Oh, honey, of course it's my business. I know you haven't been here long, but if you haven't noticed we look out for our own around here. Aiden may be new to this school, but he's part of our group. You know, the group that dissed you last year—for good reason? To be perfectly honest, you've got no chance ever of getting in with us, especially with your family's history. If you think you do, you're crazier than your deadbeat father. Or maybe you're drinking as much as him."

By this point my blood was way past boiling. I could literally feel my cheeks burning. Tears threatened to spill down my face, but I refused to let Becca think she could get to me. Screw this bitch. She needed a taste of her own medicine.

"Maybe the real problem here, Becca, is that Aiden isn't interested in what you have to offer. If you think us nobodies haven't noticed that you sit up and pant every time he's near, you're the one crazier than my 'deadbeat father.' So, let's just be real here. I've got what he wants, and you…well, you obviously don't. So, how about you take your little 'I'm-just-looking-out-for-you' bullshit and shove it up your ass." Then, before she could respond, I took off down the hallway.

I might have had the last word with Becca, but her words hit too close to home. They'd made me doubt everything that happened between Aiden and me. Was what she said true? I certainly wasn't one of them. I'd never be one of them, either. Who was I kidding? They would never accept me.

Without thinking twice, I headed straight toward the parking lot so I could get the hell out of school before I broke down. There was no way I was going to class now. My eyes were already threatening to fill with tears as I rushed the exit. I heard Sean calling my name but I didn't turn around. I knew he would want to talk about it, and since we hadn't spoken much since the play I didn't want to get into it. I needed to be alone. I was done. Done with Becca, done with Aiden's parents' strange little enclave and the Beautiful People, done with it all.

By the time I got into my car at the back of the school parking lot, tears were streaming down my face because I'd suddenly realized that if I really was done with it all, I was done with Aiden too.

I started the car and took off toward my house. School clearly wasn't in the cards for me. Not today. Neither was Aiden Wright. I couldn't talk to him. Not when I didn't know whether or not I could handle being with him. No matter how much I liked him—*loved* him—would this ever work? I should have listened to my instincts. I'd known Aiden wasn't the right guy for me from the very start. Anyone could take one look at the two of us and know we didn't belong together. I was just an average girl, and there was no denying there was something special about Aiden. Something I doubt anyone could define.

On the drive home, I set my phone to silent and shoved it deep into my purse; if I knew Aiden was calling, I wouldn't be able to ignore it. When I got home, I dried my eyes and slid back into bed. I covered my face with my pillow and begged for sleep to take me away from the feelings I wasn't ready to face.

47.

Aiden

"What the hell did you say to her, Becca?" I demanded when I finally caught up with her and her crony in the middle of the commons. I'd heard the story from Sammy, who'd seen the whole thing, and I was fuming.

Becca stopped walking and swung around to face me. Shari came to a halt as well. She took one look at my face and scrambled, leaving her friend standing alone, but Becca didn't seem fazed. She actually looked a little proud of herself.

"I did that girl a favor. You should be thanking me," she said, taking a quick glance around to make sure no one was watching us and lowering her voice so that prying ears wouldn't hear. "Do you really think for one minute that you can have a relationship with a human?"

I said nothing. How the hell was I supposed to respond to that?

"Omigod, you did. You actually thought Marcus would let you carry on this little fling with a domestic. That's sweet—but come on, get real. Aiden, it would never be allowed. You have to realize that. Just look what Marcus put Cade through, and Alli's only half human. Do you really want to subject that poor little girl to the wrath of our alpha?"

It was clear that Becca was really pulling out all the stops. There was nothing that she wouldn't say to make me break things off with Teagan, but her words were also making me think.

"You know what?" Becca went on. "Why don't we just pretend that whatever you and that girl had going on—"

"Teagan," I interrupted.

"Okay, you and *Teagan* had going on, never happened. We can fix this, Aiden. Take me out this weekend? I can make you forget all about your poor little Teagan. It'll make Marcus happy. I'm *allll* wolf."

Was she serious? My eyes widened as she took a step closer and placed her hands on my chest. She *was* serious. Holy hell, I couldn't handle this right now. The chick was absolutely crazy if she thought I'd leave Teagan for her, especially after everything that had happened before.

"Becca, are you hearing yourself? Are you so delusional that you think I would ever go out with you? You're a hateful, evil bitch that has to make others feel badly about themselves so you can feel good. You better pray that when I catch up to Teagan she realizes how full of shit you are, because if you hurt her, there will be hell to pay." Without giving her a chance to respond, I turned and hurried down the hallway. I had to find my girl.

She was nowhere to be found. I tried calling her again and again, but she didn't pick up. I couldn't figure out where she might have gone.

"Hey, did you talk to her?" Alli asked as she met me at the car after school.

"I just tried her phone again. Nothing. I wish I knew what Becca said."

Alli bit the inside of her cheek. That meant she was trying to keep herself from talking.

"What do you know?" I demanded.

"I really don't want to be the one to tell you," she replied, leaning up against the car.

Every muscle in my jaw tightened. "What did she say, Alli?" I asked through clenched teeth.

My sister moved from the driver's side over to where I was standing. She looked around quickly before spewing all the dirty details she'd gotten from Cami. After the first few sentences, her words were drowned out by the sound of my heart pounding in my ears. My sister was still talking, but I couldn't hear a thing. My anger and hurt were destroying my hearing.

I could only imagine the look on Teagan's face when Becca confronted her. The image broke my heart and made me want to rip Becca to pieces at the exact same time.

"Aiden. *Aiden.* Are you listening?" Alli asked.

"Yeah?" I said. I'd finally heard. But then my thoughts got in the way again.

I tried to calm myself down before I did something I'd regret, but it wasn't working. My vision tunneled, and I was only vaguely aware that Cade had walked over. He tried to talk to me, but once again I could only see his mouth moving; I could only hear the sound of my racing pulse. Rage was building inside of me, and if I didn't get out of there fast, the students of Red Ridge High were going to get an eye-full.

Suddenly, Cade was in my face. He grabbed me by my jacket and shoved me into the backseat of the Jetta then got behind the wheel. Within seconds we were speeding out of the school parking lot and heading toward the estate. I just sat there watching the clock on the dashboard, and as each minute passed I grew more and more desperate to change. But I knew I wasn't in control and was trying to fight it off.

"Want me to pull over?" Cade asked, looking at me in the rear view mirror. All I could do was nod.

As soon as he stopped, I jumped out of the car.

"Aiden, wait! Do you want me to come with you?" Alli yelled.

"No. I need to be alone," was all I could manage before I took off into the trees.

The change came more quickly this time, almost instantly. There was no pain, no panic, just a sense of release. I needed to run. I longed to run until my legs were shaky and numb. I needed to rid myself of the rage inside me before I went to find Teagan. She didn't need to deal with me or my anger issues; she needed to know that everything Becca said was a lie. Now more than ever she needed to know how I felt about her.

By the time I slowed down, I could tell I was close to home. I could smell the estate, the familiar scents of the pack. I was feeling better, more calm and in control. I took a moment to wander though the underbrush, allowing the cool December air and fresh smells to ease the anger and tension from my body. I only hoped that when I turned back this tranquility would stay.

Suddenly, a giggle from my left startled me, and before I knew what was happening I went from wolf to bare-ass-naked human. When I stood up, I saw two people heading my way.

"Holy shit. Aiden?" Luke asked.

I ripped a leafy branch of the closest tree and used it to cover myself. I could tell Luke was doing his best not to laugh at me, which I truly appreciated since Cami was laughing so hard I thought she might pee herself.

"Looking goooood, Aiden," Cami said when she finally managed to compose herself.

"Gee, thanks," I replied. There wasn't much more to say.

Luke handed me the blanket he carried. As I wrapped it around my hips, I noticed he and Cami were looking at each other like I'd caught them doing something naughty. I wondered what was going on. Together, we headed back onto the estate.

"Hey, Aiden, we would appreciate it if you wouldn't tell anyone that we were out here. Cami's parents don't know about us," Luke admitted as we left the woods.

"Of course, but what's the big deal?" I asked. It's not like either one of them was a human.

"They've known me my whole life. Let's just say they think she can do better. I don't blame them, either. I guess I deserve the reputation I have around here. I wouldn't want my daughter dating me either."

"Well, they won't hear it from me," I said.

We said our goodbyes as soon as we got to the lake. By then I was so cold that my teeth were chattering uncontrollably, so I held on to the blanket and ran all the way back to our house.

"What in the name of Christ happened to you?" my grandfather asked as I came flying through the front door. He was standing next to Cade and Alli. They looked at me apologetically.

It seemed like this was always happening lately. I'd come home, hoping for some quiet time, only to find that the family had guests. It was just my mom's parents this time, but they didn't fail to give me a you-still-can't-control-yourself look. I felt like shouting, "Yes, I'm naked. Yes, I shifted on accident in the middle of nowhere! Still want me to be your damn alpha?" Instead, in all of our best interests, I ignored the entire crew and went straight to my room.

On the way upstairs I could hear my grandfather telling Cade there was no way I could handle being the head of the pack. Awesome. Just freakin' awesome. My own grandfather was already planning to back Cade. I wasn't sure if I wanted to be alpha or not, but I at least wanted my grandparents to support me.

Alli had put my backpack and phone on my bed. I grabbed the latter to see if Teagan had finally called me back. Nope.

Pushing my anger and anxiety aside, I sent her a text:

Aiden: Baby, I'm so sorry about Becca. Please call me. I need to hear your voice. I love you.

Then I waited for a reply.

When I'd woken up this morning with Teagan snuggled up next to me, I thought that this was going to be a perfect day. I couldn't have been more wrong. After an hour of staring at my phone, I had a feeling that she wasn't going to respond.

48.

Teagan

The sound of the slamming front door jostled me awake. Somehow, I'd managed to drown out all thoughts of Aiden and Becca and allowed sleep to take me away. Unfortunately Aiden had haunted my dreams, and when I woke I had to restrain myself from immediately digging out my phone from the hidden depths of my purse. If he'd called, I didn't trust myself enough not to return it, and if he hadn't, I wasn't sure I could handle the disappointment. So instead I vowed to stay away from my phone for the next twenty-four hours.

All the commotion going on in the kitchen made it clear that my father had a visitor, and an uneasy feeling washed over me when I heard the voice of his new friend, Peter. Something about that guy screamed *creeper*.

Even though I was supposed to be at school, my car was in the driveway, so surely Dad knew I was home, but he didn't come check on me to see why I was in my room instead of class. While that shouldn't surprise me, it kind of did. Apparently he had more important things to attend.

Tiptoeing out of my room and down the hall, I made my way toward the kitchen. There I peeked around the corner and watched as Dad and Peter laid a huge poster board with newspaper clippings, charts, graphs, and sticky notes across the kitchen table. Next they laid out 4" x 6" pictures as well as some note cards, the latter which they aligned neatly beside the pictures.

It looked like a giant school research project, sans a laptop, but since my father had barely finished high school before enlisting in the military I couldn't begin to imagine what these two were up to. They chatted quietly amongst themselves and examined their work. Then Peter carefully unfolded something he dug out of his pocket, a crinkled piece of notebook paper. Together they glanced over the information.

My dad shuffled though a box and pulled out some blank note cards. He took the paper from Peter's hand, sat down, and began taking more notes. Peter stood over his shoulder and watched.

Of all the insane things I'd witnessed my father do, this topped the charts. It only took about five minutes before my curiosity got the best of me, so I wandered in leisurely as if I hadn't been standing there spying. "What's all this?" I asked.

Immediately my dad tried to shield their little project. Peter stood back, though, and with a wicked grin he waved his hand across the table as though to proudly present the work.

Dad reluctantly removed his body from the kitchen table, taking his cue from Peter. He stood up, but he wasn't first to speak. Evidently, he was going to let Peter do the explaining.

"Teagan, it's good that you're here. There are some things we should all discuss, and it does involve you, darling. Come on over and take a look," my dad's young friend announced.

My stomach clinched. *Darling? WTF.*

My gut was warning me to stay away, but I needed to see what this was all about. I didn't know why, but I had a sneaking suspicion that it had something to do with Aiden.

The suspicion was quickly confirmed, for I saw Aiden's picture sitting there near the poster along with snapshots of Alli and Cade picking up Aiden's car which appeared to have been left by the side of the road. Below that were pictures of Becca and Shari walking across a parking lot. But it was the bottom picture that set my cheeks aflame. That one had Aiden and I kissing outside my house.

Instinctively, I backed away from the table. "What the hell is all of this? Why do you have pictures of me and Aiden and his family and his friends?" Had Peter actually been stalking us?

He moved toward me and attempted to rest his hand on my shoulder, but I was faster and dodged his don't-worry-I'm-friendly gesture. He dropped his hand to his side and explained, "It's not what you think, Teagan. We—"

I cut him off mid-sentence. "Not what I think? I have absolutely no idea what to think about all of this. This is crazy!"

"Just come over here and look at the poster, Teagan. You need to know what you've gotten yourself into. Prepare yourself. This is no joke. These people, your boyfriend... They're not human. You may not believe this now, but they are werewolves, Teagan. All of them, and I can prove it. Just take a look," Peter explained.

Werewolves? Oh my God. They were crazy. My father had officially become mad—as in deranged, off his rocker, insane in the membrane. Werewolves? I thought again. This was all too much.

Incredulous, I glanced at Peter and then my dad. My eyes shot back and forth between the two of them, but they weren't laughing. This wasn't a joke. Holy shit, they were serious.

After a few seconds of dead silence I asked, "Have you two gone completely nuts? Werewolves? You really expect me to believe these people are werewolves? All of them? You expect me to believe that such creatures even exist? I mean, I like Jacob Black as much as the next girl, but really? What next? You going to tell me that you're were-hunters?"

Peter stared at me, and I could see a manic look in his eyes. "Teagan, this is no laughing matter. Yes, these people are werewolves. I know it's hard to believe, but just take a look at our research. The proof is there in black and white. These people are killers, and your father and I plan to expose them for what they are.

People in this town need to know that those crazies hiding out there in the woods, even their kids at your school, are vicious animals."

This rant was spoken with complete and utter seriousness. My father, on the other hand, just stood there looking as dumbfounded as I felt, so I turned my attention to him. "Dad? What do you have to say about all of this?"

Peter shot him a look that seemed to say *Well, go ahead and tell her*.

Suddenly, the man who was standing there with his mouth hanging open stood tall and spoke more eloquently than I could ever remembering him speaking. Usually he was a babbling idiot, but at this moment, he was calm and direct, two adjectives that I would never have dreamed of using to describe my father. Not in the past few years.

"Teagan…like Peter said, I know this is a lot to take in, but it's true. There are werewolves in this town, and if you just look at our work you will see them. I'm sorry, but Aiden is one. Peter saw him shift with this own two eyes. You need to stay away from these people. I mean it, Teagan. I don't want you seeing that boy again. He could hurt you."

What? Was my bat-shit crazy father actually thinking I'd listen when he forbade me from being with Aiden? My first thought was *Fat chance*, but then I remembered that our relationship might not actually be a problem anymore. Becca had made her point, and as much as I hated to admit it, maybe she was right.

Then again, this conspiracy nonsense was just that. Nonsense. There was something different about them, sure; they were cultish in their own bizarre little ways, and maybe they never would let me into their exclusive clan, but I refused to stand there and believe me that when the next full moon came around they'd be on all fours howling at the moon.

I took one last glance at their poster board and said, "This shit doesn't prove anything. So you have some silly profile and a few pics of the people that live in that wooded community, but that doesn't mean they're supernatural creatures. Sorry, guys, not buying it."

Peter's wicked grin reappeared. "So, you know about their living situation? You don't find it odd that they live like that? Away from the rest of us? You know, like they're hiding something?"

Backing away from the table, I admitted, "Well, that might be strange, but it doesn't mean that they're anything other than human. I mean, why not vampires or zombies? Oooh! They could totally be fairies. They are unnaturally attractive and all. I better not eat the fruit! I may never be heard from again!"

I was about to make my grand escape when Peter replied. "It's okay if you don't believe us now, Teagan. You will soon enough. The truth will come out one way or another."

As I turned to leave, I could literally feel the hairs rising on the back of my neck. Peter really knew how to creep a girl out! And to make matters worse, he'd somehow managed to suck my father into his insanity. That was the last thing my father needed. He'd already killed off enough brain cells since becoming the town drunk. If he started talking about werewolves, people were going to haul him away to the loony bin.

49.

Aiden

Teagan had been avoiding me for the past three days. I'd called her at least a dozen times and sent countless texts. I'd even gone over to her house, but no one answered the door. I'd worried briefly that she'd been hurt by her father, but I'd seen her at school, ducking into classrooms and doing her damnedest to avoid me at all costs.

I didn't get it. Becca had been horrible to her, and she had every right to be pissed, but I couldn't imagine how that would make her question how I felt. And what she felt for me was stronger than that, I'd thought. Maybe I'd completely misread her. Everything had been so perfect our last night together. She'd said that she loved me. How could she just write me off because of something some crazy bitch said? How was I supposed to fix this when she won't even talk to me?

Well, this couldn't go on. If I had to go to her house again and sit on her front porch all night, Teagan was going to come out and talk to me. We were going to work this out. We had to. Becca and her petty mean-girl bullshit were not going to ruin our lives. It just wasn't going to happen.

The only thing keeping me halfway sane these days was learning to manage the change from man to wolf. Ever since I'd heard my grandfather say the pack would never consider me as alpha material unless I could control myself, it had become priority number two. Teagan, of course, was still number one.

At first I went out in the trees behind our house to practice. Mom practically begged to go with me, but I flat out told her no; she had to settle on giving me tips instead. Soon, however, I moved the practice to my bedroom. It was harder inside, without the elements and the cool night air, but at least I wouldn't get caught without any pants again. I had two separate encounters that ended with me without the sweatpants I started with, and a good deal of embarrassment for all parties involved.

Being able to change at will was not as hard as I'd once thought; at least, it wasn't after I figured out a trick. All I had to do was think about my grandfather's words and that smug look on Cade's face. Apparently for me, all I needed was to be pissed off. That's all it took for the change to come seamlessly. The hard part was figuring out how to stop a shift when someone pissed me off beyond control.

Did I have this shit under control yet? No, not so much.

*****

"Hey, Aiden, I just made some brownies. Want some?" Alli asked as I came downstairs after practicing for about an hour on Thursday evening.

I'd been feeling a bit weak lately, probably from putting too much stress on my body with all the shifting. When I walked into the kitchen, the rich smell of chocolate hit me like a truck. I ran for the front door and barely made it off the porch before I lost it. I threw up so much that my entire body cramped from the convulsions. With the entire contents of my stomach on the front lawn, I staggered back into the house.

"Jeez, Ad, what the hell was that?" Alli asked as I came back inside. She looked about fifty percent concerned and fifty percent repulsed. Not that I could blame her. I'd never vomited before; werewolves didn't get sick like humans. Not usually. How did humans just throw up and go back to business as usual? I felt like I might die.

Alli handed me a bottle of water. I took it and went over to the kitchen sink. After washing the nasty taste out of my mouth, I went to sit in the living room.

"Did you really just throw up?" she asked.

Wow. Dumbest question ever. "Yes, Alli, I did. Thanks for noticing."

Now she looked about ninety percent repulsed.

I sat there on the couch for a few minutes with my eyes closed, willing my stomach to settle. When I felt like I could stand without toppling over, I made a decision. "I'm going to bed. Thanks for the water."

I had to pause a moment when I stood. My vision blurred, leaving me dizzy. Taking a deep breath, I hurried back to bed before I could pass out. I checked my phone as I lay down, a habit over the past several days. Still nothing from Teagan. I sent her a quick text telling her goodnight, but I knew that she wouldn't reply. I wondered if she'd ever talk to me again.

Two very familiar, very noisy female voices sounded outside my room. Great, I thought. Apparently it was time for an intervention. Damn it. Why couldn't Alli keep her big mouth shut?

"Aiden," Mom called as she knocked. "I'm coming in."

The door swung open, and both my mother and Alli bolted over to my bed to stand over me.

"I told her," my sister admitted.

"I see that," I said.

Before making any other comment, Mom put her hand on my forehead.

"Mom, please. You don't even know what you're feeling for," I grumbled. She had to be the worst nurse ever.

She smiled and said, "I know, but I've always wanted to do that."

That made me chuckle. Immediately, I wished I hadn't. My insides squirmed, and I worried I might vomit again. Not that there was anything left to purge.

Mom could be pretty funny when she wanted to, but it was clear that she was genuinely worried about my health. She sat down next to me and took a deep breath. "Okay..." She clearly didn't know how to say what she wanted. "Teagan and you... Are y'all... Did y'all... Oh God, of course you did."

Alli's hand flew to her mouth. "You don't think that they are..."

"Mated? Yeah, well, I mean, it *could* happen. Right? I don't see why not. It happened to you," Mom said. It was weird, the two of them talking like I wasn't in the room.

"But she's human," Alli said.

"Well, so is your father."

"Well, yeah, but unless you forgot to mention it, y'all aren't true mates," Alli responded.

"I know! I'm just trying to figure out why he threw up," Mom said.

I couldn't think straight. First I'd felt like my body was trying to eat itself from the inside out and then my mom was asking me about my sex life? Jeez. What a night.

"So? What's been going on between you and Teagan?" Mom asked, noticeably avoiding eye contact.

I looked back and forth between my mother and my little sister. I did not want to have this conversation. Teagan and I hadn't been together long, but what we had was special. I didn't want anyone to think less of us—less of her, really—because we'd spent the night together. Girls were like that. But I had a feeling they'd know if I lied.

"I love her," I finally replied.

Alli smiled, but Mom... Mom looked worried.

After a moment she gave a long sigh. "I've been talking to some of the elders and doing a little research. With Alli finding her true mate and being so young and all, I wanted to find out why that happened. I mean, after so many years without a recorded mating… Well, anyway, this is what I came up with. I think that the recent increase in 'matings' has happened because of the decrease in our population over the last few decades. There were matings in other packs this month, too. One in Colorado and one in Northern California."

True mates? Seriously? And I was having this conversation with my mother? This couldn't really be happening, could it? And, Teagan didn't even know I was a werewolf. How was I supposed to explain what we'd gotten ourselves into? If we really were mates, it would mean that we couldn't be apart. Ever. Which would explain me being sick. Would I just keep getting worse if she didn't come back to me? I guess I needed some answers.

Mom and Alli both stared at me.

"But, why are you sick, Aiden? I thought things were good between the two of you," Mom said.

I looked down at my hands. "She won't talk to me since Becca told her off. I've called, sent texts, gone to her house… She's hiding from me. I don't know what to do."

Mom and Alli's eyes drifted to the floor. For a moment neither spoke.

"You need to go to her house tomorrow and make her talk to you," Alli said. "You need to at least find out if what Mom suspects is true. If you've really mated, you'll feel better almost instantly. If you haven't…well, we need to figure out why you are sick. We don't *get* sick."

The whole room felt sad. I wanted to leave, but I felt so awful that all I could do was lie there. I nodded, though. I managed that.

"If it is true and you are mates, you need to let me know right away. I'll have to tell the elders," Mom said.

"Why?" I asked.

She placed her hand on top of mine. I must have had some sort of fever, because her hand felt cool. "You love her. If you are mated, we will have to make them accept her. If they refuse…well, I don't know what we'll do. You won't be able to live without her, and she won't be able to live here. I don't want to lose you, Aiden, but we can't hide this. A human. A human true mate." Her voice cracked, and it looked as if she might vomit, herself.

This couldn't be happening. I'd always known that there was a chance Teagan might not accept me once she knew the truth, but now she *had* to. If we were truly mated, I couldn't live without her. Literally. What would happen to me if she left? Being human, she could just walk away with no repercussions, but me…? I'd be left longing for her for the rest of my life—which wouldn't be very long because the separation would kill me.

Mom saw the panic wash across my face. "Let's worry about this when we know for sure."

She and Alli left and I tried to sleep, but I couldn't stop thinking about tomorrow. My life would change forever. My future was riding on Teagan Rhodes.

50.

Teagan

Great. Walking in the door after school, I heard my dad and his friend talking in the kitchen.

Creepy Peter had been spending an increasing amount of time at our house, and it was obvious he and my dad were still up to their plan, which freaked me out more each day. Could they really be plotting against a "secret werewolf pack"? Freaking loons. Every time I was in earshot they'd stop whatever they were doing and resort to small talk. After I'd refused to believe in "the werewolves among us," they'd blown me off completely—which was just fine with me, but at the same time I couldn't help but wonder what crazy thing they were planning. It was beginning to make me worry.

I threw my keys down on the table by the front door and decided it was time to figure out what exactly was happening. If it had to do with Aiden and Alli, I needed to know, so casually I wandered in and said, "Hey, guys. What's going on?"

My dad started to gather the papers scattered across the table, but Peter replied, "Oh, not much. Just a little research. What to join us?"

Peter's back was to my father, and Dad caught my eye and quickly shook his head as if to warn me to stay out of it. Not that I'd ever dream of partaking in this crazy crusade. But I needed to find out more information. With my Dad set against me pretending to join them, I decided the best way to uncover the truth would be some good old-fashioned eavesdropping.

Peter stood awaiting a response, and the strange glint in his eye was completely freaking me out. There was something totally unnerving about the guy. Something unstable. He kind of made my father seem normal.

Finally, I responded. "Not interested, but you two enjoy yourselves. I'll be in my room. I've got some homework to do."

"All right, dear. Suit yourself," Peter said, turning back to the table.

I headed to my room and shut the door as loudly as possible, hoping they'd get back to their "research." I'd give them a bit of time before I began research of my own.

Throwing my backpack on my bed, I lay down next to it. The last three days had been utter hell. I'd successfully avoided Aiden, but it was growing harder and harder. After a couple of near run-ins with him at school, I'd taken to staying in my classes until the last minute and then bolting to the next. When he saw me and waited, I made conversation with teachers, and one time I even ducked into the teachers' lounge on accident, interrupting their lunch break. Ignoring his calls and texts was killing me, especially when I remembered how perfect we were together only a few nights ago. When I remembered how much I felt for him. It had only been days, but it felt like a lifetime.

My backpack was overflowing, because I'd stopped using my locker altogether. The last thing I needed was Becca accosting me again, and Aiden was likely waiting for me there, too. I knew myself well enough to know that he could break down my defenses with one simple look.

Avoiding Alli wasn't possible. I'd had to endure endless questions about what was happening, and though she'd assured me over and over that Becca was full of shit, I knew she wasn't. Not entirely. There really was something about their little clique of beautiful people that screamed *Members Only*. That was why those people down by the lake were such perfect targets for my father and his creepy friend: They were beautiful and rich and exclusive. And they probably deserved to be. Not only did they have no reason to accept me, some of them would actively fight any intrusion. Even the adults. I thought again about Marcus Walker. I didn't even want to think about what he would say about me being near his recently revealed biological son. If he knew what we'd done the other night in my bed…

I threw my arm over my face and recalled the day's conversation with Alli. She'd been more persistent than ever. "You have to talk to Aiden. I mean it, Teagan. He's really hurting. He loves you, and you just up and walk out on him because of something Becca said? If you don't want to be with him, that's one thing, but he at least deserves an explanation."

She was right. I couldn't keep avoiding him, either, but I knew I'd fall right back under his spell with one word. The truth was: I was hurting too. I loved Aiden and wanted nothing more than to be with him, but I couldn't handle it if he left me because his family didn't approve, or if after a few months he left me for another girl when he realized that he didn't really love me like he thought. Someday he'd leave me just like Alex had, no matter what I believed. Just like Mom did. I didn't want to suffer that again.

After a few minutes of wallowing in pity, I got up and pulled my door open as quietly as possible. I sneaked down the hallway and peeked into the kitchen. For some reason, my dad wasn't there. Peter was alone in the kitchen, and he was talking to himself. No, not to himself, I realized, to someone who wasn't there. I flattened myself against the wall outside the kitchen to listen.

"No! Uncle, you don't understand. We will kill them, kill them all! But I can't do it alone. I need James and the others… No! Just listen to me. What do you expect me to do, take out a werewolf pack alone? They're monsters. I need help… No! James will help me. I've already convinced him that a wolf killed his wife and now his own daughter is… Just trust me, please," Peter begged.

Holy shit. The guy was completely insane. My pulse was racing, and I had to hold my breath, afraid he'd hear me panting with fear. Where the hell was my father?

Peter was hunched over the table, his head in his hands; I saw as I peeked my head around the corner. Then I heard Dad yelling at someone in the front yard, so I tip-toed over to the window and saw Aiden. My father was shouting at him, but I couldn't hear what was being said.

Aiden! I wanted to run out there and throw my arms around him, but I couldn't. Not after everything that had happened. We definitely needed to talk, but it wasn't going to happen here with my dad and his crazy friend around. Especially not when Peter was planning some sort of mass homicide. Was he really going to kill a bunch of the people down by the lake? Was he really going to hurt Aiden and Alli and their family? Was my dad really involved with that sort of insanity?

From where I stood, I could see that something was off with Aiden. It looked like he hadn't slept in several days, which made my heart beat faster. He was clearly hurting just as much as I was.

Aiden turned and headed back to his car. I was making to go after him when I heard Peter start up again.

"I *know* one of them is out there. I can't just go shoot him in the middle of the yard. We will get them, Uncle. We just need time to… No! You're not listening! It will be done, and soon."

I wanted to get to Aiden, but I couldn't let Peter know I'd heard. I moved quietly to the front door and went outside, but I was too late. Aiden's car was already near the end of the street.

"What did you say to him?" I yelled at my dad as he came up the steps.

Just then, the door flew open. Peter stood in the doorway.

My father turned, eyes ablaze, and shouted, "I did what any reasonable father would do. I told that piece of shit to get the hell off of our property. You need to stay away from him, Teagan. He's dangerous."

I couldn't believe what I was hearing. "Are you freaking serious? You think he's more dangerous to me than *you?* Drunk old you and your crazy friends? Your crazy, murderous friends?"

My dad got right in my face, and for a moment I was sure he was going to hit me, but then I saw it: the fear in his eyes. Then and there I knew. He really did believe all of the crazy werewolf bullshit that Peter had been spewing. It made me sick to think that he might really help the nutjob carry out some terrible act of violence.

I turned to leave, but Dad grabbed my arm. "I mean it, Teagan. Stay away from him. Please, I'm begging you. I can't lose you like I did your mother."

I pulled away and ran inside. I needed to get to Aiden. I had to warn him that my father had finally gone completely nuts, and if Dad and Peter were really going to act on their fantasies, Aiden and his family were in danger. Everyone was down at the lake.

I grabbed my keys and flew back past my father, who was standing next to Peter in the yard. My dad lunged for me and said, "Teagan, don't go!"

I dodged his hand and heard Peter say, "No, James. Let her."

Yes, let me, I thought. Without looking back, I jumped in my car, started it up, and sped off down the road.

51.

Peter

Peter stood with James Rhodes in the man's front yard and watched his lovesick daughter run to her car and drive off after her wolf. They had discussed this contingency, and there were things to be gained from it.

As soon as the vehicle was out of sight, they both ran inside to collect their gear. Jumping in Peter's car, they sped down the road after Teagan. They wanted to give her time to be far enough ahead so that she wouldn't see them, but they also wanted to use this opportunity to find out if there was any different route into the wolves' estate. Teenagers always seemed to know the back roads and secret entrances to places. That's how it happened in books.

Peter drove while James took notes. They couldn't afford to have anything go wrong, and so they were double-checking and noting everything. James photographed the small street sign that marked the entrance to the wolves' estate. He drew a rough diagram of what they could see from outside; then they calculated in both miles and minutes the exact distance from James's house to the turnoff. They were going to be prepared. They had to be. Later that day they were meeting the four other men they'd recruited and wanted to have accurate information to give them. The plan had been to attack under cover of darkness, and now it had to be tonight. Teagan might warn the wolves, so they had to act before the wolves could prepare.

Once they'd confirmed there was only one road that led in and out of the community—or at least Teagan hadn't shown them another—they decided that everything they needed. It was time to rendezvous with the others.

Peter handed James his cell phone to send a text to the team and let them know when and where to meet. They had a lot to discuss. Peter needed to educate these guys. He didn't want anyone to walk into the wolves' den unprepared; that would be a suicide mission. They were already at a disadvantage, since the others thought they'd be rescuing Teagan from some kind of religious cult. They needed to be ready for a fight if one should ensue. Peter was still hoping that Teagan wouldn't warn the wolves or they wouldn't believe her, and that the element of surprise might still be on his side.

With a deep breath and a brave smile, Peter drove back to James's house. As soon as they arrived, he used James's computer to check his email one last time for his last piece of evidence. There it was, in his inbox, like a blessing from above: the DNA results that he needed to prove these beasts were real. He opened the attachment and it confirmed what he already knew. These "people" weren't human. The results showed as: ABNORMAL, SPECIES UNKNOWN.

Quickly, he printed out the proof. This was just what he needed, but he decided to keep the information to himself. For now. Now was time the to prepare for the biggest night of their lives. Tonight his uncle's death would be avenged. Tonight his uncle would finally be able to rest in peace.

52.

Teagan

Pulling into the driveway at Aiden's house, I took a moment to compose myself. Did I really want to do this? If I frantically flew through the door shouting about werewolf hunters they might decide that I was really as insane as my father. I'd already been worrying about what Aiden's family would think of me, and this would seal the deal.

The more I thought about it, the more I wanted to turn around, drive back home, and forget I'd ever heard anything. If I'd thought his mother would disapprove of me before, what was she going to think when I told her my own father planned to attack her and her neighbors because they were werewolves?

I put my car in reverse, about to chicken out, when the front door of the house opened. Aiden stood there. I almost slammed my foot on the gas to hightail it out of there, but again I noticed that something was really wrong. Aiden was ill. With a pale face and deep circles under his eyes, he hardly resembled the strong, stunning guy who'd kissed and held me so beautifully only a few nights before.

He rushed my car, and I put it in park just as he arrived at my window. Backing up so that I could open my car door, he lurched forward and threw his arms around me before I made it to a standing position, taking a long, deep breath as he did, if I was were the very oxygen that he needed to breathe. With his face still buried in my hair, he whispered, "Thank God you're here."

I pulled free to answer, but before I could say a word, his lips pressed firmly against mine. It was exactly what I needed. Maybe he was my oxygen, too.

We breathed together, deepening the kiss. With his arms surrounding me, I lost myself in his lips. I drank him in, all but forgotten why I was there.

When he pulled back to look into my eyes, I was startled once more by the change in him, this time in a good way. The color in his face had returned. His eyes shone once again, and the circles beneath them had disappeared. It was like magic.

What the hell was going on? A few minutes ago he'd looked like hell, and now he looked completely normal. Maybe I was going crazy too. I started to ask, but Aiden interrupted.

"I was starting to think you'd never talk to me again. Teagan, I'm so sorry about what Becca said. It's all bullshit. I love you, and I don't care what anybody thinks. You have to believe me. Nothing is going to separate us. Ever."

He held me in his arms as if he could make his words come true, and I almost believed him. I certainly never wanted him to let me go. I was only kidding myself thinking I could ever truly stay away. He was my everything. Standing there, engulfed in his embrace, I finally felt whole again.

It was a good thing I now believed we could weather any storm that came our way. I had to tell him what my father was planning, and something inside knew it would be a hurricane.

"Aiden, I have to tell you something, and you're going to think…I don't know what you're going to think, but I have to warn you," I finally admitted.

Aiden drew back, and with his fingers he moved my chin up so that he could look me in the eyes. I couldn't do it, though. My gaze shifted to the side. I couldn't look at him. Not with what I had to say.

"Hey, it's okay. You can tell me anything."

Tears welled-up in my eyes, and I struggled to say the words without turning into a crying mess right there in the driveway. "I'm just going to say it," I began, "but please know that I think it's completely nuts. I know it's not true."

"Just tell me. It's okay, really."

"It's my dad. He thinks y'all are werewolves. And I know this is completely insane, but he has a friend Peter, and I think they are planning to kill y'all. Everyone here."

Aiden let go of me completely. Shock registered on his face, and he turned and looked toward his house as if to see if anyone else had heard. Then he turned back and said, "What?"

I reached for his hand. "I'm sorry, Aiden. I didn't know what to do. This Peter guy is crazy. When you were out front with my dad earlier, I heard him talking to himself in my kitchen about attacking you."

Aiden pulled me toward his front door. "Come on. Let's get inside. I need to talk to my parents."

I stopped him mid-stride, "No! I can't go in there. They already don't like me. I can't stand there while you tell them that my father is trying to exterminate them because he thinks y'all are some mythical beast. Then they'll really, really hate me."

"Teagan, they don't hate you." Aiden dragged me up to his front porch. "You just have to trust me. You can go upstairs with Alli if you want, but you're not leaving. I can't lose you again, and you need to stay away from this Peter guy. He sounds dangerous. Did he happen to say when he's planning on coming?"

"No," I replied. I had no idea.

"Okay, come on. Let's go inside."

I planted my feet. "Wait. What are you going to do, just go in there and tell them that my father is trying to kill them? They're going to freak out. Aiden, listen to me. You can't tell them my dad thinks they're werewolves. For heaven's sake!"

Aiden turned the knob and opened the door. "Yes, I can. I have to. They need to know."

His parents were standing in the kitchen, chatting, but they caught sight of me and stopped what they were doing. Rushing toward us, Aiden's mother asked, "What's wrong? You both looked scared out of your minds."

Aiden didn't answer. Instead he said, "Where's Alli?"

"Upstairs with Cade," Mr. Wright replied. "What going on here?"

As if she'd heard the excitement, Alli hurried into the kitchen, Cade by her side. "Teagan, you're here! Is everything okay?" she asked.

"Alli, take Teagan upstairs. I need to talk Mom and Dad." Aiden turned to Cade and said, "You should stay."

Alli motioned for me to follow her upstairs, not questioning her brother at all. It surprised me. Aiden let go of my hand and said, "Go. I'll be up there in a minute."

This was it. The moment I'd been dreading. After this, it really would be over with Aiden. And Alli. How could we go on after my father tried to kill them? I followed Alli without looking back, but the first of many tears fell down my face as we reached the top of the stairs.

Alli turned. "You mind telling me what happened down there?"

53.

Aiden

Alli took Teagan upstairs. As soon as she was out of sight, I turned to Cade and said, "Do you know anyone named Peter?"

"Peter who? No, why?" he replied.

"Teagan just told me that this guy Peter and her father…well, they think that we're werewolves," I said. Mom's hands flew to her face, so I added, "It gets worse. They're planning to come here and try to kill us."

"How does she know? Does she believe him? You didn't tell her, did you, Aiden?" Mom whispered.

"No, of course not," I said, but from the look on everyone's faces that wasn't good enough. "I swear I didn't. Why would I tell her now? Most sane people would sprint the other direction even if they loved me, and she's already been avoiding me. Sorry about the 'sane' part, Dad, but it's true."

Dad nodded. Mom said, "I believe you, honey, I do. It's just… They're coming here?"

"That's what she said. They tried to convince her that I was a werewolf. She thought they were just plain crazy. It wasn't until she heard that guy Peter talking to himself about killing us that she knew he was dangerous. She came here right after."

We all knew what we needed to do. We had to call Marcus. None of us really wanted to make that call, though.

Mom offered, and so did Cade. I said that I would do it. Teagan was my mate; I knew that for sure now. It had only taken a few seconds of having her in my arms for me to feel back to a hundred percent. I needed to be the one to tell Marcus, and there was no time to waste.

I made a call, and Marcus flew into our house five minutes later with Phillip and Luke not far behind. Our alpha looked every bit as angry and disgusted as he'd sounded on the phone.

"Where is she?" he demanded.

Mom spoke first. "She's upstairs with Alli. Marcus, she knows nothing. She thinks that her father and this Peter guy are deranged."

"She'll know the truth soon enough, at least she will if these idiots take one step on my estate."

"What do you mean? What are you going to do?" I asked.

Marcus stopped and stared at me. He didn't say anything. He didn't have to. After a few seconds he turned to Phillip and said, "We need to call an emergency pack meeting. We need to do it fast. Get everyone here as soon as possible."

"Here? Not at the lodge?" Phillip said.

"No, let's do it here in case we need the girl," Marcus said.

My chest tightened. I looked at Mom, and she mouthed, "It will be okay."

Luke and his dad left, while Marcus paced back and forth in our living room. Turning, he asked, "Do we know when they will be here?"

"No. She came as soon as she heard anything," Mom answered.

"We'll just have to be ready then." Marcus stopped pacing and pulled out his phone. We all stood and listened to his conversation, as we didn't know what else to do. "Brian? Marcus. Listen, I'm going to need your expertise. Yeah, I know, but we have a situation here. There's no other way. I'll fill you in when you get here. How long? Okay, good."

When he put his phone back in his pocket, Mom went over. "*Brian?* Is that necessary?"

"It is. Unless you would rather we expose ourselves," Marcus said coldly. After one more look around the room, he left. He didn't go far, though, just to the back porch. I couldn't even begin to imagine what he was thinking.

"Who's Brian?" I asked as soon as the back door shut.

"The Fixer," Mom replied.

"What that hell does that mean?"

"Brian has some special skills. He's called when, uh, when there's a mess to clean up."

"Stop being so damn cryptic. What does this guy do?" I asked. Cade was shaking his head, and I kept picturing fixers from television shows or books. They were not nice people.

"Okay, baby." Mom said. "I'll tell you. He makes things look like accidents, or like ordinary animal attacks."

"So he kills people?" I said, incredulous.

"No, but if someone is killed, he destroys any evidence that would point to us."

"If someone is ki—?"

Our conversation came to an abrupt halt as the back door swung opened. Marcus stormed inside, furious, and it was clear his fury was aimed at me. "If this pack is exposed, it will be on you. A human, Aiden? A fucking human? The pack will never accept you as their alpha now! You've ruined everything. You've ruined this pack, and you have ruined your future."

I could feel blood rushing to my face. I was holding back rage with every ounce of control I could muster. If I changed now, this situation would go from bad to worse. Marcus would take it as a personal challenge. A physical one.

"Well, it's my fucking future!" I said, yelling right back at him. "Isn't it? This damned pack was never going to let me be the alpha anyway. Not with the elders, Cade, and my own freaking grandparents plotting to keep it from me."

"What? No one's plotting against you," Cade interrupted.

"Bullshit. I heard you all in here the night I changed. Don't start lying *and* scheming," I snarled at him.

The room fell silent. We all just stood there glaring. I was livid, my hands shaking uncontrollably. Cade stood motionless, but he was obviously fuming as well.

"This isn't helping, guys," my mom said as she placed herself between us. "We have a situation here, and the pack is already starting to show up outside. We need to calm down and figure out how to handle this. We need to appear united, even if you two do want to rip each other's heads off. Save it for a later date."

"You're right. This will have to wait," Cade agreed, and it pissed me off even more that he could regain his calm so fast.

Marcus took one last look at us both. "Neither one of you deserves to take my place. Such a damned disappointment." He turned and walked out of the house.

My dad spoke up, slightly calmer. "Whatever is going on here between the two of you needs to end, at least for a while; then we can sit down and work it all out. You need to get your heads on straight. If these guys are really coming to kill us, we need to stick together. My family is in danger. Both of you have someone to protect, too. If something were to happen to Alli or Teagan because you two couldn't work together, how could you live with that?"

Teagan. Alli. My father's words brought me back to reality, focused me on what really mattered. Neither Cade nor I responded with words; all it took was one look and a nod and we both stood up. Together, we went outside to join the pack.

54.

Teagan

For well over an hour we were stuck in Alli's room. I could tell she wanted to talk about what was going on with my father, but when I didn't offer up any new intel, she politely made small-talk instead. Oddly enough, she didn't laugh at being called a werewolf by my dad, but I didn't bring it up again. I didn't want her focusing on how stupid my family was.

Finally Mr. Wright knocked lightly on the door, poked his head in and said, "Alli, your mother wants both of you outside."

Alli nodded, stood, and motioned for me to follow.

We made our way down the stairs and followed Mr. Wright out the back door. Huddled together around a table on the back porch stood a group of people deep in conversation, and my stomach twisted into knots upon seeing them. These people weren't your average "business partners" as Alli once described them when she explained the odd living situation here. No, these people looked more like a tribe. A very strong and scary tribe. They were all tall, well built, and clearly physically powerful, but it was more than that. They all kind of looked alike. Everyone had olive-toned skin, dark hair and eyes, all except for Alli who stuck out like a sore thumb.

This wasn't normal. I mean, they really *were* some kind strange cult, weren't they? I'd half imagined it but this visual cue was shocking; it was as if they somehow all belonged to the same family. I hadn't noticed it in school so much, but here, all together…

The word *pack* drifted into my mind, but I shook the thought away, refusing to believe anything Peter or my father had said. There was no such thing as a werewolf. And yet, it was more than apparent that something odd was taking place on this hidden tract of land.

Marcus Walker was clearly leading the discussion, two extremely burly men standing beside him. Next to them stood Aiden and Cade, and the rest of the group formed a semicircle nearby.

Aiden saw me standing there, and he took a step my way but was grabbed by Marcus and forced to stay right where he was. He shrugged his arm from Marcus's grip but made no further attempt to move.

Alli and I hung back a bit, but I could still catch some of the conversation. From what I could gather, the group was preparing for the attack. They didn't speak like any businessmen that I'd ever heard; they spoke of weapons and sneak attacks in the night, and of a man called The Fixer. Then Alli placed her hand of my shoulder and said, "It's going to be okay. They know what they're doing."

What the hell was that supposed to mean? They were used to having to defend themselves against insane werewolf hunters? None of this made any sense.

I leaned over and whispered, "What exactly are they doing?"

She shrugged. "I'm not sure yet, but it sounds like they plan to find the intruders and interrogate them. They've called in someone to help, too. Don't worry, I'm sure you're your father will be fine."

"Interrogate them?" I repeated. "Who are you people? This obviously isn't a business meeting. I mean, look at them. This doesn't look like a corporate—"

Alli patted me on the shoulder and replied, "We'll talk about that later. Promise. Now I need to find out more. Stay here with my dad for a minute." And with that, she walked away and joined the others.

Mr. Wright turned to me. "Maybe we should go back inside, let them finish up." His expression was kind, and I supposed I had no better idea. I was just glad I hadn't been tied up and thrown out of the estate for having been the bearer of bad news. I supposed it could still happen.

Reluctantly, I nodded my head. But as I turned to follow Mr. Wright inside, Marcus caught my eye. From that intense glare, I knew I wasn't welcome there. He didn't have to say it. Nor did he have to say that it was all my fault that this was happening.

55.

Peter

Peter opened the trunk of his car and began to pull out the huge duffle bags he'd been filling with his own personal arsenal. He wanted members of his team to be able to protect themselves, as they needed to kill each and every werewolf on the property. Only total victory was acceptable.

"What the hell kind of fight are we looking at?" William asked, seeing a semi-automatic handgun Peter pulled from one of the bags.

"I don't know. That's why I have this baby. We really don't know what kind of cult this is, what they're capable of, or how deep Teagan is involved. They might have weapons of their own. We think they do. Many groups like this do. They'll probably fight us for her," Peter explained.

The group looked at each other and then at James. Peter held his breath until James nodded.

"She took off this afternoon with that boy. I called her and told her to come home, but she said they wouldn't let her leave. That's why we have to do this now, tonight. If we don't get to her before it's too late, I'm afraid she'll be lost to me forever. I don't think I could take losing another member of my family."

William shook his head in sympathy and reached for one of the smaller weapons on the table. "Don't worry, James. We'll get her back."

One of the other men spoke up. "She's still a minor, right? Shouldn't we involve the authorities?"

Peter was quick to answer. "No. Not yet anyway. We don't have any proof they've done anything illegal. The cops will just say it's a case of a teenage girl wanting to be with her boyfriend, and they won't do anything without evidence. By then these cultists will know we're on to them and it will be too late. Let's just go in there and get her back. If we're met with resistance or threatened, we'll have our proof we can take to the police. And if we're *really* threatened, we'll be ready. That's why I'm helping you guys protect yourselves."

Peter had no intention of involving any authorities, of course. Government bodies were slow and stupid, and they'd be hindered by all sorts of rules and regulations. He intended to march onto this property and kill the werewolves there. It was total victory or nothing. Collateral damage would be part of the equation.

He and James quickly shared their reconnaissance with the rest of the team: the pictures, the maps, a description of Aiden. They were going to take two 4x4 vehicles, and they all needed to know the route just in case.

Peter tried his best to keep the group beer consumption at a minimum, but the team consisted of the town barflies, so as the sun started to set, the cans piled up. Peter needed these men alert and sober, but it didn't look as if that was going to happen.

"You're losing control of your men!" Uncle Raymond said when Peter stepped away to collect his thoughts.

"It will be fine. Maybe the booze will even help," Peter rationalized. "They seem more excited and less apprehensive after a few drinks."

"It's going to be up to you, Peter. You'd better get back in there and rally them. Killing werewolves won't be easy. You'll all need your heads clear," Uncle Raymond said. "Remember what happened to me!"

With that in mind, Peter went back inside to prepare for the final battle.

56.

Teagan

Sitting in the living room with Mr. Wright—he insisted I call him Paul—I watched more and more people gather on the back porch. It was already dark out when a man who must be The Fixer showed up. By his side was a strikingly beautiful girl way too young to be his wife. Paul excused himself and went outside to join them. His body language suggested I stay where I was.

I sat inside, alone, growing more and more impatient. Unable to help myself, I peered out the window. The gathering appeared ready for war, strapping weapons to every inch of their bodies. I had the urge to run out and tell them that it was just an old drunk and a young nutcase coming for them, and who knew if it would even be tonight, but with Marcus overseeing it all, I kept my butt glued to the couch. The man terrified me.

I was starting to think I wouldn't have the chance to talk to Aiden again when I noticed him sneaking away from the group. He came inside, and I met him at the door. Before he said a word, he kissed me very hard on the lips. Then: "Don't worry. We have everything under control."

"Under control? What's going on out there, Aiden?"

Aiden looked out the window. "I know this must look crazy, but they just want to be prepared."

"Prepared for what? It's just a couple of guys. Granted," I allowed, "they plan on attacking you, but it looks like you're getting ready for a three-day siege. And why do y'all even have those weapons? What kind of business is this group in? Are you gunrunners? The mob? Whatever *that* is out there, it's not normal. And so many of them look so similar…"

Aiden's eyes met the floor. "I'll explain everything later. I promise. I just can't right now. I need to get back out there."

I was seriously getting nowhere. Was I really just supposed to stay inside doing nothing? Frustrated that I would just be kept in the dark for the time being, I decided one more question was in order. "Who or what is the The Fixer?"

"That, I really don't know. Apparently he works with Marcus, but I've never heard of him before. As far as I know, he's just here to help."

And there it was: the lie. I'd known one was coming. Aiden knew more than he was letting on.

"And the girl?"

Aiden diverted his eyes to the window again. "That's his daughter, Scarlett. Your guess is as good as mine as to why she's here. I don't think anyone here knows her."

I watched the girl for a moment. "Well, she seems to have made fast friends with Luke."

Aiden chuckled, seeing the two in private conversation. "Not for long if Cami has anything to say about it."

The door flew open just as he leaned down to kiss me a final time. Marcus snarled, "Get out here, Aiden. They've come."

Aiden turned back to me. "Stay inside," he ordered. "Alli and my dad will be here any minute. Whatever happens, stay here. Please. I love you."

After a quick peck, he headed out the door.

57.

Peter

Peter and his team reached the dirt road turnoff to the werewolf compound just after midnight. They pulled their 4x4 vehicles off the main road and hid them out of sight of any passing cars, went over their plan once more then walked forward one by one, all clad in black and heavily armed. The men were instructed to follow Peter's instructions, let him do the talking, and be prepared to fight fire with fire if necessary.

As they made their way through the trees, the reality of what was about to happen hit Peter like a ton of bricks. His body quivered from the effects of all his nervous energy, and he pushed to the front, insistent on leading the way. The others seemed more than happy to let him. He had always imagined this night: he and his team of werewolf hunters moving stealthily through the night. This team didn't move stealthily, though, they more like stumbled, but they were all he had and he would make this work.

Peter signaled the others to stop when the first of many homes came into view. All was quiet in the compound.

"Too quiet," Peter said aloud. He walked in the shadow of the trees and then crept close to the house, making his way to the back door, his men following.

"It's unlocked," he announced in a whisper.

"We're just going to go in?" one of William's friends asked. Peter couldn't even remember his name. That was unimportant, though.

"You stay here and be the lookout. The rest of us will go in," Peter commanded. "We don't know which house they're holding Teagan in."

After a swift but thorough search, they discovered the house was empty. Peter stalked out the front door and glared around at all the large, beautiful homes on the lake. Seeing how well these killers lived sent his soul into a rage.

James walked up behind him and asked if he was okay.

"My uncle is dead and I was forced into a psychiatric facility, all while these monsters are living like kings. We have to find them," Peter said. "We *have* to. And your daughter."

The team searched eight houses, one by one, but they all were deserted. He began to wonder if the wolves were lying in ambush somewhere. The entire complex seemed empty, and searching the remaining buildings seemed a pointless chore. Or a deadly one.

"You don't think they all left, do you?" James finally asked.

"No, I don't. They're here. We just have to find them," Peter repeated.

"What are we going to do if we can't find anyone?" one of the others asked.

"We call the police. I want my daughter back!" James said.

They sneaked down to the lake to get a better view of the area. Everything seemed deserted, and Peter knew that a new plan would soon be in order. He just needed time to figure one out.

58.

Aiden

Marcus had chosen about twenty pack members to defend the estate. The rest of the pack, mostly mothers and their young children, were instructed to stay in the lodge until the whole mess was over. I made sure Becca was included in that bunch. I didn't want her anywhere near Teagan. She'd already caused enough problems.

Those selected as defenders waited for Phillip and Luke to return. Marcus had sent them as wolves to scout for Teagan's dad and the others. They had now come back, and while they changed to human form the rest of us stood gathered on my family's back porch.

"They're down by the lake, Marcus. It's not much of a group— six men, five of whom I recognize from town. The other guy I don't recall ever seeing. Young guy, stringy hair. They might be easy to run off, but they're also heavily armed," Phillip reported. "It's a good thing we've got guns of our own. I'm assuming you want us to take care of this little problem as 'humans.'"

"Right, Phillip," Marcus said. "Are they close enough to see us?"

"Not in the dark."

"Paul," Marcus called.

"Yeah?"

Marcus scowled at my dad. "When you go back inside, I need you to turn on every light in the house. We want them to come to us here, and we'll meet them outside. On our terms. Understand?"

"Got it," Dad said.

"Alli." Marcus continued to give orders. "Since you are friends with that girl—"

"Teagan," my sister said, defiantly, which made me smile.

"Yes. *Teagan.* Stay inside with her and your dad. If things get bad, find a place to hide her until we can finish. If we do have to shift for any reason, we wouldn't want her seeing us," he added.

Alli went to Cade and buried her face in his chest. She was suddenly realizing just how bad this could get. The night was going to be hard on everyone.

Once Dad and Alli were safely inside with Teagan, Marcus gave us more instructions: "We are all to remain in our human forms. Under no circumstance is anyone allowed to change without my order. Understood? We want these men to realize that they were wrong about us. If anything should happen to go wrong, Brian will handle the cleanup, but let's hope it doesn't come to that."

Everyone, including myself, turned to look at Brian. The Fixer. He didn't look all that tough, but according to Mom his special skills were feared as much as they were admired and he wasn't someone to mess with. He'd never been needed here before. Personally, something about him gave me the creeps, and I couldn't wait until he was gone.

It didn't take long to draw the intruders. Within minutes of the light going on, they were completely visible walking toward us. We all moved together to meet them. I couldn't begin to imagine what they must have thought. We didn't have to be in wolf form to be intimidating.

As we approached, I saw Teagan's father. He found me with his eyes, and he held a small gun in his shaking hand. It both surprised and saddened me.

"We don't want any trouble," one of the men shouted. "We just came to get Teagan Rhodes back."

Liar.

Marcus answered for the pack. "That's not what she told us. And if that were the case, there would be no reason for you to be trespassing on our property, especially not armed with semi-automatic weapons. The girl is free to leave whenever she wants."

"What did she tell you?" her father asked. From where I stood, I could see the color drain from his face. Marcus glanced over at me, and he nodded as if giving me permission to speak.

I said, "You're here because you and some guy named Peter think we're a pack of killer werewolves."

The faces of the four other men registered disbelief, and they all turned to stare at Teagan's father. Clearly they hadn't been aware of Peter and James's beliefs or true intentions, and the man who'd first spoke said, "What the hell? Werewolves? Jesus Christ, James. You told us they were some kind of crazed cult out to steal and brainwash your daughter."

Before James could reply, Marcus did. "We are not a cult, nor are we werewolves." He chuckled, as if the very thought were preposterous. "The fact is, this is my land, and all of my extended family and friends live here. That's it. You men have been duped, and this is private property."

"They're lying! They're werewolves! I know they are! I have proof," one of the members of the group suddenly shouted. Peter, I assumed. Wait a minute, I remembered seeing him before. He'd been at the diner that night I first talked Teagan into going out with me.

The four townies started slowly backing up, away from Peter and Teagan's father. They looked shocked and angry, if a little unsteady on their feet. Had they been drinking?

"If you leave now, we will not involve the authorities. If you choose to stay, please be aware that we are prepared to defend ourselves," Marcus said, pulling his jacket open so that the men could see it wasn't an idle threat.

"Look, mister," said the first man. "I'm sorry. We were lied to. We would never have come out here with these two crazies if we knew what they were planning. Come on, guys, let's leave these poor people alone. Sorry to have ruined your night."

"I appreciate that," said Marcus, keeping his voice even. "Drop your weapons, and Phillip here will show you men back to your SUVs. Your weapons will be returned to you later. After you've left the property."

The man named Peter shouted, "Wait! Don't leave. He's lying. I have proof! These beasts are not human! You promised to help us!" He pulled a folded-up piece of paper out of his coat pocket, but his army was already giving in to Marcus's demands, placing their weapons on the ground and turning to walk away. Whatever the paper revealed, the men didn't bother to look.

"Gentlemen." Marcus raised his voice, ignoring Peter's appeal. "I might not be as forgiving the next time. Not when my family or land is threatened by intruders carrying weapons. I hope we do not cross paths again. Do we understand each other?"

The four men looked back and slowly nodded; then they followed Phillip into the darkness. I wished Teagan's dad would just go, too. Nothing good would come from him standing his ground with Peter. The man was obviously out of his mind.

As the others departed, Mr. Rhodes frantically looked around. "Where's my daughter? I'm not leaving without my daughter!"

"Teagan is perfectly safe. She's inside with my sister and my dad," I said.

"Get her! I'm taking her home," he yelled.

"James, I'm Aiden's mother," Mom said, taking a step forward.

I didn't like it, and obviously Marcus didn't approve either. "Lily, get back!" he ordered.

"It's okay, Marcus," she assured him. Then, to Mr. Rhodes: "Teagan is safe. As soon as we clear up this misunderstanding, I'll have Aiden drive her home."

"No. I w-want to t-take her home now," he stammered.

"That's not going to happen. I will not let that sweet child come out here and see her father waving a gun around ranting about werewolves. Do you really want her to witness this? You've already got her scared out of her mind with all your crazy nonsense. We may live out here in the woods, but we're not dangerous. Nor are we mythical creatures," Mom stated, her voice full of derision.

Teagan's dad appeared to be thinking. The hand on his gun continued to shake, but his other hand smoothed back his unruly hair. "All right. Let's figure this out so I can take my baby home."

59.

Peter

The night hadn't gone as planned, and he was close to his breaking point. Everything was falling apart. First his reinforcements surrendered and now James Rhodes was giving up, too? Peter started to scream wildly and wave his gun in the air.

"What the hell are you doing, James? Don't you dare trust them. These aren't normal people, you idiot, they're werewolves!"

Everyone, including James, moved back from him.

"Get yourself together, boy," Uncle Raymond told him sternly. "That gun could go off by accident. You don't want this to go down like that. You want to be in control. Otherwise you'll lose."

Peter glanced around, hoping to see his uncle, hoping Ray would tell him what to do. "Where are you, Ray? The mission is all screwed up. I should have figured a way to do this on my own," he complained.

Everyone looked around. After a moment they seemed to come to a decision, and they moved even farther back. They were eyeing him even more warily.

"Pete, I think we made a mistake here," James said.

Peter's face reddened. "I made the mistake. I should have never picked a bunch of drunken cowards to help me kill werewolves." He continued to talk, getting more hysterical as he did. "All my time, my hard work, all ruined by a bunch of morons. Now I have to kill them all. I have to do it by myself. No one can be trusted to avenge my uncle but me. I won't rest until every filthy, mangy, no-good, murderous wolf is dead and its body burned to ashes!"

"Peter, you need to get control of yourself, man," James scolded, but he looked more and more nervous. He kept glancing from the group to Peter to the semiautomatic pistol Peter flailed around, back and forth, back and forth; he clearly didn't know whom to trust.

"You don't talk to me, you spineless pig. You deserve everything these animals are going to do to you, and so does that slut daughter of yours," Peter yelled.

The comment seemed to cause a stir among the crowd, and Teagan's wolfboy tried to step forward. He was restrained with difficulty. The rest of the crowd started moving forward, closing in on Peter and James. They spread out, forming a semi-circle, and that was when Peter made his decision.

"I vowed to eradicate the entire werewolf population," he announced, "and that is what I intend to do."

60.

Teagan

Alli and Paul had been trying their best to keep me distracted from what was taking place outside. I could hear the commotion from where I sat, and I noticed Alli glancing out the window every few minutes. They had cleverly positioned me so that my back was to the scene, and every time I moved to turn, Paul would distract me.

"Teagan, everything is going to be okay. Just let them handle it," he reassured me for the millionth time.

Before I could respond, Alli did. "Really, it looks like they have it under control."

Someone outside started ranting. Alli turned again to look out the window. "Don't move," she said after a second. "I'll be right back."

Her father tried to stop her, but she was out the door before he could do anything. With Paul's attention diverted, I took the opportunity to peek. What I saw out the window was my father and Peter completely surrounded, and Peter appeared to be freaking out. He waved a longish pistol in the air.

My dad, on the other hand, was standing still as a statue. In the light spilling out of the house and from the back porch, his face seemed drained of all color. There was a gun in his hand as well, but he held it down by his side. From where I sat, I could see his hand trembling.

Paul was headed back to me, but I couldn't let them hurt my father. No matter how much I hated him in that moment, he was still my dad, and I knew if Peter took one single shot, the group would attack. Cultists or simply angry businessmen, my dad wouldn't stand a chance against them.

Without hesitation, I took off toward the door. I dodged Paul on my way out, and he shouted my name as I ran down the porch steps. I plowed through the mob, and to my surprise they let me pass. It was only Aiden, who stood at the far end of the crowd, who shouted, "Teagan! What are you doing? Somebody stop her!"

I took a quick look in his direction. He was trying to get to me before I made it to my father; I could tell his intent. I had no plan, myself, no idea what I was going to do when I reached my dad, but I couldn't stop now. I needed to protect him. I'd beg the group for mercy, convince my dad to leave, something, anything to get him away from this place, these people who all looked so strange and menacing. I couldn't just stand by and watch my father destroy himself because Peter had convinced him there was such a thing as werewolves. They might not such a thing, but this group was dangerous, and Aiden had some serious explaining to do.

Somehow I beat Aiden to my father, but before I knew what was happening Peter grabbed me, twirled me around so that my back was pressed against his body and held me in a chokehold. He held his gun in one hand, which was now pointed at the crowd, and in the other hand, the one with a forearm wrapped firmly around my neck, was a knife. He threatened, "Nobody move or I will slice her open. I mean it. Stay away from us."

He tightened his grip, causing me to choke. In a whisper he added, "I won't hesitate to kill you, but these people are worse. You're my ticket out of here, so just do what I say and we might make it out alive."

Aiden froze in his tracks. For a moment he stood stock-still, but when our eyes met he slowly began inching towards me.

Peter realized. Wrapping the arm holding the gun around my body, he positioned his knife against my neck. The blade pricked my skin as he shouted, "I mean it, dog. Stay the hell away from me or she's dead."

Rage flashed across Aiden's face just before…

What? Before he shifted from the guy I'd fallen in love with to a giant, snarling, growling wolf. Holy mother of God. This couldn't be happening. Was I hallucinating? Could it be true? He was really a wolf? A fucking *wolf?*

I couldn't believe what I was seeing, and apparently Peter couldn't either. But he seemed more overjoyed than shocked. He whispered, "I knew it!" The words were more to himself than me.

Aiden's mother darted forward. "Aiden, stop!" But Aiden wasn't listening—or the wolf that he'd become wasn't listening. It hunched down low to the ground and inched closer.

His gun was around my waist, so with Aiden only a few feet away, Peter screamed, "James! Shoot that piece of shit!"

I couldn't see my father's face, but from the corner of my eye I saw his gun rise. Immediately, all hell broke loose. Aiden's mom, Alli, Cade, and Marcus shifted in unison. My brain could hardly register what I was seeing: four wolves where before there had been people I knew. Their clothes fell to the ground, torn and ragged. I felt my body swoon and feared I was going to pass out right then and there.

My legs gave out, causing Peter's knife to cut my skin. Blood trickled down my neck. The wolves had formed a circle around us, and they were snarling, but my father dropped his gun and pleaded, "Peter, let Teagan go. There's no getting out of this now. She doesn't need to get hurt too."

I regained my footing, and the pressure on my neck lightened. I could feel that Peter was shaking as he shouted, "James, you fucking coward, fuck you and your dog-loving whore of a daughter. I should have never trusted you!"

Peter switched his grip around my neck and raised his gun. Without a moment's hesitation, my dad tried to take advantage of the situation. He lunged for me, but he wasn't fast enough. Peter shot him point-blank in the head. Dad's limp body fell to the ground.

I gave a sob of horror, but there was no time for it. Peter didn't stop. He unloaded the rest of his clip at the wolves surrounding us, but they seemed to dance here and there and remain unharmed. He shrieked, "Get back! I'll kill you too. I'll kill you all!"

He'd loosened his chokehold a bit, just enough for me to elbow him in the stomach. He jerked and let go. I threw myself away from him and fell to the ground, and a second later Aiden attacked him from behind.

Aiden's mother sprang into action next. Rolling out of her way, I crawled over to my dad and gathered his lifeless body in my arms, struggling to breathe as tears poured down my face. He was gone. Dead. My father was dead, and I had no one left in the world. Both my father and mother were gone. I was alone.

I heard screaming behind me, wet noises and tearing. I ignored all of it. With trembling fingers, I closed my father's eyes. I sat there rocking and crying, not knowing what else to do.

I don't know how long this lasted before a hand touched my shoulder. "Teagan? I'm so sorry."

It was a familiar voice, and I turned to see Paul standing over me. Before I realized, I was standing, screaming, "Get the hell away from me! How can I...?" I didn't know what to say. I couldn't think clearly. I only knew I needed to get the hell out of there. Peter had been a lunatic, but he was right. This was a werewolf pack, and Aiden was one of them. He was a fucking *werewolf*, and now both Peter and my father were dead.

Shocked, crying, and completely freaked out, I scrambled to my feet and took off for my car.

61.

Aiden

I hadn't even felt the change this time. There was no pain, no warning; it was instant, automatic, and uncontrollable. The moment I saw the knife press down on Teagan's delicate neck, the need to kill that son of a bitch was too strong to prevent. I thought of nothing else except stopping his pulse with my teeth.

Teagan's scream for her father broke my heart. A second later, she flinched and tumbled out of Peter's arms. It was my opportunity, and I took it.

To be honest, I wasn't really aware of what I was doing until it was over. Suddenly Peter was dead, and Luke was pulling me away from his lifeless body. My mouth was covered in blood.

The first thing I did was look around for Teagan. She needed me right now, and I needed her to know that I would never hurt her. I couldn't. She was my mate. I couldn't live without her. I scanned the surroundings but didn't see her anywhere. I needed to find her. I had to change back. Screw modesty and waiting for someone to pass out towels.

"Where's Teagan?" I yelled as I returned to human form.

Luke walked over in his boxers and handed me his pants. His face was dark. "Dude, she freaked. She ran to her car and took off."

My heart fell. I ran up the steps leading to the house, and my mom, dad, Alli, and Cade all looked at me with such pity in their eyes as I passed. They must have seen Teagan take off, too. Was I going to lose her?

I went straight to my room and slammed the door. Grabbing my phone, I dialed Teagan's number. She didn't answer.

"Teagan, baby, I am so sorry. I'm sorry about your dad. I'm sorry that I scared you. We need to talk. Please call me. I love you," I pleaded to her voicemail.

I sat on my bed with my head in my hands. Why the hell was this happening? So much occurred today that could change my life forever. I didn't know if Teagan could ever forgive me for keeping this secret. I didn't know if she could ever accept the wolf inside me, either. I needed to get answers...but more than that I wanted to console her. She couldn't be alone right now.

I threw on a sweatshirt and some other shoes, took my phone and flew back down the stairs. I was going to find her. I was going to make her understand.

Marcus was in the living room, and he grabbed my arm. "Aiden?"

I pulled away and turned to face him. "I don't have time for a lecture right now. I have to find Teagan."

Marcus took a deep breath. "Yes, you do. Listen, Aiden, if she really is your mate, as Lily says, then you need to make her understand and accept you."

"I know that!"

"I don't think you do. You need to understand what's at stake. If she doesn't accept you, if she doesn't accept all of this...well, Brian will have to step in. Do you know what that means?"

"No, I don't know," I snapped. "What will he do?" But I was afraid that I did already know, because my heart was trying to pound its way out of my chest.

"You know what Brian does, Aiden. He will have to make her disappear. He can't leave with any loose ends. We can't have humans knowing about us."

"Loose ends! Teagan is not a fucking loose end. She's just a girl from my school—and my *mate*. Brian can't just kill my mate. I won't let that happen," I promised.

I waited then for Marcus to tell me they wouldn't hurt Teagan, that he wouldn't let Brian do anything stupid. He didn't.

"If anyone even goes near Teagan," I growled, "I swear this entire pack will pay."

My legs were shaking so badly I could barely stand upright. It was suddenly hard to breathe, too. I needed to get out of there before I did something suicidal.

"It will be okay, son," my dad cut in. His voice was kind. "Go to her and be honest. She's a strong girl. I think she can handle it. She has a lot of other things to deal with right now, so if you go and explain… Do you want me to drive you?" he asked, obviously worried about my state of mind.

I shook my head. I needed to go alone. And I needed to get to Teagan's fast.

62.

Teagan

I pulled into my driveway so fast that I had to slam on the brakes not to hit my father's car. Only then, as I sat staring at his Subaru, did everything fully sink in. I had to fight back the bile that was rising my throat. I focused on taking deep breaths, trying not to lose control.

What the hell was I going to do now? My father was dead. Dead! And my boyfriend really was a werewolf. He had lied to me all this time, and Alli had too. How was I supposed to deal with that? Was I just supposed to accept the fact that werewolves were real? And my dumb ass fell in love with one. My father was dead because of it, and I had no one. He'd tried to warn me, but I didn't listen. And I'd thought my biggest problem was that Aiden was popular.

I had to get out of town. I was almost eighteen, so I supposed I could make it on my own. Somehow, somewhere. I'd been taking care of myself for a long time, anyway. I could do that anywhere.

Taking several deep breaths, I got out of my car and looked around. Suddenly I was paranoid. Something told me I hadn't seen the last of Aiden's pack. Would they come for me? Would he? What would I say to him if he did? What would he say? Was I in danger now that I knew the secret of his pack?

Safely inside the house, I turned and locked the door—as if that would keep them out. I dashed to my bedroom and pulled a duffle bag out of my closet, frantically stuffed clothes inside. When nothing else would fit, I hurried over to my bed, lifted up my mattress and grabbed the envelope containing my life savings. Quickly, I pulled out the wad of cash and shoved it into my purse. It wasn't much, but it was enough to get me out of this godforsaken town. I wasn't sure where I'd go, though.

Fear struck me again. Could I just leave? Should I go to the police? My dad was dead. Would they think it was me who killed him if I vanished? What would the pack do with his body? How could I have just left him there? Before I knew, I was on my knees, sobbing, curled up in a ball with my arms wrapped tightly around my duffle.

It wasn't long before the need to get away returned and overcame my sadness. Slowly, painfully, I made it to my knees and then to my feet. Feeling faint and empty, I threw the duffle bag over my shoulder and trudged to the front door. I stopped dead in my tracks as I opened it. Aiden stood on my doorstep.

63.

Aiden

Seeing the tears streaming down Teagan's face, all I wanted was to wrap her in my arms and make everything okay. She was devastated, and it was all my fault. Her entire world was falling apart.

"Oh, baby, come here," I said, hoping she'd just walk into my embrace. But when she looked up at me, there was fear in her eyes.

She shrank back from the door and attempted to slam it in my face. I caught it with my hand, and she took another step back and commanded, "Stay away from me!"

I'd known that one day she'd find out about me, but I'd never in a million years thought she would be scared of me. It wasn't supposed to happen this way. Pushing the door open I promised, "You don't have to be scared of me, Teagan. I could never hurt you. You know that, right? Please, just let me talk to you."

She tried in vain to shut the door. "I mean it, Aiden. Stay away. If you don't leave, I'll call the police. I swear it."

I removed my hand from the door and backed up a step. Immediately, Teagan slammed it. But I wasn't about to leave. I couldn't give up. That wasn't an option.

"Teagan, let me explain," I begged as I heard the lock click into place. "Please. That's all I ask. Please let me just explain things to you. Give me five minutes, and if you never want to see me again I promise I'll leave."

Silence. My heart was pounding in my chest. At last the door unlocked and slowly opened. Relief washed over me. Then I saw

Teagan standing there, shoulders slumped, her tears having made dirty trails down her cheeks. A bag lay at her feet.

"Were you leaving?" I asked, horrified. She'd leave without me?

She just shrugged, and fresh tears welled up in her eyes.

I picked up her bag and carried it over to the couch. She followed, and once we were both sitting I said, "I didn't want you to find out like that. God, I'm so sorry. I should have told you the truth, but I swear that I would never, ever hurt you. I couldn't, and not only because I love you, but because you're my true mate."

Her eyes widened. "Your true what?"

"My true mate. I don't know exactly how to explain it, but it's true, Teagan. That's why I looked so sick when you came over earlier. I can't...I can't be apart from you. That happened to Alli and Cade, too. They were made for each other and can't be apart. Kind of like soul mates," I said. "But physical. It's very real for us."

"And I'm yours?" she repeated, clearly confused. "You can't be serious. Are you telling me that if we aren't together you'll get sick?"

"I'm sorry, Teagan. But, yeah." When I saw her face harden I said, "Not that that should be why you stay with me. I thought about telling you the truth about us time and again, but I didn't know how. Then I toyed with the idea that maybe we could live our entire lives without you ever finding out. If you knew I was a wolf, I worried you'd stop loving me, reject me. I just...I didn't want to lose you," I admitted. "But I knew a day would come when I had to tell or that you would find out and I planned to tell you..."

"But you *didn't* tell me, Aiden," she said when I trailed off. "You lied to me about everything. How can I ever trust you again?"

"I know, and I'm so sorry, but we've only been together a short time. If I'd had longer, I'm sure I would have found a way." Moving closer on the couch, I took her tiny hand in mine. It was trembling when I pulled it to my lips, but she didn't shrink away. "Can you ever forgive me?"

She looked at her hand in mine, and then she looked me in the eyes. My heart was pounding out of my chest, and it stopped dead when she let go of me and scooted away. "I just don't know what to think. I need some time."

Her words cut like a knife. Every guy in the world knew what those four words meant. They were always bad.

I tried to be brave, to put on a smile, to not let her know that I was crumbling inside. She didn't need guilt to go along with the grief she felt tonight. Her whole world had collapsed, and now I was asking her to forgive everything. To move forward like nothing had happened, or at the very least to just move forward.

"Okay, baby. Take some time," I said, not wanting to scare her. I was scared, though. Time wasn't something we had. Marcus's threats were real. But maybe I could hold him off for awhile. With luck it would be until she came around and realized we were meant to be together.

I stood up. "You don't need to leave home, though, not if you were afraid of the pack coming after you. Please don't run. Stay here, and I promise you'll be safe. Rest. Think. Cry about your dad." I took a deep breath and vowed, "I won't let anyone hurt you ever again."

And I wouldn't.

Wiping a tear from her face, I leaned down to kiss the top of her head. Then, feeling my own agony threatening to break free, I turned and walked away.

*****

As I pulled into my driveway, my house appeared completely deserted. The lights were out and no one was in sight. The back yard was empty.

It was more than a little disconcerting that the entire scene had been "fixed" in under an hour. The thought made me sick to my stomach. It was as if the whole bloody scene had never happened. And that's when it hit me: I'd killed a man tonight. I was a vicious, bloodthirsty animal that had needed to be pulled off Peter's bloody, twitching body. I had the overwhelming urge to run upstairs and take a hot shower, to wash away the memories.

When I walked through the front door, I knew the shower would have to wait. Marcus was sitting at the kitchen table with my mother.

"I take it things didn't go well," Mom said.

I threw my keys on the kitchen counter and turned on the overhead light. Without answering, I grabbed three beers from the refrigerator. "Why were y'all sitting in the dark?"

Mom eyed the beers in my hand and said, "I don't know. So, are you going to tell us what happened?"

I handed a beer to Mom, one to Marcus, and opened the last for myself. No one questioned me or told me I was too young. I supposed if you were old enough to kill a man, you were old enough to have a beer.

I sat down across from Marcus, took a long swig and asked, "What happens if she says no?"

Marcus looked at my mom before answering. "To you, or to her?"

"Both," I answered.

Mom set her beer on the table. "You'll get sick again. You'll grow sicker every day until you die." The look in my mother's eyes was too much to bear, and her voice was blank, like I was already gone.

Or maybe it was for a different reason. Marcus added, "Or until *she* dies."

Mom was crying suddenly. She excused herself and headed to the restroom.

Marcus gave me a stern look. "I meant what I said, Aiden. Brian won't leave here with an unfriendly domestic knowing about us. She'll either accept you or she dies. That is that. And even if Brian felt differently, I will not lose one of our own. I will not lose my son."

I just stared at him, revolted. Finally I said, "She'll accept me."

Marcus shrugged. He placed his beer on the table and walked out of the house. The door slammed behind him.

I turned and saw Mom standing in the hallway. She was still crying.

"I need you to promise me something, okay, Mom?" I said.

"No! No, Aiden, I won't. Don't even say it!"

I got up and walked to her. I held her in a tight hug and whispered, "You have to, Mom. You have to promise me that if Teagan can't accept me, can't accept what I am, that you'll help her get away from here. You can't let Marcus or Brian kill her. You're the only one who'd know how to stop them."

She trembled, holding me so tight I thought my ribs would crack.

"I don't want to live without her, Mom. And Teagan can't die because of me. Wouldn't you have done the same for dad if he hadn't accepted you? I know you would have. You would have sacrificed yourself to keep him safe, Mom. Help me do the same," I pleaded.

She didn't respond, but I felt her grip on me loosen. I thought I knew what that meant.

64.

Teagan

Aiden hadn't been gone long when the doorbell rang. I pulled myself out of the fetal position and trudged back to the front door, expecting to find him standing on my porch once again. When I looked out the peephole, I found Alli and Paul looking as if they'd been dragged through the mud.

Damn it, I wasn't ready for this. Why couldn't they understand that I needed some time alone? Was that too much to ask?

With the back of my hand, I wiped away my tears and tried to pull myself together, but I felt an emptiness inside, a void that scared the shit out of me. I was completely numb and could hardly string two thoughts together. My father was dead and my boyfriend was a werewolf, but the day just seemed like a bad dream. Maybe I would wake up and find that everything was okay.

I just stood there staring at the door, willing them to turn around and leave me alone. I couldn't do this, couldn't face them. Not now.

"We know you're in there, Teagan," Paul called. "Just open up. Please. We need to talk to you." He banged his fist against the door just as I looked out the peephole once again, and I jumped back, my heart pounding.

"Come on, Teagan. Just give us a chance," Alli pleaded.

Hesitant, I unlocked the door and pulled it open. The two just stood there without speaking. Bile rose in my throat, and suddenly I felt as if I might be sick. Leaving the door ajar, I rushed to the bathroom and hung my head over the sink. Taking several deep breaths, I looked up at myself in the mirror. All color had drained from my face, and I looked even paler than usual.

I turned on the faucet and splashed some water on my face. A tingling sensation spread throughout my body, and if I didn't sit down I...

It felt as though my chest caved in, and I fell to the cold tile floor.

"Teagan! Are you okay? Can you hear me?"

I sensed Alli kneel down beside me. My eyes struggled to open, and my vision was blurred.

"Dad, get Teagan some water!" Alli yelled. "I think she's in shock."

Paul rushed in and helped Alli pull me into a sitting position. They tilted the rim of a glass against my lips, and water ran down my face.

"Please drink, Teagan," Alli begged.

I parted my lips slightly to allow the water into my mouth. Moments later Paul heaved me to my feet, and I was surprised to find my body cooperating. They helped me to the couch, but I still didn't have the strength to remain upright. I laid my head down on the pillow and closed my eyes.

Paul rubbed his hand across my forehand, sweeping back the hair from my eyes. "Teagan, you're going to be okay, but we can't leave you like this. Alli and I will stay. You just get some sleep."

A voice that hardly sounded like my own replied, "No. I want to be alone. Just go."

With conviction in her voice, Alli said, "We aren't leaving, Teagan. We'll talk in the morning."

I didn't have the strength to respond. I just lay there, and soon sleep pulled me under.

*****

I woke to find Paul making coffee in my kitchen. It was the next morning. Alli was sitting next to me, and when she felt me stir she said, "Hey, you feeling any better?"

I dragged myself into a sitting position, and Paul placed a cup of coffee in front of me. He smiled warmly. "I'm glad to see some color back in your face. We were worried about you."

"What are y'all still doing here?" I asked. Memory returned of the night before. I fought back tears.

Alli picked up the coffee cup and offered it to me. "We wanted to make sure you were okay. You shouldn't be alone. When we saw Aiden leaving, we decided it would be best if we stayed."

Paul took a small sip of his coffee. "I know this is a lot to handle, and we want you to know we are here for you. The whole family. You have nothing to fear." After a moment he added, "Aiden loves you, you know. It's killing him to not be here. He's respecting your wishes, but he's called at least a dozen times."

"But he lied to me. You all did. How am I supposed to react? Y'all are *werewolves*, for God's sake."

Paul put his cup down on the table. "Actually, I'm not a werewolf. Just a regular ol' guy in love with one. Kinda like you."

It took a moment for my brain to register that. So, Paul was human? And he was completely okay that his wife and children were supernatural creatures out of a horror movie?

When I didn't respond, Paul continued. "I'm serious, Teagan. I'm human just like you. I fell in love with Lily a long time ago, and when I found out that she was…uh, different, I had a hard time dealing with it. But then realized I that it didn't matter. I loved her, and that was all that mattered."

Alli reached for my hand. "I'm so sorry, Teagan. I know I kind of pressured you to go out with Aiden, but it's because I wanted you to be happy. And I knew my brother could make you happy. Aiden loves you, Teagan. You have to give him a chance. He needs you, and you need him too. Let him love you. You won't regret it."

Let him love me? Aiden *did* love me. That I couldn't deny. The way he looked at me, touched me, held me, made me feel whole... No one could fake that. And he'd respected my wishes and left when I was angry at him; he hadn't tried to pressure or cajole me. He was even getting sick because I wasn't with him, but he hadn't wanted that to influence me. At that moment, I knew what I wanted. What I needed. Alli was right: I had to let him love me. Because I loved him back.

She wrapped her arms around me and said, "We can be your family now."

My heart constricted, and tears filled my eyes. "This is just all too much, Alli. My father... What happened to him, to his...body?"

Alli started sobbing, too, and scooped me up in her arms. "I'm so sorry, Teagan."

Paul stood and wrapped his arms around the both of us. "Just let us take you home. You're not alone, honey. You're not alone."

65.

Aiden

I woke up early, unable to stop thinking about Teagan. What could I have said differently? Should I have gone back over and come clean, told her exactly what would happen to us if she didn't accept me? The question had plagued my dreams. And it would be like this every day from now on. I just knew it. I would never stop thinking of her, never stop loving her. Not that I wanted to.

After a long hot shower, I looked in the mirror and could already see what was happening. My eyes were red and my skin pale. My heart literally felt broken.

I couldn't live this way. I had to fight. Calling and checking in wasn't enough; I had to go back to her house and fight for her. I had to find a way to both respect her wishes and prove to her that we were better together. Even without the threat of The Fixer, I knew that to be the case.

I dressed quickly and went downstairs. The house was unnaturally quiet. I looked around but couldn't find anyone. It didn't matter. I was wasting time. I grabbed my keys and walked out the front door.

"Going to Teagan's?" Mom asked, startling me. She was dressed and sitting on the porch, drinking a cup of coffee in the cold. She seemed distant, lost in thought as she stared across the compound. "Is that Luke over there?"

I didn't want to talk about Luke. I wanted to leave, but I needed to make sure Mom was okay first. She didn't look okay, that was for sure.

"Yeah, that's Luke," I said.

He was standing outside his house with Brian's daughter Scarlett. They looked extremely friendly, and for a moment I thought about Cami, who would clearly be unhappy at what I was seeing. Luke was going to break that girl's heart. I didn't think I would have thought about her feelings before I met Teagan.

I watched as Scarlett handed Luke a note, but he didn't read it right away; he just held it in his hands and watched her get in her car to drive off the estate. It was only when she was gone that he opened the letter, but then his entire face lit up.

I shook my head. What the hell was I doing here spying on Luke? I needed to get to Teagan.

"Mom, are you all right? Where's Dad?" I asked.

The moment the words left my lips, Dad's car pulled up. It was Dad, Alli—and Teagan!

I was off the porch and at the car in less than a second. I pulled open the door and tentatively offered her my hand. She looked so fragile, so unsure. I held my breath as she looked at me. It felt like an eternity, but finally she gave me her hand. That was it. That was all I needed. I could wait for the rest.

But she was out of the car and in my arms in a heartbeat, and she wrapped her arms around my neck. I buried my face in her hair. I knew that I could never let her go, and I never would. Never again.

I could hear quiet sobs against my chest, so I held her tighter. We stood there for the longest time, and I barely noticed my dad and mom and Alli going inside to give us privacy. When Teagan finally loosened her hold, I looked down at her beautiful face. I couldn't find the right words to say, so I did the only thing that conveyed all of what I felt. I kissed her.

They were small tender kisses at first, but I needed more. She was my oxygen, and I had been deprived of her for too long. The kisses became desperate and needy, on both of our sides. Finally she pulled away, and I took a deep breath, bracing myself for what she was about to say.

"A werewolf, huh?"

I nodded my head nervously.

"I'm still mad at you for lying to me. And it's going to take time for me to get used to all this," she added.

I gave her a tentative smile. "Does that mean you love me again?"

"I never stopped, Aiden. I was just so scared."

Upon hearing those words, I felt a huge weight lift off of my shoulders. I wrapped her in my arms again and raised her body up so that we were eye to eye. "I'm sorry that I scared you," I said. "I'm sorry that things are as crazy as they are, that yesterday was as crazy as it was."

Her eyes began to tear up again. She didn't say anything.

"But the important thing is that I love you, Teagan. I will love you always."

"You'd better," she teased. "If we're going to be 'mates.' Weird."

At that word, my heart glowed. I swung her in circles and carried her toward my house. Everything was going to be okay.

"Put me down!" she laughed.

"Never," I said. "I'm never letting you go again."

66.

Teagan

Sitting in the living room, surrounded by my new family, I felt completely content for the first time in ages. We'd gathered near the Christmas tree the Wrights put up, and Alli played Santa Claus, passing out presents for each of us. My stack was overflowing, which was crazy. It had never been like that at home.

Aiden wrapped his arm around me and pulled me close. He whispered in my ear, "You're going to share some of that with me, right?"

I glanced over at Lily, who shrugged. It warmed my heart. The family was overcompensating, but I knew they were doing it because they cared. They all cared, and they were treating me like one of their own. Just like they'd promised. And I had Aiden.

In the last few weeks, so much had happened. Not only had we pulled everything together for exams and finished out the semester, the Wrights had held a proper funeral and burial for my father. I was able to say goodbye, which had made a difference. Though it still hurt, Aiden and Alli were by my side to help me through the pain. The official story had been close to the truth: Peter had come on the estate with him, insane, making crazy allegations and waving a weapon. Peter had killed my father when he balked, and then he was killed by a family attack dog. Brian took care of all the details, including providing the attack dog. The lab work matched our story, and after a couple interviews, the police finally closed the case.

I missed Dad. He might have been an awful father, but he was the only one I'd ever have. And he hadn't abandoned me. I'd always love him.

I realized I'd soon love the Wrights, too. They'd taken me in and hadn't looked back. Neither had I, much. It was clear now that Aiden and I belonged together, whether or not Marcus approved. Every day our feelings grew stronger. It was like we were becoming one unit, one person. Aiden loved me, and I loved him. The family promised to give me rundown of what things would be like, what it meant to be a werewolf, but that didn't matter. Werewolf Aiden might be, but nothing could change the happiness I felt when I was in his arms. That's what mattered.

Aiden nudged me gently. "You okay?"

Placing my head on his shoulder, I said, "I'm okay."

"Just okay?" he teased.

"I couldn't be happier," I replied. Because it was true.

67.

Aiden

I couldn't believe how much my life had changed in the few short months since I moved to Red Ridge: switching schools, finding out that I was a werewolf, the fight with Dylan, the bombshell about Marcus being my biological father, all the pain, all the hardship… Everything was worth it if I got to spend the rest of my life with Teagan. Which I did.

Just as I leaned down to kiss her forehead, the doorbell rang. Dad made his way through the mess of wrapping paper in the living room and opened the door. There stood Marcus with Cade by his side.

Alli rushed over and threw her arms around Cade. "Merry Christmas!" But then she pulled back and saw the worried look on his face. "What's wrong?"

Marcus entered the house. When he stopped in the foyer I was already standing, but I remained in the living room next to Teagan. Marcus looked from me to Cade and replied, "We have a problem."

Cade's grim expression punctuated his father's statement. I grabbed Teagan's hand and maneuvered us through the stacks of open presents, my mother following close behind. I pulled Teagan close, knowing that Marcus's arrival could put a damper on what I had hoped would be a perfect day. She deserved a perfect day.

Everyone stood staring at each other. It made me impatient.

"Well, what is it?"

"Brian called. There is word that a neighboring pack plans to try to overtake us. It's apparently gotten out that we don't have an heir, that there's no second alpha chosen to step up and take control in the event of my demise. This makes us look weak, vulnerable, easy to defeat. It needs to be handled."

Alli started to say something, but Cade raised his hand. She fell silent.

"I will not endanger this pack because you two can't get your shit straight," Marcus continued. "You boys need to figure it out. Fight if you have to, but I need one of you to step up."

As I turned from Marcus, Cade's eyes collided with mine. His fists clenched at his sides, and there was fire in his eyes.

"All right, bro," he said. "Let's do this."

ABOUT THE AUTHORS

Sara and Staci are native Texans who began writing together about five years ago. After teaching in classrooms next door to one another for several years, they decided it was finally time to try their hand at writing the type of fiction they love: YA paranormal romance. As well as being avid readers, they are close friends, teachers, wives, and proud soccer moms. *Circle of Lies* is their third young adult novel.

CIRCLE OF LIES

Life has always been easy for Aiden Wright. He's smart, athletic, funny, and the ladies adore him. But when tragedy strikes, Aiden discovers the truth about who he really is and his whole world comes crashing down around him. Aiden thought that being a teenage werewolf was going to be awesome, but it might just cost him the one girl who could make him whole.

Since her mother's disappearance, Teagan Rhodes's life has been littered with her father's empty beer cans and his hollow promises to change. Convinced that others would only let her down, she keeps everyone at arm's length—but resisting Aiden's charm is proving to be more difficult than she thought. Throw in a psychotic werewolf hunter out to terminate the species, and one wrong move, one wrong decision could destroy everything.

Boroughs
Publishing Group

Did you enjoy this book? Drop us a line and say so! We love to hear from readers, and so do our authors. To connect, visit www.boroughspublishinggroup.com online, send comments directly to info@boroughspublishinggroup.com, or friend us on Facebook and Twitter. And be sure to check back regularly for contests and new releases in your favorite subgenres of romance!

Are you an aspiring writer? Check out www.boroughspublishinggroup.com/submit and see if we can help you make your dreams come true.